Praise for Elizabeth Gill

'Original and evocative – a born storyteller'
Trisha Ashley

'A wonderful book, full of passion, pain, sweetness,
twists and turns. I couldn't put it down'
Sheila Newberry

'Elizabeth Gill writes with a masterful grasp
of conflicts and passions'
Leah Fleming

'An enthralling and satisfying novel that will
leave you wanting more'
Catherine King

Elizabeth Gill was born in Newcastle upon Tyne and as a child lived in Tow Law, a small mining town on the Durham fells. She has been a published author for more than thirty years and has written more than forty books. She lives in Durham City, likes the awful weather in the north east and writes best when rain is lashing the windows.

Also by Elizabeth Gill

Available in paperback and ebook

The Foundling School for Girls
Miss Appleby's Academy
The Fall and Rise of Lucy Charlton
Far From My Father's House
Doctor of the High Fells
Nobody's Child
Snow Angels
The Guardian Angel

Available in ebook only

Shelter from the Storm
The Pit Girl
The Foundryman's Daughter
A Daughter's Wish
A Wartime Wish
The Hat Shop Girl
The Landlord's Daughter

. . . and many more!

Elizabeth Gill

The Runaway Children

Quercus

First published in Great Britain in 2020 by Quercus
This paperback edition published in 2020 by

Quercus Editions Ltd
Carmelite House
50 Victoria Embankment
London EC4Y 0DZ

An Hachette UK company

A CIP catalogue record for this book is available
from the British Library

PB ISBN 978 1 78747 342 3
EB ISBN 978 1 78747 340 9

10 9 8 7 6 5 4 3 2 1

Typeset by CC Book Production
Printed and bound in Great Britain by Clays Ltd, Elcograf S.p.A.

Papers used by Quercus are from well-managed forests and other responsible sources.

In memory of Bill Proud, who is always the man in my books

Author's Note

When I was eighteen months old my mother had another baby and Lavinia Proud, who helped in the house, took me off her hands as much as possible because by then there were three of us.

Min and Bill and their tiny home have invaded my stories. They lived beside the Palace cinema. You went down a small dark passage from the main street into the back beside the Palace wall and there Min and Bill shared the yard with Gert next door.

The house had one room downstairs with a pantry, and two small bedrooms via a narrow staircase, and in this little haven I spent a good deal of my childhood. They put up a rope swing which was anchored to the pantry wall at one side and just outside the door on the other, and there I would come to most days when it was dinnertime at school and sit on a cushion and swing.

Bill was tall and lean and to my mind always wore a beautiful dark blue suit and a cap. They both loved me very much. I was often there at teatime and Min would say 'Here he comes, hide' when we heard his footsteps through the passage at the end of the day and I would run into the pantry, or crouch behind the green settee under the window and they would play a game for me.

'Where's the little lass then?' he would say as he stepped up into the house.

'She didn't come today, Bill,' Min would say and then I would shout out and run to him and we would settle down at the table and have tea. Min made the most wonderful custard pies and egg and ham pies.

Bill died when I was quite young. It was one of the biggest losses of my life but being a writer I can bring him back again and again so that he lives on in my stories.

One

It was spring on the fells of County Durham and bitterly cold when Sister Madeline rose. She'd woken very early because there was so much to do. The sheep and lambs in the fields looked as though they were sitting on a small white cloud and then the sun came out and the frost dazzled. It was her favourite time of day.

She looked herself straight in the eyes when she made herself neat for the day. She had been a lovely good-looking girl who had been left alone when her father died when she was in her early twenties. Before his death she had wanted to marry a businessman, Jay Gilbraith, but her father had refused to allow it, Jay being well beneath them, having no family or background. Since then Jay had begun to build this new village and she had been there to help him.

Maddy's father had been dead for ten years and she was well past thirty. She thought about her beauty now only as she might have thought about somebody she didn't know very well, as though it had nothing to do with her. Her hair was black and her eyes were silver black and her skin was pale but all that denoted to her was that her health was good and that God had been kind to her. Though she wished she was taller and bigger, she was slight and small-footed and had been thought of as beautiful and elegant. And a fat lot of good it is now, she thought briskly, dismissing all thought of her physical appearance.

Three years had passed since she first came up here from the Newcastle upon Tyne convent to begin a school for children who had no parents and were in need of a home and education. It was mostly girls because, as Maddy knew, boys always came first in a family and if there was not enough to eat the girls would go without. If anybody was to be left it would be the girl.

She now had forty children at the school and only six of them were boys, which said a lot about value and lack of it, she thought with a sigh, but then she was here and so were the two nuns who helped her to run the school, Abigail and Hilary. Hilary came from landed gentry in Northumberland, while Abigail had been a street child in Newcastle, and they both had good and varied skills to offer and, best of all, love and compassion.

Hilary was a big bluff countrywoman with a loud voice. She was fresh-faced with a lot of brown unruly hair, which thankfully was mostly hidden under her boat shaped hat. She had brown eyes, a straight nose and a generous mouth, which was given to laughter, and powerful arms from vigorous country exercise such as shooting and helping calves into the world, as well as turning sheep on their backs for the shearing. She ruled the kitchen and anybody who got in her way.

Abigail was the opposite, a street child who had been starving in Newcastle before the nuns found her. Although she ate a lot she never put on an ounce in weight and she was tiny, almost like a child. She looked like a bird, as though her arms and legs might break under any pressure, but she had a will of steel and had learned a good many useful attributes and cunning measures which came in very handy up here in the wilds.

Most of the people here were runaways, having fled from oppression, from famine, from families who wanted them to be other than they were. Maddy had run from the home which was empty after her father died. Hilary was called Darling, the most beautiful name Maddy thought she had ever heard, and was from a country estate which she would never inherit. She had run from the family who did not want her but wanted instead her sister, the pretty girl, who had married for money. Jay, who had financed and built the village, had run from the person he had become, getting rich for the sake of it, and had learned to help others. And the children who came to her were lost, abandoned, ignored, abused.

Jay was typical of a Border man, tall and lean and brown-faced with thick hair and fine dark eyes. He was clever and far-sighted and ambitious.

Maddy loved Jay, but not as she had once loved him. Their relationship had gone beyond that now and she was glad of it. Now forty years old, he was trustworthy, dependable and intelligent, and these things mattered less since they had learned to accept one another on a much bigger scale, creating something new in this village, giving men jobs and women and children homes, education and skills.

Always there were problems and at the moment Maddy's main one was that they were halfway through building another house so that they could take more children, but until it was ready she was having to ask people to take the lost ones in among them, wasn't always easy.

Just yesterday Mrs Pinner, whose husband was a carpenter, had got very upset when the children she was asked to look after did not follow her religion. Maddy understood that, people here had very little education and tended towards being insular, but she could not afford to allow people to turn the children away.

Mrs Pinner had wrung her hands and not invited Maddy into her house. It was a pretty house, stone with a backyard and a bit of garden, one of the first which had been built, and it looked out across the fell top. The ones that had come later were not as large, Jay having by then seen that outside space was the most important thing, he would need to fit in as many houses as he could without making people feel cramped. Not that that pleased Mrs Pinner.

'I can't hang my washing out, it blows all over the place and now you come here telling me I have to take two Methodists into my house. I can't do it, Sister, I've got four bairns, where am I supposed to put them? We've only got two bedrooms, you know, and my bairns are lads. I can't see the lasses being in the same bedroom, you know what will happen then, don't you, or maybe you don't, Sister, in your position.'

Nuns, Maddy reflected ruefully, were meant to know nothing about sex, children and, worst of all, it was assumed that they had a private address for God and were constantly in touch with him.

'It's only for a few weeks until the new house is built.'

'My Fred says it will be months before that building is fit for folk to live in.'

Maddy knew very well that a lot of couples slept in their front room and, although she wouldn't have called it ideal, it was so in places like these where people had large families.

'How about if I ask Mrs Temple to call and do your washing and ironing and help with the cleaning?' she said and then Mrs Pinner, who was really a decent woman, reluctantly agreed.

Now all Maddy had to do was tell Mrs Temple that she would have even more work. She needed to take on extra women to help. Widows and single women were best, everybody else was too busy. Mrs Temple was widowed and had only one child but if she was not at home she had to ask her neighbours to take her offspring since she was out at all hours aiding other women.

Single women were a godsend. Maddy knew that sounded wrong and that it was considered less than respectable not to be married but they had more time and energy. However, in a village like this there were few women unmarried. Why ever would they come here? Single ladies – and they were thought of as ladies – had shops. There was a dress shop, a shoe shop and a shop which did clothing repairs and made hats and gloves. Women ran all of these. There was a butcher who was a married man. He did the butchering and his wife made sausages and pies, and she was always there to greet the customer and make each woman feel that she was getting the butcher's best attention.

That morning, however, Maddy was thinking of a scheme so that she might entice girls from the dale. The trouble was that she would have to house them; she could hardly expect them to travel six or eight miles a day in bad weather.

Her office door always stood open and she heard a noise. When she looked up Jay was standing in the doorway. Having loved him but been unable to marry him, she didn't feel like that any more. He had since lost his dearest friend in a pit accident here in the village and had loved though not married another woman. Maddy had done work she considered more important than marriage and was content with it, so she thought they were comfortable with one another.

She indicated he should shut the door, after which he came and sat down where they relaxed and called one another by their first names. The only people who might interrupt were Hilary or Abigail, nobody else would have dared as these meetings were known to be more important than anything, other than an emergency. Hilary and Abigail would just be bringing them tea or coffee. They would leave straight away and often without speaking, smiling because these meetings had long since become the norm and usually occurred halfway through the morning.

'More on your plate than you can manage?' Jay said. 'I heard you sighing from halfway down the hall.' He sat across the desk from her.

'We need the new building now.'

He looked vaguely irritated and she knew that he was as keen as she was to get on but the winter and early spring had been very wet. Since the autumn there had been nothing but snow and they had not been able to get the roof on so that the building would be warm and dry.

'We just need a week of good weather.'

He had been saying this for about two months and they were no further forward.

'We can't take any more children,' he said and then he looked at her. 'How could we turn them away? Jim,' this was Jim Slater, his right-hand man, 'suggested wooden buildings for now but they would never stand the first good storm.'

Hilary had come in with the tea while they were talking and she had a brainwave. Mr Nattrass, who owned a farm not far away, had several good rooms and lived alone.

She was the one Mr Nattrass spent the most time with. They went shooting together and Hilary, having come from farming stock, helped him on the farm when she had time because they were so grateful for all he did for the children.

He was good with the smaller ones, taking them to the farm

to see the animals, especially lately since the new lambs were on their feet. He also supplied the foundling school with rabbits, pigeons, game and he grew vegetables for them.

Mr Nattrass could have been married many times, Maddy thought now, with the neat farm his parents had left him. He had neither brother nor sister and, as far as she could observe, no family at all. He was clever and prosperous and also so attractive that she had seen women stop what they were doing as he went past. He was wonderfully unaware of his fair hair and green eyes, his brown face and hands. He farmed a great deal of land, some of it being up on the fell so only fit for sheep, but he cultivated as much of it as he could. On the slopes below his house he had made a garden, part of which held flowers of all different kinds and the rest was for vegetables. He had a couple of dairy cows so that there was plenty of milk, four which were being fattened for beef, half a dozen pigs for pork and bacon, two dozen hens which ran about outside to their hearts' content, and even a duckpond where khaki Campbell ducks, brown and placid and very friendly, floated at their ease making a tremendous mess.

Jay's new project was an orchard. Maddy wasn't as keen on this, such things took a long time to grow, so for now they bought in their supplies when they were at their cheapest and stored them, something else which took up space.

'He'll be in later and I'll ask him,' Hilary said of Mr Nattrass. 'I could always go over there more often and help.' She blushed slightly when she said this. Maddy ignored it. It took more than a nun's habit to keep emotion at bay but Hilary was always to be trusted and Mr Nattrass's saving grace was that he was shy and avoided the eyes of those who fancied him.

'You're needed so much here. We need to find somebody

who can be there most days to do the cooking and cleaning.'
Back to the original problem, Maddy thought, sighing again:
not sufficient of anything and more children needing help
every week.

Two

Ella McFadden had never intended to run away, not at first.

Saturday was always the best day of the week because that was the day when her mother visited. Ella would stand, watching down the back lane from when she first got out of bed. Her grandma got cross with her for not eating her breakfast but how could she eat on such a special day, so her grandma would give her a thick slice of bread and dripping, well salted, and let her go. The waiting felt like days though her grandma told her it was usually only an hour or two. When you were seven an hour or two could feel as long as a week.

'She will come,' her grandma said, reassuring, and she did but she was always in a hurry.

'He will be waiting for me.' It was almost the first thing her mother said when she got in the back door, as though she already wanted to be gone, couldn't wait to get back to That Man, as her grandma called him, her other name for him being the Fancy Man. Ella had met him once and once had been enough. He was large so that she couldn't see around him or above or below him and he had a loud voice.

It was, she knew now, a long time ago. Her mam had been gone a long time from the house. She had been small, she thought, or so her grandma told her when her mother left. She tried hard to remember the time when her mother did not come to see her just once a week. All she remembered was waiting for her coming back and watching her leave.

At first, when Ella was much smaller, her mam had come to spend time with her and sometimes took her out to the shops to buy her sweets. In those days Ella would ask when she could go and live with her mam, when could she leave her grandma's house. She wouldn't have said such a thing in front of her grandma because she loved her very much and her grandma said how lonely she would have been had she not had her lovely little Ella to keep her company.

Ella had liked being seen in the streets of the small town with her mother, it made her feel as though she belonged in a different way than with her grandma. When your mam didn't live with you Ella thought that people thought less of you, but if they could see her mam there she would be proud.

In the early days her mam would stay all day and read to her if the weather was bad. She would have her dinner in the middle of the day, sitting down with Ella and her grandma to eat. Sometimes her mam and her grandma would chat just like other people did, about what they were doing and what had happened to the people they knew.

Gradually, however, her mother curtailed her visits. They got shorter and shorter so that Ella became aware of minutes rather than hours, how precious they were. She would go to bed at night and store up the images of the three of them and the two of them and of her mother coming and going and of what kind of sweets she had been bought – the sticky ones which clung to the bag, or the peppermint humbugs which could be sucked for minutes, or the special chocolate at Christmas and at Easter. She held on to the memories because the memories grew longer tails and now there were some Saturdays when her mam did not come at all. It hurt like somebody had twisted her arm until it broke. Chinese Burn, that was what it was called in the playground, and it hurt. This was the worst Chinese Burn in the history of the whole world, Ella decided. The outings, the storytelling and the sweets had long since gone. Now she would go into the back lane and because she was scared that her mam would not come she would fill the day with the idea that she hadn't expected her to, hadn't really wanted her to, didn't care, she was fine with her grandma. But on those occasions when her mother did turn into the street her heart lifted and soared like the seagulls who came into land when the weather turned bad. Ella tried not to get excited but it was too much to endure and yet those precious moments went by so very swiftly that it was as if she needed somebody to draw pictures she could look at in bed. Her memory was so full of all those times so long ago when she had been very little and her mother had loved her.

Those times when her mother was late her grandma got cross and when her mother did get there she pounced on her like a cat in the back street.

'I wish you'd make your bloody mind up if you're her mother or you're not. The times when you take all morning to get here she stands there hour upon hour whether it rains or snows or a howling gale comes down the back lane. She sometimes gets up in the thick blackness and stays there until it's dark again and I have to go and bring her back inside. One of these days the bloody bogeyman will get her. Then where will we be?'

'You shouldn't swear in front of her, Mother. I come as soon as I can. It isn't always easy.'

'Swear? You think swearing makes it worse? Words don't hurt. It's you and your Fancy Man. Sometimes I think it would be better if you never came at all, rather than going on like this and upsetting that bairn every week.'

'I keep you, don't I? How would you live if it wasn't for the money he makes? He's keeping us all. That has to be enough. I did it because it was the only way, you know that, and it doesn't help with you going on and on about it.'

'You did it because you care more for him than you do for your own child, may God forgive you.'

'Do you want to starve?'

'We were getting by.'

'We had nothing. What else was I supposed to do?'

When there was a row like this her mam didn't stay, no matter how late she had got in being there. Ella hated those Saturdays most of all because her mam just walked out and talking about it in that daft way made it all seem worse somehow.

Her mother would throw money into the middle of the table and go. Her grandmother then always said,

'It's a pity the Fancy Man doesn't go back to where he came from like yer dad did.'

Her mother would try to give money to her grandma but she would turn away. It was a kind of pattern with them, her mother would offer it and her grandma would pretend that she hadn't noticed. Her mother would stand for a few seconds, still offering the money, and then she would put it down in the middle of the table. There it would lie long after her mother had gone.

When her mother walked out she didn't stop or look back. Ella would run after her, watching all the way down the back lane until she turned into the front street and then was no more to be seen. Sometimes Ella went back inside but other times she waited, hoping the money would be gone before she went back into the house. But it didn't matter how long she waited, it would always be lying in the middle of the table. Her grandma would be in the pantry, singing and washing up, as though nothing mattered or as though she would never let it.

After that, throughout the early months that year, her mother would come maybe twice a month and then once a month until Ella started to lose hope and think that there would come a day when her mam did not come back at all. Did Ella not matter to her?

The Fancy Man. How important he was to them. It made him sound like God. Ella knew what God was like, she went to St Mary's, at least she had until her grandma's legs could not carry her that far. The priest, Father Abraham, had come and tried to persuade her grandma to be there and her grandma had cried so that in the end Ella said,

'God can't expect Grandma to walk all that way when her legs are filled with water.'

The priest stared at her.

'They are,' Ella insisted, 'that's what the doctor said.'

Their doctor was the man that Ella most admired, not least because he had a wife, and a daughter named Charlotte. Ella had seen her at school though had not dared talk to her. He had not gone away and left them like her father had. He wore such nice clothes and he had a soft voice. He always said such lovely things to her so she believed every word that he told her. Sometimes she pretended that the doctor was her dad and she was called Charlotte Waters because Charlotte wore nicer clothes than everybody else and Ella couldn't think of anything to say to her. She couldn't understand why Charlotte had such a nice dad and her mam looked nice when Ella saw her on the street. They had a lovely big house with the surgery on the end of it and they had a garden where Charlotte played. They had an orchard, so it was said, a place where you grew fruit on trees. It must be wonderful, Ella concluded, being able to reach up and gather plums and pears and apples. Also they had a greenhouse with tomatoes and a back garden full of radishes and lettuces. Ella had heard that some of the local lads would go in at night and steal the succulent fruit but that the doctor did not complain.

'It hurts having your legs full of water, Grandma cries in the night. She cannot go to your church.'

'It's not my church,' Father Abraham objected, 'it's God's church.'

'Well she can't do it for him, either,' Ella said.

After that she marched out as though waiting for her mother and it was some comfort to think of her even when it was not a Saturday, because the vague hope remained that she would come. Otherwise it would be five weeks since Ella had seen her and she had never not come for that long before.

Father Abraham must have gone out the other way, she thought after a good long time. She waited to make sure he had gone and then she went inside.

'He went out the front way.' Her grandma sounded appalled. Nobody ever went out the front way. The door usually stuck in bad weather, one of the reasons they never used it, but also because of the front room. They only sat in the front room when visitors came and since they never had any visitors it wasn't often used.

'Can't he bring God to you, Grandma?'

'He will have to, my pet, because there's no other way it will work.'

She loved Grandma to call her 'my pet', it was the best thing that had ever been.

Ella had realized a long time since that her grandma was far from well. She had hoped to begin with that her mother would come and take them both back to the house where she lived with him but it didn't happen. Ella kept saying that she would go and bring her mother but her grandma wouldn't let her and she had an awful suspicion that her grandma didn't know where her mother was or surely she would have sent for her. But then maybe her grandma was too proud to ask her mother to be there or maybe her grandma hated the Fancy Man so much that she would ask for nothing more than the money she was given every Saturday. Since her mother had now been gone for five weeks the money had dwindled almost to nothing, even though they had been ever so careful with it.

Right from being very little Ella had gone to school and she had liked it. Her grandma somehow knew that it made Ella happy to be there so as soon as she had been able to she had gone. The schoolmaster, Mr Hewitt, was kind. She learned to read and write and it felt really good, it made sense of things.

The books were old and torn but the letters were big and there were lots of brightly coloured pictures. Mr Hewitt was really old, maybe as old as her grandma. He spent a lot of time reading to the class and it was always something exciting so she got to the point where she didn't want him to stop reading.

Writing was more complicated but she mastered it because again he told her how well she was doing. They were all doing well. Then there was adding up and taking away. He put sums on the blackboard and the person to answer first got a sweet. Ella soon reached multiplication and that was really hard.

Her grandma took to her bed. Ella hadn't known that having an upstairs could be so difficult. She knew that people wanted more rooms but now she was going up and down the steep stairs so very often and it was a trek.

It was particularly hard because her grandma was filling the po under her bed with a kind of enthusiasm so that Ella had difficulty getting it down the stairs without spilling it. Also her grandmother's guts gave out so very often that the whole place stank and Ella had to clean it up. The sheets and pillows and blanket on the bed and her grandma's nightie and the po and the rug by the bed reeked so that in the end she threw it all out, it smelled so awful. Her grandma told her over again and again how sorry she was. When her grandma cried Ella would get into bed with her and say,

'It doesn't matter, Grandma, all that matters is that you are all right. Go to sleep now and in the morning Mam will come and everything will be better.'

She did ask her grandma for her mother's address. She kept on asking where she lived until her grandma got cross and pretended not to hear and then pretended not to understand. Ella got to thinking that maybe it was as she had thought, that her grandma had no idea where her mother lived.

It began to matter now that her grandma was ill and she thought she would ask her mother for the address the next time she came back. That Saturday she waited by the back lane once again and looked up the unmade street all day but her mother didn't come. Her grandma wouldn't have the doctor or any help. By the time that Saturday had come round again Ella was really worried because she had nobody to ask what to do. Her grandma didn't like the neighbours and nobody spoke to her. Ella had the feeling it was because of her and her mother but whatever it was there was nobody about and there was still no sign of Ella's mother.

They lived in Consett and the ironworks ruled the town, so her grandma said. If the works ruled the town and everybody lived there, where was her mother? Did her stepfather not work at the ironworks where everybody worked?

For a long time Ella had thought that her father must be the man who didn't want her but it wasn't true. Somehow her father had never existed and the man her mother was now married to was somebody else. She found that very difficult to understand.

She no longer had time to go to school but she didn't like not to tell Mr Hewitt. Also she had to pay to go to school and now as never before they needed every penny they could get. She felt awful because she had the feeling that Mr Hewitt needed the money too. He wore shabby clothes and there was a Mrs Hewitt and probably children, though they must be tiny because they did not come to school.

She felt grieved about the whole thing. Surely her mother and the Fancy Man should be taking care of her grandma and Ella's schooling. On the Friday she went early before the other children arrived and Mr Hewitt smiled at her. He just nodded when she said that she could not come any more because her grandma was poorly and they had nobody to look after them. He said he was sorry. What else was there to say?

Ella managed. She had long watched her grandma clean the house and for the last two years or more had helped her so that she knew how to scrub the floor, wash the pots, keep the fire going so that the water she put into the boiler would heat. If she kept the fire going they could put pans and a kettle over it and the oven grew hot and her grandmother made wonderful Yorkshire puddings from that oven every Sunday. She had learned to do that as well but they were not as good as her grandma's. Her grandma said that people only cooked well when they did it with love and this was not love, it was desperation.

She did the washing and hung out the clothes and she polished the horse brasses which her grandma cared for so much.

She began to worry about money so much she couldn't sleep. They had very little left even though she had eked it out like her grandma had taught her. The next day she bought potatoes and carrots and butter and yeast. She had flour so they could have soup and bread and that would be good so she was quite satisfied when she got back. She called up the stairs but there was no answer and she wished she had not shouted because maybe her grandma was asleep.

She got the flour out and she put the yeast to rise and then she trod up the stairs to see whether her grandma wanted a cup of tea. The curtains were still closed in the bedroom so she drew them back and spoke to her grandma, who must be very tired indeed because she didn't move.

Ella spoke again and touched her but still her grandma did not move and then she was frightened. The old lady did not stir so in the end she ran next door for Gert, their neighbour.

Grandma did not speak to Gert but this was an emergency so Ella dashed across the yard and Gert's door was open. Their doors were almost always open because the big fires made so much heat that except in bad weather it became too hot in the kitchen.

Gert came carefully to the door, several children trailing behind her. Her grandma always said that Gert bred like a rabbit and she had said it in some disgust, but Gert was always nice to Ella if they met in the yard or in the street.

'There's something wrong with my grandma,' Ella gasped out.

Gert picked up the smallest child, told one of them inside to see to the others – Ella presumed she could not afford to send them to school because Ella hadn't seen any of them there – and then they trod back across the yard. Ella made her way up the stairs. Gert came quickly after her, took one glance at the old lady and then looked at Ella in a kind way.

'Oh, hinny, she's dead.'

Ella gazed at her grandma.

'She can't be.'

'She is, love. I'm sorry.'

The baby that Gert was carrying began to scream and Gert said that she would have to go and feed her so off she went, saying,

'Your mother is due isn't she, tomorrow?'

Ella wished somehow that her grandma had gone straight to heaven and it was all over. But since it was not she didn't know what to do.

She couldn't go upstairs where her grandma was dead so she let the fire die down, but then she couldn't sleep because of how cold it became.

On Saturday she waited and waited. It was almost teatime when she made herself accept that her mother would not come and she went slowly back into the house.

On the Sunday, unable to bear it any longer, she went and banged on the doctor's door. He lived on the main street among the workers, and visitors seemed to be welcome all the time. It was opened quickly now and a small maid looked enquiringly at her.

'Is Dr Waters in, please?'

'He's at church,' the maid said.

'Well, when he comes back could you ask him to come and

see us? My grandma is very bad and dying. My name is Ella McFadden and we live at number ten, Back Railway Street.'

There was nothing to do but go home. Ella couldn't bear to be in the house. She sat outside on her swing and waited for the doctor to arrive.

It was a very long time before he came. He hesitated when he saw her. She took him inside. There was a distinct smell of what she knew by then was dead Grandma, but the doctor didn't flinch. He went across to the bed and looked at her.

'My mam usually comes on a Saturday,' Ella explained although it had turned into a lie. 'I thought it best to wait for her.'

'Can you go to your mother?' he said.

'I don't know where she lives.'

The doctor nodded as though he knew how things were.

'Right, well. Have you anybody else to go to, any more family?'

Ella shook her head.

'Gert next door has a lot of children, she can't take me in.'

'You had better come along with me.'

'What will happen to Grandma?'

'She will have to be buried.'

Ella was afraid. She had the horrible thought that the doctor would take her to the workhouse. People had been known to kill themselves rather than go in there so she lingered. The doctor strode out and did not stop until he reached the door of his house and he went in by the front way though there was no surgery on Sundays. Here he paused.

'Come along then, Ella,' he said so she followed him into his house.

She didn't know what to think. Was he given to taking children into his house when their grandmothers died? If so he would soon have no more space.

Mrs Waters came bustling through and Dr Waters said,

'Ella has come to stay with us,' as though it happened every day. 'Her grandma has died and she has nowhere to go.'

'Oh dear,' Mrs Waters said. 'You poor child. Come in and sit down.'

Ella was surprised at all this. The doctor went out again.

'He always has so much to do,' Mrs Waters said, as though Ella was an adult, and then Charlotte came into the dining room and she said,

'Hello, Ella. Sorry about your grandma.'

Ella was astonished. They had never spoken before and now she started to think that maybe it was her fault because Charlotte Waters was so kind. She smiled at Ella and offered cake.

'Thank you but I don't think I can eat it.'

'You must be so upset,' Mrs Waters said. She gave Ella tea in a pretty cup with a saucer. It was red and white with gold around the rim and Ella admired it a great deal before she actually drank the tea. Then she was hungry and Mrs Waters offered her dinner which they had had a couple of hours ago and would reheat.

She made Ella sit at the table and she was given a big plateful of beef with vegetables and gravy and even Yorkshire pudding. Ella demolished the lot and then a large piece of plum crumble with a small ocean of custard around it. She was after that very tired. She hadn't slept well since her grandma had died and so she fell asleep by the fire and was left to her dreams.

In the early evening the doctor came back and he sat down beside her on the settee as she came round. He told her that they had taken her grandma from the house and that she would be buried.

'Would you like to see her?'

Ella considered.

'No,' she said finally, 'I don't think so.'

'Father Abraham has promised a funeral but you don't have to go unless you really want to.'

'I don't think I do but I think my mother should know.'

'We will sort that out.'

'You'll be able to find her?'

'I'm sure we will.'

She stared at him. He could find her mother while all this time she hadn't known where her mother lived? But then it was nothing to do with him or with anybody else. Would she get to see her mother? Would she get to go and live with her mother? What about the Fancy Man? He had never wanted her.

In the meantime the doctor had to go back out again. She had not known that doctors were so busy, even on Sundays. Mrs Waters played the piano. Ella had never heard music before in somebody's house and was entranced. Charlotte smiled at her as they sat by the fire and listened. It was the most pleasant evening that Ella could remember and then she remembered that her Grandma was dead. It had always been the two of them, her mother dropping by on Saturdays. Now she was beginning to realize that those days would never come again.

She wanted to panic and run out but she couldn't do that. The music was soothing and the fire was warm.

'It must be awful without your grandma,' Charlotte said and Ella was amazed that Charlotte knew she was hurting.

'My mother died when I was little,' Charlotte said.

'I thought—'

'This is my father's second wife. She's very nice but . . . she isn't my mother and she has such different ideas than my mother had.'

Mrs Waters, seemingly oblivious, played on. Ella didn't like to say that Mrs Waters was lovely but then she hadn't known Charlotte's mother and perhaps there were in the world mothers who were even better than Mrs Waters.

When they went to bed Charlotte said,

'You are to sleep with me. You won't mind?'

'No,' was all Ella could manage though she thought it strange. She had only ever slept with her grandma.

The bedroom was so pretty, all done out in pink and white, and there were two beds in it. Ella had a bed to herself and there was also a white nightgown which had been laid on the bed for her. She felt shy but Charlotte left her alone to undress and when they were both in their beds with a candle between them she was so pleased to have a girl of her own age to talk to.

'Do you think that we might become friends?' Charlotte said into the almost darkness.

'I don't know what will happen to me now.'

'Can't you stay here?'

'I don't suppose so.'

'That's a shame. When I think I would have liked to know you all this time but I didn't know what to say.'

'Neither did I.'

'Tell me about your grandma. I never had one. Both of mine died long since, I don't seem to have anybody except my father.'

So Ella talked about her grandma and it made Charlotte giggle. All the wicked things her grandma said and how kind she was and how she made lovely Yorkshire puddings and custard tarts. She even told Charlotte how her mother would come on Saturdays but how she had not come for a long time now and so she didn't know Grandma had died.

'She would have come, I'm sure she would, if she had known,' Charlotte said and it occurred to Ella that Charlotte was the kind of person who always said the right thing. She felt healed that Charlotte had wanted her to talk about her grandma. To talk about her meant that she was not far away, that part of her would always live in Ella's heart, and she did not miss her so very much when she could talk about her.

Ella went to sleep when Charlotte blew out the candle and said goodnight. She felt so comforted, so tired and so sure that her dreams would not trouble her and that when she awoke in the morning she would be back in the little house which she shared with her grandma and it would be Saturday and her mother would be coming to visit and she would be out there in the back lane watching and waiting for her and everything would be all right again.

Three

'You aren't supposed to call me "Neddy",' seven-year-old Edward Waverley objected to his sister Julia.

'I don't see why not.'

'Because it makes me sound like a donkey.'

Julia thought for a moment and then she said,

'Isn't that Noddy?' and they both subsided into giggles.

They weren't supposed to be up there in the schoolroom together. Ned could never understand why it was called the schoolroom because he did his lessons in a comfortable down-stairs room next to the library with a big fire while Julia was left up here with a nursery maid. He hadn't realized for a long time that Betty was a nursery maid and nothing more until he saw that he was being taught stuff and Julia wasn't.

He had moved out of the nursery a long time ago and had a big bedroom on the floor below, but Julia still slept there with the room next door full of toys long since discarded.

Neither of them liked the schoolroom, it was almost a different world from the rest of the house, an area half forgotten. Julia, being used to it, he presumed, didn't seem to notice that the fire was kept low even on the coldest day and there were no books.

The rooms were both gloomy, being at the side of the house with trees all around. Ned had tried to open the windows in summer but they had been painted shut. There was no decent furniture, just a rickety desk and chair attached, and next door just a small single bed with a cupboard for Julia's clothes, and few they were. Big Fat Betty, as they privately thought of her, slept in the room next to Julia's bedroom on the other side. Ned hadn't been in there so he didn't know what it was like. Julia took all her meals on a tray in the nursery, sitting at the desk. Betty took her meals downstairs with the other staff so Julia ate by herself. Ned didn't understand why.

He knew that his sister was different. She could be very funny, it was one of the things he liked best about her. They had been born on the same day but although he knew that people born of the same mother on the same day were said to be twins it was always pointed out to them that they were nothing alike.

But they knew that they were alike in all kinds of different ways. Julia knew when he was thinking of her and the other way round. They liked being together better than anything in the world, though Ned knew that it was being deliberately arranged that they should spend as little time together as their parents would allow.

His schoolroom was called the study. It was very like the library and all the walls were crammed with books. They weren't the kind of books you read, at least he wasn't allowed to. According to Thomas Blake, his tutor, most of them were in German. Ned thought that was daft. He wasn't allowed to say the word 'daft'. His world was full of words he was allowed to say and words he wasn't.

'Why are all the books in German when we speak English?' Ned asked.

'I don't know.'

'Can I learn German?'

'It wouldn't be so bad if you could understand English,' Mr Blake said with a sigh, and though it was funny in some ways rather than daft, Ned knew what he meant.

Even though Mr Blake was a very nice young man, at least Ned had overheard his mother say so, learning was boring. He came from the village of Rothbury in Northumberland. His uncle had been a schoolmaster and given him a good education because his father was poor and he had a big family, Mr Blake had told Ned.

Everything that happened without Julia was boring and since ninety per cent of his time was spent away from her there wasn't much help for any of it.

It was, he thought as he got older, a very strange life that they led. They lived in the same house as their parents but rarely saw them. There were lots of servants to look after the house but despite this, or perhaps because of it, it seemed to Ned that things were badly done because there was nobody to say 'Have you done this?' or 'What happened to that?'

If it wasn't your job and you didn't do it, it got left. So if Evan, the boy who was meant to see to the fires, didn't see to them the fires were left to go out. And they were left out, since for some stupid reason it seemed to have nothing to do with anybody else. Julia, being at the top of the house, fared badly and often had no fire. When Ned spoke to Evan about it the boy just looked sullenly in front of him and nothing more was done.

Also, although Ned caught glimpses of the dining room when the servants were going in and out laying the table and bringing food in or taking it away, neither he nor Julia was allowed in there. He and Mr Blake had their meals in a little room just off the kitchen, which was good in some ways – the food was always hot – but it had just a small table and two chairs, nothing more.

Very often there were lots of adults staying and in the hunting season the men and some of the ladies went hunting. The ladies who didn't hunt sat over the fire in his mother's sitting room, another room he was rarely allowed into. Sometimes he caught sight of the dining table full of elaborate dishes and he might observe the ladies when they came down to dinner having changed after hunting. They wore dresses which glittered, their hair shone with sapphires, rubies and emeralds, and they sounded so gay, so happy.

His mother was the most beautiful of them all and she wore the Darling diamonds. These stones had been in the family for as long as anyone could remember. His father had sometimes said that they should be locked up in the bank but then his mother would never get to wear them. There was a necklace with at least a dozen stones, drop earrings and a bracelet which shone when his mother moved her wrist.

Another thing Ned noticed as he got older was that his sister grew thinner and thinner so that he said to Betty, on a rare day when he had ventured as far as the nursery and could find no evidence of food or drink,

'Has Julia not had her tea?' Betty, putting her chins in a way that he couldn't like, and looking hard at Julia, said,

'Of course she has, haven't you, Miss Julia?'

Julia just stared as though she didn't understand, which was more than possible, so he squared up to Betty and said,

'No, she hasn't.'

'How do you know? I've cleared away.'

'Don't mess around with me, Betty. I will go and tell the master and you will be dismissed.'

'Please yourself,' Betty said and walked into her room where he dared not follow her.

Ned therefore barged into the kitchen. His temper was, Mr Blake said, his worst fault but he was too angry to care. He was not meant to go there either, another blasted place with no room for them. It was full of people because there was some kind of dinner that night and there would be several courses if the place was anything to judge by, piles of pots and pans, heat and various smells, sweet and savoury. One maid was chopping up something green on a big wooden board, there were various dead birds which he tried not to look at, especially since at that point one woman was vigorously chopping the head off what looked like a chicken, and various other people kept appearing from the dairy and the back rooms where the pots were washed and the back doors were open to take away some of the heat. He found the cook peering at something on the stove.

'Has Julia had her tea?' he asked.

The cook ignored him.

'Mrs Fennel?'

She went on ignoring him so when he tugged hard at her skirt she turned around, looked appalled and said,

'Master Ned, get out of here.'

'Julia hasn't had her tea.'

'I've got sixteen people to feed tonight, come out of the way before I tell the mistress you was in here asking daft questions.'

'Why can't she eat with Mr Blake and me? Wouldn't that be easier?'

'It's nowt to do with me, it's the mistress commands here.' And she bustled away and he could see nothing more of her, she disappeared amongst the steam and among others who were chopping and stirring and arranging stuff on plates. So Ned took hold of a big plate which was on its own and a bottle of something and he left, one of the maids shouting after him,

'You can't take that!'

He went straight up the stairs and into the schoolroom and put down the plate and the bottle on the desk. Julia stared at it.

'What is it?'

'I don't know. Something to eat.'

Julia went on staring at it.

'I thought you were hungry.'

She glanced at him.

'No,' she said tentatively.

Betty was hiding in her bedroom. Ned picked up one of the round bits of toasted bread with something on it and he ate it. Julia watched him.

'Is it all right?' she ventured.

'It tastes like meat paste only better. Have one.'

Julia didn't like to eat white things but the bread was toasted dark so hopefully she wouldn't notice. She didn't really like new things either but if he could just persuade her to try one she might fancy another.

She nibbled a tiny bit, wrinkled her nose and then ate it. Ned opened the bottle. It was fizzy like the pop they sometimes got if Mr Blake had been to the village shop.

They ended up eating the whole plateful of food and drinking most of the bottle of pop and then they fell asleep on Julia's bed.

Ned came round to hear Betty screeching,

'Master Ned, what have you done?' so that he got quickly out of there, taking with him the huge oval plate and the empty bottle.

*

Having thought about Julia being stuck up there in the cold with nothing to eat and no lessons, Ned decided to go and talk to his father. He had never done such a thing before but he didn't see how he could do anything else so he decided to be bold. His father also had a study. For some reason it was known as the office. He went and banged on the door and when he heard his father's voice he went inside.

He was afraid of his father. It was not that his father hurt them, he would never beat anyone or anything. No animal was ever put in any distress, except of course for foxes. Foxes were vermin apparently. Ned thought there was something very wrong about people who chased small animals and then saw them torn into pieces but no adults shared his view as far as he could tell.

His father had never even spoken sharply to him but, considering that they met infrequently, this was hardly surprising. He noted that his father seemed taken aback to see him, as he well might be.

His father sat behind the huge oak desk where he was busy with some papers. It was known, Ned was aware and proud of it, that his father was seen as a good master and a good man – just and fair. Nobody on his land ever went hungry or did not see a doctor when they had need of one. The houses were sound, warm and tight; the animals had good shelter. Ned, aware of all this, still found that he disliked this man. He didn't want to but somehow he couldn't help the feeling and it was nothing to do with how his father looked because he was a fine man, tall and lean and elegant, well dressed, dark-eyed.

He sat back in his chair and almost smiled.

'Well, Ned, what can I do for you?'

Ned might have been encouraged but he knew his father too

well for that. He was not going to run away, he felt as though he had stood enough.

'I am concerned for Julia,' he said.

His father frowned.

'And why is that?'

His voice was cold and not encouraging but Ned ploughed forward.

'She never has an adequate fire, she doesn't have enough to eat, she has no books and there is nobody to teach her.' His father said nothing for so long that Ned was afraid but he didn't care, he went on looking straight at his father until his father met his eyes.

'I doubt she needs books,' was all his father said.

'Why is that?' Being given nothing but this to pick up on, Ned made the best of it.

'She will never read.' His father looked down, at what Ned was unsure but he did.

'Why not?'

'She is backward.'

'Backward?'

His father caught his gaze again and Ned did not forget the coldness and disillusionment in his father's dark eyes.

'Your sister is an imbecile. You might as well know it.'

Ned was even more furious at this casual announcement. He had known his twin was different but to have this put into such cruel words was so awful for him that he could barely breathe for a few seconds. Then he said,

'So because she is different she needs no fire, no food, no comfort?'

'She has everything she needs.'

'No, she doesn't. Have you been up to the nursery recently?'

'You forget yourself.'

'Do I?'

Ned thought his father would shout. He had forgotten that when his father was angry he softened his voice because he knew he was so powerful here that everybody was beneath his touch. Ned hated him for it now. He hadn't felt hate before, it was odd but very satisfying. He had somebody to blame for Julia's neglect.

'I'm sorry, Edward,' his father said, 'she will never learn to read or write. She will never make progress or become an adult. You do understand?'

Ned thought about it and made himself breathe carefully and then he said,

'And so she is condemned to cold rooms and not enough food and no joy?'

'Betty sees to her.'

'Betty does nothing of the kind.'

'You go too far.'

Ned didn't answer. He felt ice form around his heart. He understood now why things were as they were. He and Julia were never held, they were never beaten, they were never in company, and his parents were ashamed of how Julia was. Could it have been her fault? He didn't see that it could be. His parents cared that he should have a tutor and do well but they tried to pretend that Julia was not there.

He wanted to get out of the room but his lips quivered and the tears dismayed his eyes and it was not for himself – as least he hoped not – it was for the small girl upstairs who was his only care. He loved her as he knew he would never love again.

He said nothing more. He could have asked for permission to visit her but then it would have put the whole matter up for refusal so he didn't. He said,

'I didn't mean to offend you, sir.' This was what Mr Blake had told him to say and he could tell that his father was easily appeased. His father nodded and after that Ned despised him as never before; he thought the man weak and stupid.

Four

Back at the foundling school, as spring turned into summer, things were better in some ways. A spell of fine weather ensured that Jay got the roof on the new building, which would be three-storeyed. There would be dormitories for the children on the top two floors and a small clinic and dispensing room on the ground floor for Mr Gray, who was the doctor here and in Wolsingham, and the several nurses he had recruited, along with rooms which would serve as dining room, kitchen and living space.

Jay was planning a big field around it so that the children would have plenty of places to play. He wanted formal games for them, cricket, football and rounders. He also wanted to add another large room at the back of the building for indoor activities. So the work was going well.

Maddy was very pleased. Mrs Pinner was not doing so well. She came to the school and complained about the two girls she had taken in. She had brought them with her and they sat outside the room while she went into Maddy's office.

'They upset my lads with their airs and graces. They will eat this and they won't eat that and the bigger one is always showing her knickers to the world. It's disgraceful, that's what it is. She keeps sticking out her tongue at me, there's gratitude for you.'

Maddy had no choice but to take the girls into an already crowded dormitory. Alice, the smaller child, had some kind of problem and was always throwing up food and Sarah, the older girl, was sullen and silent. Maddy could hardly blame either of them. Their father had drunk himself to death and their mother had had to give them up because she had six other children and couldn't afford to feed or keep control of them.

Hilary tried to give Alice different food but she had no way of knowing what the child could keep down until Abigail suggested that maybe goat's milk might help if Alice could be persuaded to drink it.

'I don't like it, it tastes funny,' the child complained.

Hilary was running out of patience by then – she had tried milk puddings, different kinds of tisanes and teas. She gave Alice mint but the child spat it out.

Mr Nattrass had been experimenting with cheese. He gave the little girl goat's cheese and she liked it so they were thankful and the poor girl lived on goat's cheese and bread.

Sarah kept running away back to her mother who lived in Sunniside, which was only about a mile away. Her mother kept bringing her back, the girl crying and somewhat bruised, but nobody said anything. Her mother could not afford to keep her and that was that. Maddy had tried to leave the child there, offering help to her mother, but once she had been inside the house she had changed her mind. There was one room up and one down and the children, who didn't seem to go to school, were huddled by a tiny fire. The place was filthy and the mother didn't even meet her eyes.

Maddy would have asked if the children could come to school – she envisaged clean clothes, decent food and at least the rudiments of education – but she could see that it would never happen. The woman was heavily pregnant and her husband had been dead a year so God knew who the father was.

She wished that she could somehow include the little village of Sunniside in her ventures but it was impractical. She told herself that you could not save the whole world, even this small world here. She had enough to do but she felt guilty and tired and frustrated at the awful lives that people lived. No doubt one day long since that woman had been a young girl hopeful of a better life, and here she was weighed down by poverty and too many children and unable to get herself out of it even with what help Maddy could offer.

One day Maddy would look for somebody in Sunniside, or for somebody who could go there and set up some small kind of school at least, but with no money to do this and unable to spare anybody she pushed it to the back of her mind. If she managed Sunniside then she had Crook and Willington and soon the whole world and nobody could hold that much together, she knew it.

Sarah wouldn't go to lessons, she barely ate and at night she would get up and wander about outside until Maddy thought that she would fall over something in the darkness and be badly hurt.

Hilary had taken Abigail and some workmen to sort out Mr Nattrass's house so that boys could live there. Hilary and Abigail scrubbed the rooms and the workmen mended broken windows and doors and made sure everything was sound against the weather and then they moved in furniture.

Miss Proud, Jay's housekeeper, had a cousin who lived in West Gate but who could come and lodge with Mr Nattrass. No woman could lodge there by herself but she had a friend who happened to be losing her house. This friend had a small child so it was a very useful arrangement for everyone, as she could work and keep her child. The farm itself was pretty, being set into the hillside halfway down, and was a long house with various barns and byres. It had an exquisite outlook across the fells.

Mr Nattrass was to teach the older boys farming but they would also come to school two days a week. Maddy would have crossed her fingers had she not been a nun, so she asked God in her prayers if he could help because she was unsure it would work. The boys clamoured to be there, not just the older ones; they all seemed to love milking and mucking out and collecting eggs. Everybody loved Mr Nattrass's dogs who looked after the sheep but were pets too.

Miss Proud's cousin, Vera Plass, and her friend Irene were a big help, putting three meals a day in front of the boys, keeping the place clean and making sure that nobody felt lonely or left out and Miss Proud reported to Maddy that it had been an excellent idea. Jay hoped in time that some of the older lads would be taken on at other farms to provide them with a home and an income.

Hilary taught the girls to cook and bake, Abigail helped them to sew and make clothes and they all had general lessons. When they came to leave Maddy wanted them to have skills which would give them the kind of work in the world which was pleasurable as well as useful and necessary, not an easy thing to manage.

The nuns had so much to do these days that there was not sufficient time to do everything and Maddy found this frustrating. They did get together four times a day for prayer but she became impatient and wished it gone so that she could get back to more practical things. Her mind would wander and yet without the prayer, without the quiet moments, none of the rest meant anything. She had to tell herself this, that the quietness of their small chapel and the moments of singing or praying were a necessary part of each day. Without it none of them would be here and they would have no purpose. She was inclined to excuse herself to God but it was no good and so when things got too much she would find herself on her knees by the altar, emptying her mind and not asking for more when she already had so much.

Their little chapel was always open and she knew that if Hilary or Abigail was missing they too could be found in quiet prayer to get them through the day or the night or a particular problem. Prayer could not be allowed to lapse because if it did everything crumbled around the nuns.

She knew also that Hilary, having been brought up in the country, needed time to breathe beyond the village. Abigail, having been brought up in the town, was happy there. She had been lifted from a life of poverty and was joyous remembering how lucky she was to be there, to have good food, a bed and friends and the children. She rarely ventured beyond the village and took herself into the quiet chapel when she needed more space.

Maddy could see another problem arising, though she was not sure it would come to anything. She had the feeling that Mr Nattrass had done what here was called 'taking a shine' to somebody and he had taken a shine to Sister Hilary. It was hardly surprising, Maddy thought, because they were in one another's company a good deal, but while she had no doubt Hilary would make an excellent wife for Mr Nattrass she selfishly did not want to lose somebody who was such a good nun and had so many skills. She looked carefully at Hilary and didn't see that Hilary was aware of Mr Nattrass except in a general way, but when Maddy went to bed at night it bothered her.

*

Mr Nattrass had never been in love. He had thought it was a stupid idea until he met Sister Hilary. He was a typical countryman of the area, sparely built but very strong, wiry, that was what they called it. He had nobody after his mother died and he had begun helping at the foundling school.

It had seemed ridiculous to him that he should learn to love not just a woman well past her girlhood, but a woman who was taller than him and as strong as him, and a nun at that. He was ashamed of himself but he couldn't hide it. He longed to be with her and so when it was suggested to him by Mr Gilbraith that he should do a lot more with the children and have plenty of help, he was glad. Mr Gilbraith would pay generously and the farm would become another school. Mr Nattrass enjoyed teaching the children all the skills he had always taken for granted, like shooting and fishing and milking and helping animals give birth. He could shear sheep and teach his dogs to round up sheep but best of all he was known as a good farmer who never neglected an animal or let a piece of land go to waste.

Everything of his bore fruit and now his thoughts had turned to love. At night he envisioned Sister Hilary as his wife, having his children, being there for him so that they could run both the farm and the farming school together, but he dared not broach the subject.

He had to give the project with the two women and the boys time, and be glad that he was getting to spend a lot more time with the woman he loved.

It was untrue that Hilary was unaware of Mr Nattrass but she hid her feelings because she thought she was being false to her role in life. She had taken that on with gratitude when it had become clear there was no place for her at home and she wanted to be faithful to it when it had done so much for her. God had called her and she had replied. Mr Nattrass was just a man, she told herself. The trouble was that he was the kind of man she had always liked, a countryman. They talked about the animals, they talked about land and crops and fishing and shooting. She loved his whole way of life but she determined that she would keep on with the place God had so kindly given her. She would and could manage her feelings, she would come about, she felt sure. It was a passing whimsy, nothing more.

Five

For some reason, which was not explained to her, Ella could not stay with the doctor. She assumed, though nobody said anything, that they had not been able to find her mother. She was a nuisance, she was a problem to be solved, so after two days she was taken by the doctor to a house on the edge of the town. It was quite a nice house really, nothing like the small place on the back street where she and her grandma had lived.

It was a stone terrace and had a tiny garden and four stone steps up to the front door. The doctor knocked smartly on the door and when a woman opened it he said, as though Ella was a parcel,

'Here we are,' and off he went. Ella tried to look forward instead of back but it was not an easy thing to do.

'Well, howay in then,' the woman said.

It was gloomy in the hall. Halls were new to Ella. The doctor's hall, which she could not help comparing to this, was much wider and bigger and it was full of light because somebody clever had made little windows at the tops of the doors which led off into various rooms. She longed for Charlotte and the way of life she had known so briefly.

The woman led her into the back of the house where there was a tiny kitchen.

'You can wash these pots,' she said and she poured hot water from the kettle into the sink, threw washing soda after it and gave Ella a cloth.

This was easy, Ella had done such things for a long time now for her grandma and she longed to tell this woman about how her grandma had died and she had been left. After the pots were done she was set to scrubbing floors and all day after that she worked without a break. Nobody spoke to her, the woman did nothing but bark orders, until the early evening and then she was ushered into the front room, the woman saying to her,

'This is Mrs Henderson who was kind enough to give you a home here. She is a widow and has nobody and she is the lady of the house so you must call her "Ma'am" and be very respectful towards her.'

It was just as dark as the hall, there were curtains no more than half open and it smelled of old lady. Ella knew that smell, it reminded her of her grandma but it was not the same. It was mixed with other smells, soot and as though the room had not been cleaned and crumbs and dust had lain there undisturbed for a long time. There was, too, an odd smell of some kind of medicine so she decided that the old lady was ill. Large bottles in a variety of colours stood on a table at some distance.

'Come where I can see you,' the old lady said and Ella went around to the front of her.

'You're not very big, are you?' the old lady said. 'They told me you would be able to work for me and read to me. You can read, can't you?'

Ella nodded.

'Well, speak up, child.'

'I'm hungry.'

'There will be tea shortly. Sit down over there.'

Ella sat and then she was required to read chapters of the Bible. She knew the Bible reasonably well, having gone to school and church, but it was really boring and the old lady nodded off straight away and snored.

Every time Ella stopped the old lady woke up again so she was glad when the tea came. The woman from the kitchen brought it in and the tray held several different kinds of cake and sandwiches and it smelled very good.

Ella was ushered into the kitchen, given a slice of bread and butter and then was required to clean brasses and bring in coal. It was not until she was quite worn out that she was shown into a bedroom at the top of the house, three storeys up, where there was one iron bed. It creaked when she sat on it and was the most uncomfortable bed she had so far experienced. She huddled there beneath a blanket, trying not to remember how lovely the doctor's house had been, how she had been spoken to nicely, had good things to eat and how Mrs Waters had played the piano and she and Charlotte had talked before going to sleep.

Six

On the evening after Ned had gone to his father about Julia, his father got to thinking about it as he sat by the drawing room window which looked out over the sea. The beaches there, he believed, were the best in the world. Few people were ever on them and here beyond the city, the shipyards and the mining towns, there was no industry other than fishing as you reached this part of the Northumbrian coast.

The sand was golden and the tide washed up and down in such a reassuring way that it made Edmund Waverley feel so much better. He had been born in London but here he felt was his true home. He had long since been advised to spend as much time as he could there because his health was not good and the sea air was the best it could be, according to his doctor. He liked to take his wife to London for the season and to visit various friends throughout the year but he didn't think it did him any good. He became tired and coughed a great deal, and was always best resting at home, though he knew she grew bored faster than anyone he had ever known.

His wife, Jessica, whom he loved more than anyone in the world, came over to him as he pondered by the window. It was late and they were about to drink their coffee, having finished dinner some time since.

It had been a big dinner with several guests, some who were staying over, but now it was quiet, everybody having either gone home or to bed. He liked opening up his house to other people but he also liked the late evenings when there was just the two of them.

Had it been warmer he would have opened the windows to hear the waves. In summer he liked walking the dogs down there when it was late and every evening if he could he liked to watch the sun going down.

It being spring the sun rose late and sank early so sometimes he did not manage to see either and it was a form of distress to him, at least it had been of late. He was getting older, he thought, and such things had come to matter.

Summer sometimes did not arrive here, and there would be rain and wind all season. He loved the place dearly but thought that if he had been born in Italy his health would have been better.

Jessica touched his shoulder from behind and he turned to smile at her.

'Aren't you feeling well, Edmund?' she asked.

He had been what the doctor called a little under the weather lately and got short of breath and coughed more than usual. Cook recommended warm water, which took away the pain and shortness of breath.

'You're troubled,' his wife said.

'Edward came to me today asking why his sister was so badly treated. I didn't think we treated her badly.'

His wife came around and looked into his face.

'Our children both have huge advantages, especially Julia.' She looked down at this point and he knew that even now she was ashamed at having given birth to an idiot child. It did not help that Julia was beautiful. She looked like a fairy child, slender, with long golden hair, wide blue eyes and flawless skin. She looked just like her mother, whereas Ned was tall and dark like his father but also blue-eyed. Sharp eyes, they were, his father recalled uncomfortably; he had had to meet that all-seeing gaze from across his own oak desk earlier that day.

'She must stay out of sight,' Jessica said, faltering at having to talk about this, he knew. 'I cannot bear that people will point and stare and perhaps even laugh at us behind their hands. I wish more than anything in the world that she had been normal.'

'It was never your fault,' Edmund said and he wondered how many hundreds of times he had said this to her. It didn't make any difference, she could not get beyond it. 'Edward was like a little old man, he was so polite. I didn't mean to tell him that his sister was mad but I suppose he had to be told sooner rather than later and he was questioning me so I felt that I had to say something.'

'I think it was probably the right thing to do,' his wife said soothingly.

They clasped hands. A lot of children would have been sent away to some kind of institution which dealt with mad people, but they had not done that, they had tried to make things work at home. Edward would go on and be a great man and Julia would stay upstairs with Betty and not be seen. It was the very best they could do for her but sometimes Edmund wished their consciences had allowed them to send her away so that they could have washed their hands of her. It was affecting Ned more now than ever before, something his father had dreaded. He felt now as if he could not win, doing his best and seemingly failing on all sides.

*

Julia felt like a maiden in a tower. She listened to Ned telling her stories and the best one of all was about the girl who let down her hair and the prince climbed up to rescue her. It was such a lovely story. But she liked them all. She even liked the one where the princess went to sleep for a hundred years, though it scared her for a few nights, thinking that if she let herself sleep she would never wake up.

She also liked the one about the princess who slept on a hundred mattresses and still felt the one pea, beneath the lowest mattress. It was most unlikely, Julia deduced: the princess would have fallen off the mattresses and ended up on the floor, regardless of any vegetables under her. Julia decided that she must talk to Ned about it, he would think that if the princess had had a turnip under her she would have felt that right enough.

Julia was the princess in the tower. She never got to go outside, or so she thought. Betty said there was nothing good outside but from her tower she could see the gardens. Then came the day when Ned told her that he was taking her downstairs and outside. Betty had remonstrated, but in the end she let them go because it was easier for her.

So Julia went into the garden and felt the sunshine on her face.

'Have I felt the sun before?' she said.

'Many times. You must remember.'

'It doesn't feel like I have,' she said. 'The flowers are pretty.'

'The weather's been awful for months so we couldn't come out until today,' he said.

She thought hard and tried to remember but since it had been so long it was like something new. Always things felt new. Each flower was a surprise and the colours were all so different, yellow and blue and white. She felt safe with Ned at her side as though he was some kind of extension of herself. She hated how he was not there at night though of late he had started creeping upstairs and into her bed and there they would lie very close, clasped together, and she thought they had been born like that, two people but one self.

She knew how he breathed. She knew when he was hurt. She remembered him having some kind of horrible disease when they were quite small and how she had thrown herself at doors trying to get to him because she thought he would die and she would be left here alone. The servants had tried to talk to her so that she would move and in the end had carried her away but she screamed and shouted and wept.

She hoped for nothing now. She had endured so much for so long. She didn't care whether she got out of the room or the windows were not opened as she liked. She didn't mind not being offered food. There was no variety of any sort, she was just left there as though it didn't matter. Was it because she was different? Was it because she was a girl? Were girls always like this? She didn't know. All she knew was that she had no variety to her days. They took on a pattern and that was all she had except when Ned came to her.

Ned was the only person who mattered to her. Betty she despised and her parents she barely knew and the other servants did not come near, though she knew they were around because Betty talked to them. Often she went downstairs and was gone for hours. Julia had heard Betty say that her charge was difficult and how hard it was being stuck up there with an idiot day in and day out, which of course she was, and how she never got to see her mother or her sisters.

So there was nobody and her parents didn't seem to notice anything for a long time. They didn't even know that Ned had begun to sleep in her bed every night. She and Ned talked and left the curtains open and looked out at the stars. They saw the way that the hill beyond the window went down and then up, and how there was the seashore beyond. Sometimes, when the weather was mild as it soon became, they would climb down the backstairs when it was late and go down to the sea and they would take off their shoes and dance in the waves.

The North Sea was cold even in July, Ned said, when it had had all spring and early summer to warm up, and they would squeal from putting their toes into the sand where it sucked at their feet. But it was home, it was theirs, it was the very best that things could ever be.

They would never leave this place, it was the most important thing of all, that they should stay and live here which was their inheritance. The family had lived there for thousands of years, at least they hoped it was that long, or hundreds, as Ned would say when he was feeling like he should speak what he thought to be the truth, but Julia hoped it was not.

The truth held so little, the room upstairs was what mattered to them away from the noise of the parties, the laughter, the glittering dresses and the music and dancing. She had ventured to the top of the stairs and seen it all and had known that it would never be hers.

More and more often now Ned would sit there beside her, gazing through the bannisters and they would watch the glint of glasses on trays and the servants offering drinks and silver platters and the ladies who were dancing who had dresses like gossamer.

'It is "gossamer", isn't it Ned?' Julia would say, 'like the fairies' wings in stories. Have I got the right word?'

'That's it,' he said, 'like cobwebs in the morning with rain on them.'

'They never last.'

'No, well, I suppose neither does the dancing or the people or the night.'

But the night lasted for them because, when the music stilled and the people began to break up their party, the two children went back to the nursery and Betty was always what Ned had discovered was called 'spark out'. Not even bothering to close her bedroom door, she would lie like a great dead fish across her bed.

'Does she drink?' Julia said, remembering he had thought so.

'Beer.'

Julia choked.

'But she'll be pissing her pants all night,' she said and he said,

'Let's hope so,' and they went off to the bed which was Julia's only luxury and they lay there and watched the stars. Betty would have closed the curtains but Julia hated the idea of being shut up so Betty had ceased to do this long since, though she did say that it was indecent.

'The stars move, you know,' he said.

'Oh, don't. I can't bear that everything moves. I want the moon and the stars to stay still for me. Just for a little time. Just for now.'

So even though he had discovered that the moon and the stars moved around all the time he told her that they did not and nobody in the heavens would change it. And so he listened to her go to sleep. He liked to hear her breathing so that she was free from this world that was so unfriendly towards her.

Seven

Sister Hilary had not been to see Mr Nattrass for several weeks after everything had been put into proper working order. She did not like to admit to herself that she missed the sight of him. She did go to the farmhouse but he was out helping the boys or the animals, usually both, and she was inside with the women. She was pleased that her project was doing so well. It was nice to think that she had been the first one to mention it and was glad that the others had helped her to bring it into fruition.

The women who ran the place, Mrs Plass and her friend, were very good, it was spotless. Maddy had sent help because there were ten boys staying there now who they needed to feed, clothe and keep right and it took a lot of doing. Two rooms had been given up for them, with five beds in each. The farmhouse was still big, the barns and byres on the end having long since become part of the house, with new byres and barns built just further along. Hilary was glad of Mr Nattrass's dad for his vision; he'd built as much as he could afford to just a few years before he had died. It was making things so much easier for the foundling school, now that boys had a place.

At the moment they went back to the school for lessons but Hilary was hoping that the teachers might go to them, it was much easier moving two people than moving all the boys. And because so many of them had never had a home she wanted consistency for them, a place they did not have to leave until they grew a great deal older.

Every time Maddy and Jay ventured into something new there were problems, she thought, forgetting to remind herself how much they had already achieved. Jay had what they called vision and, Hilary thought, that essential ingredient, money, but Maddy had the practical ideas. These things together made progress not just possible but gave them the drive to move forward. Jay looked at the bigger picture, Maddy was good at detail and things like how light came into the buildings, how they were situated. Lately Jay had been taking more land to build bigger houses. He wanted each house to have a garden as well as a yard because, after lodging, food was the first essential and a lot of these men were natural gardeners. Perhaps two generations since they had been country dwellers and had worked on farms.

Hilary longed to go shooting, it had been her only pleasure, but there was so much to do that she barely got to speak to Mr Nattrass and she really missed him. She pushed down the feeling. Without his help they would have had much bigger problems – other than Jay he had been the most important person they had met here and she was truly thankful. She had been a farmer's daughter, she thought, and that was difficult to shake off.

She felt as if she had taken charge of the farm project and therefore should spend a lot of time there. Thankfully she had too much else to do and so she was always fretting now, trying to do the work of two people and never being satisfied with what she was doing.

Mr Nattrass had good help, she knew, but she was the person who pulled the whole thing together. Every time she went there he had questions and Mrs Plass and her friend had problems, and the children also had to be dealt with, but in some ways Hilary thought it was the best project they had thought of this far and she was quite proud of it. The boys seemed happy, nobody complained or cried or said he would be glad to be elsewhere. It occurred to Hilary that Mr Nattrass would have been a good parent and she was of the opinion that few men made good parents. It did not come naturally to them as she believed it often did with women.

The farm buildings were so pretty and some had been extended into rooms for the boys to work and eat in. Mr Nattrass had one room where he had tables and benches and lots of paper, ink and coloured pencils so that soon the walls were covered in pictures of the animals the boys saw day to day on the farm. Dobber and Bonny, his two sheepdogs, figured hugely here but also there were sheep and hens and rabbits and pheasants, and the pheasants were given wonderfully colourful bodies. There were also pencil sketches and when Hilary asked Mr Nattrass blushed and said that he had done these. It was the first time he had ever done such a thing and Hilary told him that she thought they were very good and that it might be nice for a lot of the children to join in with these sessions. Art was something that was not often made time for with children, but Mr Nattrass was doing well here. The boys were largely unsupervised, he said, but nobody threw ink or attacked anybody else's painting, they all joined in. It was a kind of release for them – some of them had been city lads and had never seen a rabbit or a hen before they came here.

Eight

Ella was there with the old lady for what felt like a very long time, the days dragging past. She had very little to eat and became more and more tired while the woman in the kitchen was always telling her what to do. Ella almost ran away but she had nowhere to go to. The doctor had not wanted her so she could not go there, and she knew that somebody would now be in the house where she and her grandma had lived.

No matter how much she tried, and how much she did, she was never thanked, or given a little time to herself. She lived on bread and a scraping of butter and yet Mrs Henderson did not seem to understand that Ella was even a person, never mind a child who was lonely, and there seemed no way in which Ella could say anything for fear that she might end up on the streets. Ella was required to read to her several hours a day and all the rest of the time to work hard in the house. She was cold at night even though the summer was arriving. She hated it. The kitchen woman began screeching at her so that the evening came when Ella thought that she could not do worse beyond these walls, she would find something else. She lay down to sleep and slept better than she had since arriving here. Her decision made, she would go in the morning.

The following morning her mother turned up. Ella wanted

to cry out and go to her and was astonished that she had been found so easily. Her mother was very polite to Mrs Henderson and Ella went with her as everybody somehow expected her to.

Her mother didn't speak, she walked very quickly away from the house and through the town. She didn't say anything.

'I haven't got my things from my grandma's house, I thought I might have had my books and clothes and the horse brasses,' Ella pointed out.

'Nothing would make me go back there,' her mother said.

Ella couldn't think of a reply to that and then her mother stopped and she said,

'Do you know what you've done? He had to pay for my mother's funeral. Can you imagine that? Can you imagine the problems that causes for us? And for us to have the doctor at the back door and for him to explain what had happened? She's always caused problems. Your grandfather left because she treated him so badly and called him names. Bill wouldn't go where she was and he wasn't happy about me going. She was a nasty difficult woman. I don't know how your grandfather put up with her, she called him all the names under the sun. He could never do right. None of us could ever do right for her.'

Her mother walked on and there seemed to be nothing to do but follow. It was quite a long way but then it was a big town, Ella concluded.

When she got there she was amazed. It was Monday and her mother's washing was all on the line in the sunny day. Her mother must have got up really early for that. They went up the yard and in by the back door. Ella stared. She had never seen a house so clean and tidy and her mother kept saying,

'Don't touch anything. He doesn't like it.'

Ella stood in the middle of the floor. She had no idea what to do and she thought of her few books and her clothes and she wanted to say that she would go back for them but she didn't know how to get back and she had the feeling that if she protested any more her mother would put her out and have nothing to do with her, despite what Dr Waters thought. She wished she could have stayed with the Waters family. She thought of the short time she had spent with them. It was a golden world. Did Charlotte know how lucky she was?

'Do you have any books?' Ella asked, glancing around her.

Her mother made a face as though Ella had sworn.

'What on earth would we have such things for? Nobody has time to read.'

Ella did not make the obvious answer.

'If my mother had read fewer books and concentrated on her family she would have done a lot better.'

'What am I to do?'

'I don't know. It's bad enough that I have had to take you in. He won't like it.'

Ella wanted to ask whether he liked anything but she didn't. It was a long time until tea. She got nothing but a sandwich for her dinner and though her mother made something that smelled nice Ella got another sandwich and was told to go upstairs and into the back bedroom and stay there before he came home. She was terrified by then and glad to go. She closed the door of the little room and slid down and leaned against it in case he should come in and murder her.

The room was white. Ella had never seen anything like it. The walls, the bedcover were all the same colour. There was a little fireplace, empty and black, and the room was stuffy. She had nothing to do but wait and listen.

When he came in she heard him but he didn't seem loud or

difficult. His voice was soft and she thought she even heard him laugh. She could smell the dinner. It smelled lovely. She had not known that her mother was a good cook but then she knew so very little about her mother.

Eventually she went to sleep, lying there against the door.

She dreamed that her mother's house was filled with snow to match the curtains and the front step. Was that what it was about, how dirty people were, how clean they might be? Did she see her man come home and scrub him or put out a bath with hot water and towels and let him whiten his skin to where it was supposed to be? Ella didn't understand it but she had known a woman who had filled her house with rubbish until she had to sleep in the back lane so maybe it was like that, only the opposite but the same sort of thing.

There was no middle ground and she saw now why her mother did not want her there, she would clutter up the house. She was a living and breathing extra person and, just as some people didn't like cats or dogs because they weed and pooed and left their hair on the furniture, so some people thought that children did likewise, that they were too dirty to bother with.

Had her mother always thought that or had he somehow taught her and if he had how had he done it? Did he not smell good or bad? Did he not wee or poo? Did he not breathe out onions as men did, her grandma had always said. Steak and kidney pie and onions and the house stank for days. At least her grandpa had, farting and belching and then laughing. Ella thought her grandma had laughed with him because it was part of life but not for her mother.

She wished and wished that she was back in her grandma's house where she had understood what was going on. Was her mother doing this cleaning because she did not want Ella there?

It seemed a reasonable enough explanation, that her mother never had wanted her and did not want her now and the cleaning was a way of keeping Ella from belonging to the house. She thought nothing had ever hurt as much as that, not even on those awful Saturdays when her mother did not turn up and the time when her grandma had lain still and gone cold and died.

Ella awoke very early the next morning and the first thing she realized, after where she was, was that she was very hungry. She thought she might sneak downstairs before either of them was awake and steal something to eat.

The day was dark with rain and she could hear it banging against her window but it was not until she got halfway down the stairs that she knew somebody was up. There was a light burning and she thought she could smell the warmth of the fire.

She didn't know what to do but her hunger won. Surely it would be her mother, making sure everything was right for the Fancy Man. Could her mother begrudge her breakfast as she had begrudged her dinner? Ella tried not to think about it.

She made her way even more softly down the rest of the stairs and then turned into the room and the sight that met her eyes. It was him, the man she had been so scared of, the man she had imagined the size of a monster. He had his back to her but, the fire being well lit, he was stirring a pan on one of the arms which went over the fire for cooking. It was porridge, she could smell it.

She gazed at him. He was not much taller than her mother and quite wide. He wasn't fat, he was just short and heavily built, and when he turned she could not believe that he smiled, his eyes warm as he said,

'Hello, lovely. How are you?'

Ella had been warned by her grandmother about men who interfered with little girls so she hung back. Just at that point he took the porridge off the heat and put the pan down on the mat before he went into the pantry and brought forth two bowls, scooping the porridge equally into them. He then brought milk and sugar and told her to help herself.

'Wasn't some of this for my mother?' she said, feeling guilty.

'She never gets up at this hour. She spends too much time working as it is. She told me you were here and too tired to stay up to see me. How are you feeling, after your grandma died? It must have been so hard when you had lived together for such a long time.'

Ella was astonished and could do nothing but stare.

'I can understand that,' he said, taking his spoon and rolling sugar into the porridge and milk too, so that it made a lovely mess, and then he laid into it so she did the same. It tasted like heaven.

She thought he would go on and on about paying for her grandma's funeral but he said,

'It was a shame that your mam and your grandma didn't get on. I always thought it was a bad idea to keep two houses but they couldn't live together.'

Ella stared even more.

'You wanted us here?'

He looked at her.

'Keeping one house is a lot cheaper than keeping two. I had no money for beer,' and then he smiled at her and the smile reached his eyes.

They ate the rest of the porridge in silence and then he pronounced that if he stayed any longer he would be late for work and he said,

'You will wash up? Your mam will expect it,' and when she nodded he went, winking at her so that she was more confused than ever.

She took some water from the boiler and washed up the pan and the spoons and the dishes and then she went back to bed. She fell asleep, stomach now full.

It was a lot later when she woke up, the sun was high in the sky and when she got downstairs her mother was doing the washing. Ella couldn't work out why there was more washing and why it had to be done now. Most women did their washing on a Monday and their ironing on a Tuesday and so on all week, fitting in different household tasks until it was done before Sunday.

Ella had always hated washing day, the house full of steam, the line outside filled with wet clothing, the way that it had to be brought in and it kept the warmth of the fire from you because it had to go on a clothes horse and everything was damp. But this was Tuesday.

Her mother laboured without saying a word and soon the washing was outside on the line. Since it was by this time a good fine day her mother looked pleased and then she began on the house. Her grandma had never done as much as this. First her mother washed the floors, then she polished the brasses, although they seemed to Ella very bright. She went upstairs and presumably washed the floors up there and she came down with the sheets and proceeded to wash these too even though the sunshine was beginning to go.

They had nothing but a cheese sandwich at midday and then Ella was told to keep out of the way and go upstairs so she went.

Later her mother was ironing and had also put something delicious on to the stove but she said to Ella that she was to go upstairs and not come down again.

'Am I to have no dinner?' she said.

Her mother glared at her.

'He doesn't know you are here. When he does you had best watch out.'

'He does know I'm here. We had porridge this morning, at least two hours before you got up.'

Her mother paled.

'What do you mean?'

'I came downstairs and he had made porridge and he gave me half with sugar and milk and I needed it. I'd had nothing yesterday but sandwiches.'

'You think you deserve more?'

'I think everybody deserves more.'

Her mother's eyes glittered.

'You spoke to him?'

'He talked to me, he gave me porridge.'

'He doesn't want you here.'

'And do you think I want to be here? I want to be back with my grandma.'

'Yes, well, none of us chose this,' her mother said.

That night Ella stayed downstairs when he came in, her mother saying nothing more. Ella still could not get over the idea that he was not enormous and shouting. Where had she heard the shouting and who had been so tall and threatening? Was it her dad or could it have been her grandpa? Had her grandpa left because of her grandma or had he left because of his daughter or had he just died as people did? She couldn't work any of it out.

And something else which astonished her even more. He came back with a big sack and in it were her clothes and, even better, her books.

'I got the woman next door to show me what you would want,' he said. 'I took everything I could carry.' There were also the horse brasses. Ella thought that her mother, having already had some of these, would want them too but she said that she didn't.

'Can I keep them?' Ella asked.

'They'll make good money,' her mother said.

'We don't need it,' he said, 'let the lass keep them. She has a room all to herself.'

They had tea. It was egg and chips, her mother complaining that she had had no time to do better, but Ella loved it. She stuck the huge soft chips into her eggs, two of them. It was strange how he sat sideways at the table as though he was unsure he should be there, or as though he might have to go back to work. And he drank his tea from the saucer, a skill which Ella was keen to learn but she didn't like to suggest it. She wondered what he did. He didn't come back black like the pitmen did, she had seen them. He was relatively clean when he came home, pausing only to wash his hands in the pantry. They were workman's hands, rough, and the nails were uneven, but he didn't talk like a workman and he didn't sound Irish to her, though a lot of the people did.

'Where do you come from?' Ella asked, nervously.

'Don't talk with your mouth full,' her mother told her.

'I'm from the Lake District.' Ella had never heard of such a place. He told her that he had lived in a big town there and there were lots of mines and that silver had been mined there since Elizabeth's time. Ella had no idea who Elizabeth was but she didn't say so.

After tea he went back out. Her mother said that he had gone to the pub and would come back drunk so she had better go to bed so she did. She read for a long time and she heard him come back. She didn't know what it was like when men came in drunk, she thought he would shout and swear. Would he throw things? Would drink make him so that he couldn't get up the stairs? But she barely heard him come in and when he did she could almost see them sitting over the fire together. Their voices came softly through the ceiling and she blew out her candle and lay down to sleep and was almost comforted.

Nine

And so the summer arrived and it was hot and Ned asked Mr Blake if Mr Blake might teach Julia to read and write. His tutor looked uncomfortable.

'That's not part of my remit,' he said. 'Remit' was another word which Ned particularly cared for and it was always obvious from Mr Blake's language what the word meant. He had never had another tutor but he didn't think he could like a man better than he liked Mr Blake.

'Is it because she's . . . slower than I am to understand things in some ways?'

'I don't know why it is, Edward, I think it's just that boys have tutors and girls don't. Some people don't approve of education for women.'

'Do you approve of it?'

'Nobody's asked me.'

'I'm asking you now.'

Mr Blake looked clearly at him and he was smiling and that was when Ned was afraid and he knew instinctively that he was right to be afraid. When you led the life that he and his sister did you had to be afraid because things went wrong with startling regularity. He had the feeling that the last wheel was about to be pulled off the wagon, as the old song said, so that it skidded down the sun-baked dusty road beside the farm turning over and over and over until it ended up the wrong way on the beach where he saw the tide coming in and the water going all over it, washing and washing and washing.

'I'm not in a position to air my views.'

'Would my father get rid of you?'

'Dismiss me,' Mr Blake corrected him.

'And would he if he knew?'

Mr Blake took a deep breath and for the first time it occurred to Ned that his tutor wasn't very old. He was an adult of course but he wasn't old like other people were, like Betty and Cook and his parents.

They were people of another time and another country and perhaps another world and another universe and so on and so on beyond the stars but Mr Blake was real and, though he was not a child, he was sympathetic, that was the word.

He was not paid to be sympathetic but just to get Ned through whatever was meant by education. Though Ned had the feeling that education didn't necessarily have much to do with libraries filled with books which nobody could read and the way that Julia was stuck upstairs like an unwanted rat.

'Edward,' Mr Blake said after Ned had thought he was going to stand there until the cows came home, as Cook would say. He hesitated and then he stopped looking at Ned and he said, 'I will be leaving soon. My time here is finished.'

Ned stared at him and he saw that Mr Blake wasn't looking at him. Mr Blake liked him. It had not occurred to him before that his tutor liked him, he had thought that Mr Blake's manners carried him forward, but no, the man liked him. It made Ned very proud for the past and worried for the future. How would he manage without the kindest man he had known?

'I don't know what you mean.'

'You will be going away to school in September,' Mr Blake said.

Ned knew all about the idea of a world crashing around you, and his had had several wobbly turns before, but this was on a different level entirely.

He stared.

'I will be going away?'

'Of course. All boys of your age go away to school and I have to say that I think you will do very well. I know I don't say so to you but you have a very fine mind on you. You will get a great deal out of it. You will make good friends there and learn all sorts of games and there will be different masters for different subjects. You may even learn German.'

Ned knew that Mr Blake meant him to smile but he couldn't. He couldn't leave Julia. He couldn't even discuss leaving her. He would never leave, he could never leave. Here was where he was meant to be, here with her forever and ever.

That night he couldn't sleep. He took food upstairs and then couldn't eat and Julia was not slow about things like that, she was not stupid, but then she knew him so well. She was his twin and you couldn't get much closer than that.

'What is it, Ned?' she asked when the candle was blown out and he lay there, feeling like a stone had settled right in his middle and it ached.

'Nothing. Go to sleep.'

She laughed very softly, he only just heard her, and he heard her say,

'Oh Ned, you can't hide anything away, I can almost see it. I can hear it in your voice and feel it in the way your body quivers with hurt. What is it?'

He didn't want to tell her, he couldn't let go any more, she knew all these things but neither could he tell her what was wrong. She was the last person he could tell but then who could he talk to? In the end, though he didn't want to, he went into the library and ventured close to the desk. His father looked up immediately and even smiled.

'Edward,' he said, 'are you all right?' He put down the pen he had been using as though it was a welcome interruption, which was encouraging.

'No,' Ned managed.

'Oh dear, what is it?' His father frowned, and on his behalf, Ned thought.

'Mr Blake is leaving.'

'Yes, of course he is.'

'I didn't know.'

'I was going to tell you. It's not yet. I was going to ask you whether you wanted him to stay here over the summer, though he says you are doing very well in all subjects and should have no problem fitting into school. But I know that you like him and his next appointment is not yet and I think he needs the money.'

It was the longest speech that Ned had ever heard from his father so he had to test himself, to think that perhaps he had misjudged his father and his father was always friendly and helpful. Or was his father aware that he did not want to go away and was telling him as politely as possible that he had no choice?

'Can he not stay here and teach me?'

'His knowledge is limited and I think you have reached the end of his use. You will have to earn your living one day so you need to go to school, then to Oxford, and when you come home you will be grown up sufficiently to be able to achieve a great many things in your life. School is your opportunity to fit yourself for becoming a man. You never know what you might want to be and that way you have choices.'

'Did you have choices?'

'My father was poor but he made sure that I had opportunities and then I met your mother and we married.'

Ned didn't quite understand.

'Didn't you grow up here?' Ned saw that it was the wrong question to ask because his father's manner changed and he looked down and he said,

'This was your mother's family estate.'

'Did you go away to school and to . . . to Oxford?'

'No, I couldn't go to university though I did have some education. Boys like me didn't go and that's why I want the best for you and it is the best. You will make us proud of you.'

'Can Julia come with me?'

His father showed the first hint of impatience.

'Don't be silly,' he said, 'Julia can't go away to school with you.'

'We cannot be apart.'

His father so obviously didn't understand this, so Ned wished and wished that he had never said it. His father frowned.

'My father came up from very little and I had few advantages. For you it's different, you will be able to go on and do astonishing things with your life. You will go to school the first week in September. Now, do you want me to keep Mr Blake here over the summer or not?'

Ned considered. He thought of how shabby Mr Blake's clothes were. He had the feeling that his tutor had a family somewhere, perhaps he too had a sister he had had to leave and he sent money back. So although it wasn't what Ned wanted he managed to smile and thank his father and say that he would be very grateful if Mr Blake could stay for the rest of the summer and his father smiled and told him he was a good boy and would make them proud.

Ned staggered out of the room. He didn't think his father noticed.

'I'm so glad you talked to him about it. I'm already proud of him. I think he will do well.'

'He will.' Her husband kissed her and then, since they had guests staying, they went down to dinner.

It was their favourite time here, when they left London at the beginning of August they could begin to think about the hunting season which would begin in November. They both adored hunting, it was what had brought them together in the first place. Jessica had had the estate and Edmund had had the money and both families were pleased at the union. Although he was socially below her he was very rich and their estate and their daughter needed a rich man so everybody was happy.

The trouble was that she had given birth to twins. The boy had been delivered easily but the second, the girl, had been so long in coming and her mother had gone through such pain. There had been an interval during which the child did not breathe and did not cry, and her mother said for months afterwards that it would be better had she been taken.

Julia didn't walk until she was two. She rarely spoke until she was five and her eyes gazed beyond people when they spoke to her. It was a tragedy, everybody said. Jessica felt responsible and cried and cried over it until Edmund said that it was not her fault, they must be glad of their son and take care of her as best they could but not talk about her in public. She must not be seen.

The trouble was that she looked like a fairy child, she was so beautiful. Every parent wished for a daughter like that. Her hair was so fair it was almost white. Her blue eyes were like china, her skin was pale and peach-coloured and her limbs were straight and lovely.

Her voice was soft and sweet when she eventually found it, and her smile could have affected anyone. Being in her presence moved her mother to tears so often that her father had the girl sent to the nursery at the top of the house where she bothered no one. Edmund got a maid to look after her and when Jessica did not have to deal with her so very often she was better.

He thought of getting in specialists but it would have looked bad and he knew that his wife would not have been able to stand it. The girl had what she needed and the boy grew and he was perfect. His teacher said he excelled himself in every subject, he was a natural horseman, he was polite and liked all outdoor things. He was a fine shot and a good fisherman and could run in wet sand for miles without hesitating. His parents were so proud of him that it almost made up for the daughter who would not do.

Ten

Ella did not feel that she belonged with her mother and the Fancy Man, even when she had been there for a month. She had been in so many places lately and all she really wanted was to go back to live with her grandma where she had been happy for so long. Now that she had what she had longed for she found that she didn't want it, but then she had always conjured up such wonderful ideas of what life with her mother would be like. She had envisioned them all together, it had been a happy picture. She had not thought things would turn out this way though, that the choice would be made for her when her grandma died. She had loved her grandma more than all the world put together.

She had been but two days with the doctor and not long with Mrs Henderson but here she felt so out of place that all she wanted to do was run back to the little house on the dark street which was the only place she had ever known any happiness

She still thought of him as the Fancy Man. She wouldn't have risked 'Bill' or 'Mr Wilson' so she thought of him but in a good way as her grandma had called him because he was so much better than she had ever thought he would be. In a lot of ways he was a fancy man. Having imagined him loud and angry for so long, she found it difficult to keep him in the frame of what he was really like.

Every time she went to bed she thought she would wake up in the morning and he would become the person her grandma had so much hated. She wondered whether her grandma had really hated him or if it was just that he had taken her daughter away, that he paid for everything, that her daughter had left her only child with her mother and nobody was happy.

Ella tried to look at her grandmother as different, the way that her mother had to view her, as somebody who had failed because there was nobody to provide for them. Had she married the wrong man and had her daughter married just such another, so perhaps when a decent man came their way they could not accept and did not want to think that there might be good things about him?

The more Ella thought about these things the more her head ached and the more difficult everything became. After the first day or two she thought that she might be happy there but no place was made for her. Her mother even seemed to forget to sit her at the table or put down a knife and fork for her.

Sometimes she made enough dinner for just the two of them, as though she could not count past that or did not want to. Her mother was for ever saying,

'Come away out of my road,' impatiently, though Ella was not aware of being in it. She stayed out of the way as much as she could but since her mother did not allow her to go outside and would not hear of school she had no place to be.

Ella had never seen a house so clean and wondered why on earth it had to be like that. She didn't think the Fancy Man noticed. He seemed grateful for his dinner but since his wife rarely sat down to enjoy it and would take it away if Ella was not finished as soon as he was, he got himself out of the house. Ella wished she could go with him.

'It's only the pub,' her mother said, watching him put on his coat and disappear beyond the door.

Ella was there five weeks before her mother took ill. She feared illness, she thought that everybody would end up like her grandma. Her mother did not take to her bed but soldiered on, washing every day, scrubbing the floors every day, peeling the vegetables and cooking and putting water into the boiler and throwing coal on to the fire and all the other dozen things which were never done so very often as her mother did them. And then Ella thought, what if everybody went on like that and it was just that her grandma was what they called 'a slattern'? If she was it seemed to Ella that she herself could be just the same because the amount of work her mother put in was huge.

When her mother was not doing the housework she sewed and knitted, but when Ella asked to be shown how to do this, for her grandma's eyes had been too old for such things, her mother said that she had not the time.

It was when her mother was doing the washing that she began to cough. Ella thought it must be the steam from the poss tub but then she began to sneeze and her nose blocked and she looked very hot. She fought it for a couple of days more while the Fancy Man implored her to go to bed.

'I don't have time,' she wailed and he didn't contradict her. Ella thought he had learned not to. If you contradicted her mother she shouted and screamed at you so he merely ate his dinner and went out. Ella missed him, he was so little at home and she was beginning to see why.

On the third day, however, her mother could barely get out of bed. Ella crept downstairs when it was very early before the Fancy Man got up and she raked the fire which had been settled down for the night and as it began to burn she put newspapers and sticks on it. She loved how fires worked, how they came to life almost from nothing.

By the time he reached the bottom of the stairs she had the kettle boiling.

'Well, aren't you a grand little lass,' he said as she poured him a cup of tea. 'Howay and sit down.' So she poured tea for herself and put lots of sugar and milk in it as she had done for him and they sat down together at the table and she liked her mother's absence.

'Do you go to church on a Sunday?' she asked him. It was just for something to say really and church was a way of getting out of the house, though it was a work day today.

'I haven't for years. Did you want to go?'

'Can I?'

'I don't see why not.'

'Would my mam take me?'

'She doesn't like it,' he said.

Ella was shocked. Liking had nothing to do with church. You went because it was what you were supposed to do but she hadn't been in a long time because of her grandma's legs filling up with water. She had liked it when they went and she had liked going to school.

She gave him eggs for breakfast, fried until crisp which she knew he liked, with lots of brown bread dipped in the fat of the pan. Her mother made good bread. Ella made and packed his sandwiches and filled his bottle with cold sweet tea and saw him out of the door and he smiled and thanked her.

Then she went to see how her mother was and to take her a cup of tea.

Her mother didn't speak at first so that Ella thought could her legs be filling with water? Then she knew that it was silly, her mam had a cold but a bad one.

'Can I get you something to eat?' she asked. 'Would that make you feel better?'

'What on earth are you doing?' her mother asked in a gravelly voice which told Ella she had a very sore throat.

Ella by now knew better than to answer her. She left the room and then began on the housework. Later on, having been told not to go upstairs again, she went for a walk and it was the first time she had been outside since she got there. She began to wish her mother was ill more often and then she felt guilty.

Why was her mother so bad-tempered? Did she not like the Fancy Man any more? And yet he seemed nice. Did her mother like anybody? Or was it just that Ella had upset something wonderful by being there and she was not wanted? She had tried not to think this but it would not stay out of her head, that this was all her fault and they had been happy before she had come to live with them.

It was a lovely day and Ella determined not to spoil it by worrying about things she could not alter. She would take her opportunity and enjoy it. She greeted everybody with a smile and a lot of people smiled back at her so that she felt better. She had been gone only about an hour but she came back to find her mother scrubbing the floor. Ella stared.

'Where have you been?' her mother said, not stopping what she was doing.

'I'll do it.'

'You won't get it right. Come out of the road,' her mother said and so she did. She went upstairs and into her bedroom and there she read one of the three books she owned which she knew off by heart.

She stayed up there until she was hungry and by then her mother had retreated to bed, the kitchen floor presumably being clean enough to suit her.

Ella peeled vegetables and made broth and she made bread too. She was rather pleased with herself, it had been part of the life she had had with her grandma. Her grandma had shown her how to make a quick loaf with one rising. And the bread puffed up in the oven and browned. She loved the smell.

Her mother did not come back down but Ella kept waiting for her to. When she didn't Ella ate the broth and the bread while it was still warm. She lavished the bread with butter. She also made little meat pies after cooking the meat very slowly. Her grandma had prided herself on her pastry and Ella thought hers would be just as good. She scrubbed potatoes and carrots and she made the dinner for when the Fancy Man came in, pouring the gravy from the meat cooking all over the pies.

'Eh,' he said, very impressed, 'I didn't know you could do owt like this.'

'When my grandma was poorly I had to because she couldn't do it any more but she showed me and I like doing it.'

'How's your mam?'

'She came down and scrubbed the floor.'

He pulled a face though, just a bit, as if it was something which could not be altered. Ella thought he might go upstairs to see how her mother did but he merely went to the pub as ever. He came back late and was singing. It was the first time he had done that but he managed the stairs and then crashed into her mother's room. Ella lay still but everything went quiet and in the quietness she thought she could still smell the good broth and the pies she had made and she was proud of herself.

The next day her mother did not get up and Ella asked him whether she might send for the doctor.

'You can try but she won't see him.'

'Has she been poorly like this before?'

'I don't know. She doesn't like me anywhere near when she doesn't feel very well,' and off he went to work.

That day was the hardest of all. She half convinced herself that her mother would die and kept walking into the bedroom offering food and tea while her mother shouted at her.

'I'm frightened you'll die,' Ella said at last.

'I'm not your grandmother,' her mother said, 'just get out and leave me alone.'

She told herself that she must try to live up to her mother's standards since it was her house but in the end she was so tired that afternoon that she fell asleep on the old green settee which stood under the window. When the Fancy Man came in she was just waking up.

'There's no tea ready,' she said.

'Dinna worry, hinny. I'm not that hungry. Have you done all this?'

All this presumably being the ultra-clean house.

'Why don't we get the frying pan out?' he said. 'I love egg and chips.'

So they did and it was one of the best meals Ella ever had. He turned out to be as good as she was at peeling potatoes and making fried eggs and his chips were big and fat and tasted wonderful. The strangest thing happened, he didn't go to the pub, they sat over the kitchen range and drank tea and he told her about what it had been like when he was a little lad with his mam and dad in the Lake District. They had lived in the country and his dad had grown potatoes and they had a donkey. Ella could have listened to him for days.

She heard her mother's footsteps coming down the stairs as the brass rods clinked under the slight weight and when her mother got to the bottom of the stairs she peered into the room and she said,

'What a mess.'

'It isn't a mess,' he said, 'the little lass has toiled all day to make it right. There's only the washing-up to do.'

'Come away and I'll do it myself,' and when he got up and approached her she hit him really hard across the face.

Ella was horrified but even more so when he put his hands around her mother's throat. Her mother caught at her breath and whimpered, putting up thin hands to stop him, which flailed in the air as her breathing became laboured and harsh. Ella was afraid that he would kill her. She saw now why her mother had not wanted her here.

When he let go and took his coat from the peg behind the door and slammed out, her mother fell to the well-washed floor.

Ella dared not approach her. She tiptoed out of the room and went to bed as soon as her mother was revived and Ella knew that he had not killed her. She lay there and shook. She couldn't stop the shaking. Ella knew now that she couldn't stay here, her mother and the Fancy Man were waging some kind of war and she did not want to live in the middle of it. There had to be a better way than this. She knew now that she had been happy with her grandma.

This was the very opposite. She would live in fear that the Fancy Man would kill her mother, that her mother would drive him to it with her ways and her lack of love for anything but her clean house.

In the morning Ella got up and took with her the little she had and left. She had no idea where she was going, she had stolen a little money out of the big jug which lived on the mantelpiece and she went. Nobody was up. She hadn't heard the Fancy Man come in. Maybe he would not come back. Maybe he would come back late and kill her mother but as far as she knew he had not come home at all. Her mother had coughed all night and presumably she could not sleep because of it. Ella thought her mother's throat had been bad before now but it certainly would be covered in big bruises from the impact of his hands, almost choking her.

She didn't know whether to be pleased that he had not come back because she didn't know what would happen then or if he'd be glad that she was leaving. She didn't know where to go. She certainly had nowhere to go here, nobody to help her, nobody wanted her. She imagined herself dead and her mother being sorry and the Fancy Man being sorry. That would learn them, as her grandmother would say.

Eleven

It was August when Sister Hilary at the foundling school for girls up on the tops of Durham had a letter from her sister. She and her sister did not get on. This was partly to do with the fact that Hilary had never married, and partly to do with the fact that her sister had married a man with money and no breeding, and had all kinds to do with the fact that Hilary had never had a suitor, had long since given in and become a nun and her sister had taken over the family estate, which Hilary had loved so much, and her sister and brother-in-law had altered it to suit themselves and the twins who were born to them.

Hilary rarely went back these days. Her sister appeared to have everything – a handsome rich husband, a daughter and a son, lots of money, a wonderful social life – and also she had something which Hilary, tall and well built, had never had. Her sister was dainty and pretty and could smile the sun into the sky.

Hilary tried not to envy her, which she knew was a sin, but she liked being away from the Northumberland farm which had become an estate somehow with added farms and acres and now was huge. Hilary hated how it had been altered, she hated going there and seeing how her childhood was lost. Her parents died and she went back then and even the few days there convinced her that she had no place. So she went back to Newcastle and then to the Durham fells and was grateful for them.

And then a letter from her sister arrived.

My dear Hilary,

I hope this finds you well. I am writing to ask whether you will take Julia into your school. Edward is to go away to school this September and Julia will therefore be left alone. I am hoping to secure some kind of education for her. I am sure you are aware that she is a most unusual child. (yes, if unusual meant mentally subnormal, Hilary thought, having seen Julia on a number of occasions by then. Though Julia's parents pretended she was normal, at least when Hilary was there. She was in the nursery because she was very young was the silent agreement.)

We will of course be happy to pay for this (I should think so, Hilary thought) *and I hope to hear from you soon.*

Yours affectionately,

Jessica

Hilary made her way along to Maddy's office. The door was always open. Maddy heard her and looked up at once. Hilary still had the letter in her hand.

'That bad, eh? Close the door,' Maddy said.

When that was done they both sat back in their chairs and Hilary handed the letter to Maddy and waited while she read it.

'Oh,' she said and Hilary appreciated that 'oh'.

'Yes,' she said.

'Well of course we will take her.'

'I don't think we should.'

'Why not?'

'Because she isn't normal.'

'What's normal?'

'Oh, come on,' Hilary said. 'The only person who ever heard her speak before she was five was her brother. He is going to one of these ghastly places boys go to so that they can never relate to womenkind again and this poor wretch will be left with no one and she will be in the way so we are asked to take her.'

'Might not that be a better idea?'

'I don't know.' Hilary got up and wandered about the room. It wasn't a big room so she didn't have far to go but it looked out over a tiny garden and it was a good place in which to think, but she couldn't think at the moment, all she could say was, 'I don't want to impose my family on you.'

'Oh Hilary, as though you would,' Maddy said and she smiled.

'We don't have the room,' Hilary protested.

'The new building is almost ready, they are putting in the windows today and the doors and the inside is coming along really well. The floors are down and all the rooms divided up so I think two or three more weeks and it will be usable and what a relief that will be for all of us. I worry, you know.'

'I know.' Hilary sat down heavily. 'If children keep coming and coming like this because they are having a bad time, wherever will we put them all?'

'Sarah Smith ran away again this morning. I'm tired of having to send somebody to fetch her, her mother has given up and the men don't have time to waste away from their work.'

'But Alice is better,' Hilary said, 'she can manage eggs and potatoes. It has become my ambition to try and get a vegetable down that child so that she doesn't throw it back up the next second.'

'Write and tell your sister that we will be happy to have Julia.'

'As long as she pays,' Hilary said.

Hilary went off back to the kitchen. It was *her* kitchen, her favourite place. She loved how people ate three times a day, she loved to fill them up and make them feel good and how it was a constant. She didn't have to go where she didn't trust anyone but now her peace was shattered.

She had seen Julia, she was so beautiful, almost of another world somehow. She would find no happiness here, Hilary was convinced. What child would want to be away from its natural environment, never mind one who was not normal. Hilary veered between wishing her sister had not asked her to do such a thing and feeling that she ought to help.

She could not get beyond the sense that, since Julia would be alone when her brother went away and since Hilary disliked her brother-in-law and thought her sister self-absorbed, she must take this child. Sister Maddy was right, they should take her but there were so many children who had nothing. To think that a child who should have been given everything was now being cast out and for money and lack of love was so awful. She had never liked her sister but she had not despised her before now.

She was not a mother but she felt that having given birth, as difficult as it was, the gift was so great that she didn't understand why her sister wouldn't want the child. But she knew nothing of such things and so she replied when she and Maddy had talked it over and said that they would be glad to take in the girl if she would be willing to come there.

Hilary knew, of course, that the boy was favoured but then boys mostly were and since the children were twins and Julia was strange to some extent she had been hidden away, as though they were ashamed of her. It was not going to be an easy thing to do, partly because Hilary didn't get on with her sister or brother-in-law and partly because she had not met a backward child she would have to take on and had no idea how to treat Julia.

Twelve

To Ned's joy, early in the summer, his parents went away to stay with friends to the south. His mother was always talking about the south as though it was a better place. She talked about how much warmer it was and how she had gone there as a girl to friends and how nicely everybody spoke and how there was no cruel north wind and never any snow. His mother loved summer in other places. Ned had not thought until now that he could make use of this and do what he liked.

He had not seen before then – maybe he had been too little to see it – that if there were sides to be on, the servants were definitely on his side.

Having seen the parents off with great ceremony and a lot of fuss, since his mother seemed to want to take her entire summer wardrobe, it was as if the whole place gave a sigh of relief.

Julia now came downstairs and spent her days there. Ned tried to get Mr Blake to teach her but he found himself becoming impatient because Julia could not equate the words on the page with her mind in any way. Neither could she write. She couldn't work out why one and one made two but, when Mr Blake recited poetry to them, she remembered it, and though the poems Mr Blake read to them were very long, she could recite every single word once she had heard it, though

Ned wasn't convinced she would find recitation terribly helpful with anything.

He had also found that there were certain kinds of food which she would not eat and, since these included anything white, this ruled out sandwiches, chicken breast – not so difficult because he liked chicken – and mashed potatoes. She liked all the things he didn't like: broccoli but not cauliflower, carrots in butter were her favourite. Eggs had white outsides so she would eat omelettes.

The weather was hot and they spent the days on the beach. Mr Blake showed them how to play cricket but, though Ned asked him privately what rugby was, he had no idea and had only played football. Ned found out that his mother lived in Rothbury and they were very poor. His father had been a clergyman and had died, leaving his poor widow with nine children.

The servants also decided to have a holiday and they ate and drank and sat about in the gardens and Cook relaxed the meals so that they were informal. She would not have Ned and Julia eating with them in the kitchen but, if it was wet, they would sit in the little dining room, watching the rain pour down into the gardens. The fire was always lit and Ned and Mr Blake had big discussions about the world and Julia listened intently to all that was said. And she remembered all this too. Ned was so pleased at this that he forgot about going away. He let himself believe that it would always be like this, that his parents would never come home and that he and Julia would always be together.

His parents came back at the end of August and the day after this Ned found a trunk open in his room with two of the maids dealing with his belongings. In it there were a great number of clothes. He knew because he had been measured for them. His father had been there – he had been enthusiastic and told him how well he would do. There were socks and blazers and sports kits and things like rugger boots, which he had never seen before and which frightened him, and a great many other things. The trunk filled up and his heart gave out. Did they not understand that if he could not stay here he would die?

He said nothing to Julia and, although he was aware that she suspected treachery, he couldn't actually say it. He was to go away on the fifth of September. Mr Blake had been there all summer and, as if aware of the fact that Ned had kept him on, he became a companion to both children and would take them outside and talk to them and read to them and recite poetry, since Ned had requested it and since Julia apparently loved it.

Mr Blake thought that Julia would have loved anything that Ned suggested but it didn't matter. Mr Blake had a very fine voice and so the poetry flowed as the tide flowed that summer and to make things worse it was fine and dry. They spent most of it on the beach and Cook gave them a hamper to take with them and, as if she knew it was their last summer, she put into that hamper all manner of fine things. There was cold chicken with good brown bread and thick yellow butter, and cheese which the local cheese-maker made, almost orange, and with that dates from the glasshouses on the estate and some drink which Mr Blake was pleased about, which was pink and fizzy.

He let them taste it but neither of them liked it because it was sour. Mr Blake laughed a lot at this and he said it had come from France and was very special. Also Cook made pies for Julia, somehow knowing that she would eat them because they were brown. Cheese and bacon and egg open-topped pies. Ned had never tasted anything half as good.

The sand was warm and the sea was as warm as it would ever get there and when the icy bubbles reached their toes they would run back to Mr Blake, screaming and laughing. Ned told himself that it would be like this forever and he would hear his sister screaming in delight and laughing on that beach and Mr Blake would ever be there, for them to run on the beach towards, such as no parent ever was.

The summer went by so quickly it was like a flash to Ned and then the tutor had to go off to his next pupil and Ned had to say goodbye to him. He had not imagined how hard it would be. He could not look into Mr Blake's face but he knew that he had done all he could for his tutor and that his tutor had done all he could for Ned so he looked up and thanked the man. As the train left the station he watched, long after it had gone out of sight. He had the feeling that things would never be as simple again.

He asked his father whether it was a long journey to the school and his father said it would take all day and therefore they must set off very early. His father was going with him. His mother cried at the idea of him going away but Ned knew that they were crocodile tears. Had she wanted him there with her as usual he knew that it could have been arranged but also he saw that his father would not give in. He was determined that things would be as he had decided and nothing would change his mind.

It was not until the day before they went that Ned decided to tell Julia. She listened carefully to him but so obviously did not understand. Julia lived in the moment. She didn't care about yesterday, she had no idea how to plan for tomorrow. It was in some ways a very nice way to live but his parents would have said that it would get her nowhere. Nowhere would have been a very good place to be right now, Ned thought. He explained very carefully that he was going away in the morning and would not be back until Christmas but Julia only said would he be back that night and when he said no, he would not be back for four months, she couldn't work out what a month was.

In the morning he felt as though his heart was so heavy that it would clunk out of his mouth. In his own room he dressed in the new and very strange-looking clothes. They were purple and brown and grey and quite disgusting. His blazer was too big and the sleeves almost covered his hands.

He had to wear short trousers and a stupid cap. Julia was upstairs, apparently fine and playing with a doll, but when he went up to say goodbye she did not speak to him. He wasn't sure whether this was because he was going away and she understood the parting, or because she was so upset that she could no longer say anything.

She did not look at him, she went on pretending that the doll was running in and out of the waves and that Mr Blake was in the background and she began reciting the poem that she had loved best. It was 'The Eve of St Agnes' by John Keats. She remembered every line.

She was in the middle of it when Ned could stand no more. He ran away, down the stairs to the front door. His trunk had been loaded up into the carriage. He was urged in by his father and they set off. His mother would not come to see him off, she said that she couldn't bear it. She could of course bear hardly ever seeing him but that was not the point.

His father was excited. He had never been to a school like this and said it was one of the best schools in the north east. His father said he was pleased to be able to give him such wonderful opportunities. Ned couldn't speak, he felt sick, and at one point they had to stop the carriage for him to go and retch into a hedgeback. His father became brisk and told him to stop his nonsense and come along so he did.

It was the longest day of Ned's life. They arrived in the city of Durham in the middle of the afternoon and he was obliged to get out. The ground came up to meet him and the next thing he knew he was sitting on the road and his father was bending over him and saying,

'Come along, my lad,' so Ned got up and followed his trunk inside. He thought he had never seen such a dismal place. Everything looked grey, a clutch of buildings seemed to huddle together. There were lots of what looked like fields, only very well kept, and further up a hill there was what looked like a small church. Ned could see a much bigger grey church and lots of streets running into one another.

He was scared. There were a lot of boys walking about and talking together. He wished he could run back to his home.

Betty had left that summer so there was no nobody to be there with Julia after Ned went to school. By the end of that day Cook became worried when Julia did not go downstairs. At one time she had considered Julia her mother's problem but she had come to understand that her mistress did not see the problem. So in the evening after the day that Edward had gone she went upstairs. Julia was lying on the bed in the last of the evening light.

'Miss Julia? Would you like to come down and have some broth? I made it yesterday and it is at its best.'

Julia did not respond and, clasping her doll to her, turned away. Cook offered to bring up the soup for her but Julia did not move and in the end Cook was so worried that she went downstairs and into the mistress's sitting room and there she said,

'I think we might have the doctor to Miss Julia. She isn't well.'

'I'm sure it's nothing to worry about,' her mistress said. 'She's probably sulking over Edward leaving. She's just trying to draw attention to herself. She will be gone by the end of the week.'

'Gone?'

'Oh yes, my sister is coming to collect her on Friday. She will be going to a school which the nuns have.'

Cook was appalled. She couldn't think why rich folk had children at all. They never seemed to want them or see them and they sent them away. What a very strange thing to do to people you were meant to love.

Thirteen

Ella hated leaving almost as much as being there but all she could think of was the way that the Fancy Man had put his hands around her mother's throat. She had to get out of there. She had to find somewhere better but by now all she could think of was her grandmother dying, leaving the doctor's and how badly she had been treated at Mrs Henderson's house. Would nobody ever want her? Was this what it would always be like?

She knew that Durham City was about thirteen miles from here, which sounded an awfully long way, and what would she do when she got there? She knew nobody, she had never been out of Consett, she didn't even know which road would lead her where. She knew also that if she went the opposite way the road eventually led to Scotland and that didn't sound like a decent prospect either. But there was a third way out. She had no idea where that led so she took that and soon regretted it. It was nothing but hills and she was not used to walking a long way.

She dreamed of her mother finding that she had gone and being distraught about it, but then her mother hadn't wanted her there, had made it obvious that she didn't care and also Ella had the feeling that her mother did not want the Fancy Man liking anybody else. She was like somebody trying to grab a toy from her. Ella remembered Gert's children fighting over such things.

The Fancy Man was hers and nobody else should have him and he must like nobody else. So it could be that her mother was pleased she had gone away and would not care or try to find her.

The Fancy Man had been very kind to her but she was nothing to him, could be nothing when he and her mother fought like that, when their lives were so horrible that anything new made them want to kill one another. Ella had the feeling that she had made things worse and that maybe it was the first time he had done such a thing but she wasn't sure. She knew now that somebody else in their house could never be thought of as anything more than a nuisance, somebody unwanted, and nobody else could be there where they were having this awful life. Nobody else could do anything about it and maybe they couldn't either.

It was a very nasty thought, Ella felt sure, and she had come to understand that nasty thoughts were usually right. She didn't make much progress that day, it took her all her time to find her way out of Consett and she was tired with not having done that sort of exercise before. It rained most of the day so she stopped and sheltered in shop doorways, reluctant even to leave. Several times she reconsidered, thinking that she must go back, there was nothing else for her, but she just couldn't make herself.

The rain got even worse. Ella was right on the edge of town by then and there was a farm with a white notice saying 'Berry Edge Farm' so she took shelter in one of the buildings, ate and drank what she had and finally fell asleep. She stayed there overnight, she didn't hear anybody or see anybody so she thought she was as safe as could be – though she had the feeling that nowhere was entirely safe for her. It was such a dispiriting thought that it made her cry.

*

The next morning Bill was contrite. He told Lydia how sorry he was. She didn't tell him she was sorry, she just pretended nothing had happened. He went off to work and they didn't talk about it. She ignored the way that Ella didn't come downstairs for breakfast. She tried not to think about her and then she felt guilty. They had behaved so badly, more badly than ever before because, although they did fight, it was not generally like that.

Lydia wanted to blame Ella for the fight, she didn't like that he liked the child and she knew how mean that was but she couldn't help it. She had never had anybody of her own before. She had always kept her mother and Ella away from him, she could not manage them all together, she could not live in a house where they were, where Ella and her mother would get in her way. He was all hers, he had to be all hers, and yet she was ashamed that they had fought like that and in the end she made her way up the stairs and opened the door of Ella's room.

It was empty. It had never looked so empty. Even before Ella had come to them the room had not been so quiet, so still. Lydia tried to think about it. They had frightened her and it was hardly surprising and this was what she had not wanted. She had never wanted the child and now this. She felt resentful against Ella, she was glad she had gone, it was good riddance to bad rubbish.

She closed the door again, assuring herself that Ella would come back. The girl had just taken a huff about what had happened. She had nowhere to go and rain was beginning to fall. It got heavier and heavier.

Lydia would have nowhere to hang out the clothes she had been planning to wash that day so she set to scrubbing the floors and polishing the surfaces. By the time Bill came home she had turned out the cupboards and made bread and cakes and broth with ham and pease pudding. He would have nothing to complain about at all.

They barely spoke. Nobody apologized. He washed his hands and face and they sat down to eat. It was only then that he said,

'Where's the bairn?'

She couldn't look at him, she had been dreading this moment. 'I don't know.'

He stared at her and now between them the food was forgotten and went uneaten.

'She hasn't been in all day. She'll come back when she's hungry.'

'Did you see her go out?'

'No.'

'Or hear her?'

She shook her head. They sat there. Bill managed half a cup of tea, she couldn't even get liquid down her, until finally he said hoarsely,

'She's run away because of the way we went on.'

'She can't have. She's got nowhere to go. Eat your tea. She'll be back before it gets dark.'

He glanced out of the window at the rain.

'It's never stopped all day. If she's out in this she'll catch her death.'

The day grew darker and darker until finally Lydia went into the pantry and started to cry. Bill followed her in there.

'We did it,' she said, 'now what?'

'I'll go and look for her.'

'There's no point in this.'

'First thing in the morning. I'll talk to the boss and see if I can have the day off.'

'There are so many places she could have gone.'

'I'll go back to where your mother lived first, she'll likely have gone there, and then I'll go and see the doctor and the priest. She can't have got very far, not in this.'

Ella found the farm a good place to stay. After her first night's rest the sun came out and she ventured to the back door and when she knocked on it an old lady came and opened it. Her face was tiny and wrinkled.

'Now, my love?' she said.

'I wondered if I might have a slice of bread and butter? I have nothing to eat.'

'Oh dear,' the old lady said, and Ella thought how very different she was from Mrs Henderson.

'Where have you come from?'

'The other side of Consett.'

'All on your own?'

'I'm on the way – I'm following the road because I have an auntie who lives up on the hill and she has said she will take me in if I can find the way. She isn't very well and has nobody to send for me and it's a lot further than I thought it was,' Ella managed.

The old woman ushered her in and there was a step down, a dark hall and then a little kitchen off to the left which was lovely and warm. An old man was sitting sideways at the table. It reminded her of how Bill sat and she wanted to cry. Bill had been so kind to her but he was a . . . a violent man, that was what they called it. He wasn't a nice person at all, her grandma had been right. The old man stared at her but he said nothing when she was told to sit down and then she was given a big plateful of bacon and eggs. She was amazed.

'I was just about to have mine, you have that, lassie, and I'll make some more,' the old woman said.

Ella wanted to be polite and refuse but she was too hungry. The old woman ladled thick white bread covered in bacon fat on to her plate and gave her a huge mug of tea. Ella ate and drank and the sun came out in the yard beyond the window and she could see various red and brown hens foraging among the cobbles and over the way were various barns, including the one she had slept in.

The couple didn't seem to think that she should move on. The old man offered to show her the pigs and the hen house and how the cows were milked. He took her down to the river and showed her the cows which had names and then he introduced her to his collie dog, Mary. Mary lived by the back door and wouldn't come inside even when it snowed. He had tried to get her in but she wouldn't have it.

Everything went well for a week and Ella was just starting to think that things were improving when she saw a middle-aged man come into the house. The old lady explained that he was their son and he had apparently been away buying stock, whatever that meant. He scowled at her and when they were by themselves in the kitchen together he said,

'You have no right to be here, bleedin' off old folk. You get yourself away. And don't come back. If I see you again you'll have big trouble.'

Ella was so scared that even when they offered to have her stay for a few more days she couldn't, she was too afraid of him. And so when they went to bed, she left the little back room she could have fallen in love with and set off into the night. It was cold but not raining and all she could do was walk.

She walked until she could walk no further but by then she could see that she was now on the top of the fell and she thought she could see some kind of houses. She had no idea what to do, she just had to keep on going, so as soon as she had slept as best she could in the cold she set off again.

When she came to she could feel hot doggie breath on her and a man's soft voice.

'Come away, Dobber, there's a good lad. Now then, little lass, what are you doing here?'

Ella did not think any man would be kind to her now but she looked up in to the man's face and tried not to cry.

'Can you walk, hinny?'

She got quickly to her feet, saying that yes, of course she could.

'Are you going some place in particular?' he asked as they went along, though it was slow going since Ella's feet were hurting, her shoes were almost worn out and she could feel the road beneath her feet.

'I just need to get away,' she said.

'Aye, I know what you mean,' he said and then Ella found herself stumbling until she hurt her foot and fell and then he picked her up and carried her the rest of the way.

She kept saying she would be all right, she was so afraid of what might happen, but his voice was reassuring. When he put her down it was at the entrance to a very big house and she saw the door being opened by a nun, a tiny nun, but that made her feel better. Things could not be that bad when a nun greeted you at the door, she knew.

'Oh, poor lass,' the nun said, in an accent that Ella had not heard before – she had a sing-song quality to her voice which Ella liked. She liked even better that the nun led her into a little room and took off her shoes and socks and then bathed her feet in warm water and put some sort of thick cool stuff on her feet and then big socks.

The man and the dog came with them so that Ella wondered whether they lived here and he explained he had found her and the nun told him how good he was and the dog sat by Ella while she had her feet dressed. Ella liked the way that the dog licked her hands as though it was doing its part.

'You must keep off your feet until we get you some new shoes,' the nun said.

'I'll see to that,' the man said.

'Thank you, Mr Nattrass, what would we do without you?'

'When is Sister Hilary back?'

'Today, we hope. She is bringing her niece with her. We thought you might come and greet them. Hilary will be so pleased to see you and the girl will need the kind of care that only Dobber and Bonny can give.'

Mr Nattrass looked very pleased at this, Ella thought, and she imagined that he cared for his dogs very much, which made him especially nice.

Ella was only sorry when the dog and the man went away.

The nun didn't ask her anything but went out for a few minutes and then came back with sweet tea and an egg sandwich. Ella tried to eat slowly in case it was all she would be given but the nun assured her that there was plenty of food.

'Did you get lost?' the nun asked when Ella had eaten.

'No, my mam doesn't want me and the Fancy Man doesn't really either and they had a fight and I got frightened so I couldn't stop there any longer. I don't know where I'm going.'

'There's no need for you to go any further. We are here to help folk like you, especially little lasses. This is a school for orphaned girls.'

'I'm not orphaned. I lived with my grandma until not long since but I can't find anywhere now that my mam won't have me.'

'It's all right, my pet, you don't have to worry. Nobody will hurt you here. That was Mr Nattrass who found you, he's a grand lad, kind as they come.'

Ella blinked. She didn't think she had heard of a man being called a grand lad before but she liked it. She wanted to cry now that she was safe – or at least she felt safe. The feeling continued. She was given a clean bed in a room with several other girls but nobody was nasty to her and nobody made her feel left out either. She had meals and she liked it when she first went into the classroom. She had always liked school and the lessons were lovely. She was proud to display how good she was at reading and writing and adding up. The nun who took the classes, Sister Madeline, praised her and said what a clever girl she was and Ella hadn't been praised since her grandma had died.

That night she thought long about her grandma. They were very kind but she badly wanted to go back to her old life where her grandma was and everything had been all right. Things would never be all right again. She hadn't known how happy she was until she was unhappy and now she thought that feeling might never lift.

Fourteen

'Two hundred pounds,' Hilary had said when she reached home to collect Julia.

She had been loath to go and had to make herself, and it must have been obvious because Mr Nattrass told her that he was worried about the idea of her going all that way by herself.

How kind of him, she thought, to care. She had taken to blushing when he was around. In vain did she tell herself that it was nonsensical. She told herself that it was worse than that, Mr Nattrass was what was known as a catch in the area. Many a woman had looked at him and seen what she liked, and thought of the farm and the pretty land around it. He would never think of Hilary in that way. She regretted how large and energetic she was. If she had been vulnerable it might have been easier, and yet she did not want to display vulnerability, much as she would have liked his company.

She must stay at least overnight and a man's presence would complicate things. When she was around Mr Nattrass she could not help looking at him and liking what she saw and wondering what it felt like when he put his arms around a woman. Jealously now, she watched when other women were there and hoped that he didn't like any of them more than he liked her. She wished she was at the farm and she wondered whether the two women there, Mrs Plass and her friend, were attractive to him. She had lost her mind, her faith and her body. The whole thing was silly.

'I don't think you ought go all that way by yourself,' he had said, looking hard at her and smiling into her eyes so that she could not help smiling back and telling him that she would be fine. In the end she had managed to dissuade him but he'd looked so worried that she'd been pleased.

After setting off she spent most of the journey thinking about him and it was only when she reached home that she understood her feelings for this place had changed. It still hurt that she did not belong here but her mind was moving on and giving her images of Dobber and Bonny and Mr Nattrass's strong brown arms. It was not hers and probably never would be, she told herself.

She tried to pretend this wasn't home, that she had never lived there, while her mind gave her how it had been in the old days before her sister married and they got rich. It had been nothing but a lovely farm then and she had been involved in all of it. Jessica had not liked animals or the barns and byres. She wouldn't even ride a pony – that at least had altered, Hilary thought, since her sister now spent a lot of time riding to hounds.

Even the house itself had been changed so that she barely recognized it. There were endless rooms, sweeping stairs, lots of servants she didn't know and not a cat or a dog near the house. She tried to put this from her mind. It was not her home any more, it didn't look anything like her home, and when she found her sister, sitting in the drawing room in a dress the like of which Hilary had never seen – it was silk and full – and wearing beautiful jewels, with her hair done and her face made-up, Hilary barely recognized the woman she had known. But they had never got on so did any of it matter now?

Her sister stared at her.

'Two hundred pounds a year to look after a small child?'

'It isn't that,' Hilary said calmly, 'it's to help the poor children who would have been taken on at the school if we hadn't had to have Julia there and we are building another house for the school which costs a great deal of money.'

'You make her sound like a burden.'

'And isn't she?'

'Of course not. Children go away to school all the time. Edward has gone to a very reputable school. He is clever, of course, whereas nobody could call Julia clever.'

Hilary was dumbstruck when she saw the child who was contained at the top of the house. Hilary was horrified. This room had been her and Jessica's nursery and schoolroom but it hadn't been like this. There was no fire, there was no light, there were no toys, no books. She wondered what had happened to the rocking horse she had so much liked. There was hardly any furniture. Did this child sleep here at the top of the house all by herself? It was darkly shadowed and the trees which overhung near the windows made Hilary feel uncomfortable.

Why had her brother-in-law not had the trees cut back? He seemed so keen on changing everything, why not these? The branches were like fingers as they tapped at the windows, and since it was autumn and had been very wet the leaves clung dark and sodden, drooping and about to fall when the next icy blast came from the sea. You couldn't see the sea from there, something Hilary had always missed, and because the room lay at the back of the house there were other buildings which kept out the light.

There were empty shelves where her books had lived. The room next door, which had been her sister's bedroom, was completely empty and another room where the nursery maid had slept was also vacant. It was as though nobody considered this child a person at all, she did not matter, she was like an outdoor cat, a stable animal, and all she needed was somewhere to exist. Julia was unmoving, she clasped to her a doll and her face was so white you could almost see through it. Hilary spoke to her but nothing happened. Hilary touched her on the arm and then she moved. She gazed at Hilary and then she screamed. She screamed and screamed and screamed.

Hilary watched her. She had never heard anything like it. She tried to talk to Julia, tried telling her that everything would be all right though she knew it for a lie. One thing was certain, the foundling school would treat Julia a great deal better than she was treated here at home where she was meant to be safe.

'Don't worry, it will be all right. You will like it. There are dogs and cats and nice people and you will have pretty surroundings and we will look after you, our speciality is looking after people. Come on, Julia, we will take care of you.'

She attempted a small embrace but Julia backed away, still screaming until Hilary didn't know what more to do but wish that her sister and brother-in-law had found at least some love and compassion for this poor little soul. She went back downstairs where her sister was apparently deaf and was sewing by the window in what light there was on that dark September day.

'Can't you hear her?'

'She always makes a fuss. It's nothing important.'

'I can't take her like that.'

'She'll be quiet eventually. She cries herself to sleep. Come and have some tea with me, you have had a long journey.'

Hilary wanted to throw tea in her sister's face but she was forced to stay there overnight so she couldn't. She had not thought she could hate this place. She tried to tell herself that it was not the place she hated, it was what had been done to it and what had been done to the children who were meant to inherit it. She had been put out and now it seemed that Julia would be as well, but then Hilary had been a usual kind of a child. She didn't think that Julia was. She was a troubled soul.

'You know this is not what I wanted,' her sister said.

Hilary, intent on her tea, looked into her sister's face and wondered why they were so different. They had been good friends as children, they were almost the same age, but it seemed to her that the year between them had been used by her sister to take everything.

That wasn't fair, Hilary reminded herself now. She was tall and built well like her father; her sister was small and fair like her mother. Jessica had all the good looks, she was the elder child and had found the right man – though on a hunting field, Hilary thought with a shudder. But then he had been very wealthy and looking for a woman with breeding and God knew they had breeding.

They had been mouldering away in the middle of nowhere for several hundred years in an old pile of a house which she had loved with a love she could not forget. Even now when she saw it she remembered it as it had been and not as it was. She told herself that she must think of it as it was now and that it was no longer anything to do with her. Her sister had changed everything. The threadbare curtains were gone, the old chairs where the Labradors had slept out their days were probably in the attic, everything was bright and new and shiny clean.

'You know that I wanted several children,' her sister said and Hilary nodded. She knew that her sister was ashamed at having given birth to an idiot child. She had tried over and over again to have another child to make up for it. 'It has ruined my health.'

Yet Jessica could still hunt all day, dance all night and spend the season in London doing God only knew what stupid activities rich people got up to while everybody else struggled to live, Hilary thought.

What upset Hilary most was that her sister and brother-in-law had never offered the convent in Newcastle a penny. Her father, of course, had paid to get rid of her and by then she'd been glad to go because she was nothing but a burden to them. They did not know what it was like to be without anything. But her sister's womb had failed. Hilary wished her sister would get over it but she had the feeling that you did not get beyond that kind of failure. It followed you, no matter how hard you tried to shake it off.

'I know,' she said gently.

'How could you? Shut up in that dreadful school of yours. You smell of the kitchen, Hilary.'

'I spend my life there.'

'It's a very strange life for a woman to live.'

'Aren't they all?'

'It's a woman's job to marry and have children.'

'It occurs to me that it's the most selfish thing anybody can do,' Hilary replied. 'It's a bit like people breeding puppies when there are starving dogs on the streets.'

'That's not the same thing.'

'It amounts to the same thing. As though we need any more children in the world.'

*

Hilary couldn't sleep. She was glad that her brother-in-law was not there. He and her sister had taken everything, she had had not a penny, nothing from this place. She had been put out and now both these children had suffered the same fate, though of course Edward would come back and inherit and no doubt in time he would send Julia away.

Julia did not have to wait that long, she was being sent away now. In the morning they were due to leave and Julia was not screaming. She clutched to her the doll as though it was all she had. Her mother had had her belongings packed several days ago, Hilary thought, to judge by the efficiency and speed with which the child was despatched. But she made no plea. Julia did not look back and, when her mother would have embraced her, she looked through the woman as though she did not recognize her.

Hilary knew better than to talk to her as they drove away from the only home that she had ever known. She hoped that the girl would sleep but she didn't. She just sat there by the window, seeing nothing. To Hilary it was the same as the first time she had left her home to go to the convent in Newcastle. She had felt as though her life was over, that she had left the only place she would ever care for, and even now she hated that she could not relinquish her feelings for that beautiful spot where she had been born and grown up. How many hundreds of people had played on that beach and gone away and never seen it again?

How many of them, when they lay dying in combat or from disease, remembered how the waves went back and forth across the sand and how the seagulls gathered and how when the tide came in birds of all kinds would gather to party at teatime? Hilary felt sure there was nowhere in the whole world that mattered as much and she did not pretend to herself that this child felt any better than she had.

When they were almost back to the Durham fell tops Julia finally let go of the doll in sleep. Hilary picked it up and when they reached their destination she carried the child out of the carriage. She weighed virtually nothing, she was so light, as though a decent wind might get up and float her away to some place where children did not feel the pain of leaving, the horror of letting go of the one person who mattered to you. Was that so? Had anybody mattered to Julia?

The girl didn't stir, as though she was quite worn out and why wouldn't she be? Hilary finally put her down on a cot in the same room where the three nuns slept. It had not always been like that. When Sister Bee was there she had slept in her own room, apart from them, but Maddy thought differently. They were worried that the little girl might wake in the night and be scared and she would be. She had never seen this place before and she had lost everything.

By now it was late and Hilary was exhausted. She felt bad that she had landed them with her niece. They were sitting over the fire in Maddy's office while Abigail told her about Ella, how Mr Nattrass had found her.

'He's a lovely man,' Abigail said.

'Isn't he?' Hilary said and she couldn't help but blush. In one way she was ashamed that she thought so much of Mr Nattrass and in another she felt honoured that he seemed to like her and that he would do anything for the nuns. No man had ever seemed to like her before so she thought that she might as well enjoy it now. There was no harm in it. She had her life mapped out before her but her days were the lighter for his presence.

As for Julia, Hilary told the others about the dreadful nursery, the darkness and the way that nobody seemed to care for the child.

'She's awfully skinny,' Abigail said which made them laugh because Abigail was as thin as a stick. 'Yes but it's natural to me. That child has suffered because she is different. She's been neglected.'

'Well, she won't have that problem any more, we'll make sure of it,' Maddy said.

Hilary went upstairs from time to time in fear that Julia would awaken but she didn't and, after she had done this three times, she came back to the fire to find that Maddy and Abigail were having tea and biscuits. They were the biscuits that Hilary made and all the children loved them – nothing but sugar, butter and flour with a little ginger. It made her feel as if she had come home.

'I feel as though she is the child I might have had had things been different,' Hilary said. 'Oh, I almost forgot.' And she dug from the pocket of her skirt the money which her sister had so reluctantly put into her hand and nobody said that it was too much. They needed it if they were to go on providing food, lodging and schooling for children who had nothing and they had now all learned that these were not necessarily poor children. Also Maddy had said to the others that she wanted them to become more independent from Jay Gilbraith who had built the village and oversaw everything. She wanted them to take decisions for themselves, even though he had always been very good. Independence was never a bad idea.

It was difficult for Maddy to say this because Jay was her rock but he had so many responsibilities that she was reluctant to push any more on to him. The less she asked him to do for her the more he could do for other people. The trouble was that every time she thought she could get through a problem without him she found that she needed the comfort of his confidence in her.

It seemed, too, as though he intuitively felt that she was pushing him slightly from her because that day he asked her to walk around the village with him as he pointed out the possibilities for the future.

'You're very quiet,' he said.

'I was trying to get by without your help.'

'That's all well and good but how would I get by without yours? You know more about architecture than I'll ever know.'

Maddy's father had been a brilliant architect.

'I'm not my father.'

'To me you are. You always think of stuff I haven't given the least consideration to. Every building in the village has your stamp on it one way or another. You think about light and position and exciting things like drainage and water.'

She laughed. She knew that he liked to hear her laugh. Why was it that men clowned for women, even those they weren't married to but for some reason wanted to amuse? She thought it was the most charming thing about men and particularly about him. He always let her know how much he admired her and what she was trying to achieve, and she knew that he would do anything for her. It was by far the best friendship she had ever had with a man.

'You still went ahead with your orchard,' she accused him.

He had. He winced now. She had told him it would never stand up to the gales that howled across the tops and he had ended up with a lot of broken saplings. Now the orchard was sited a lot further down the hill in the shelter she had chosen, and she longed for the day when there would be apples and pears and plums. Also down there he would be erecting greenhouses and there was the promise of tomatoes and cucumbers next summer. They were beginning to grow a lot of plants from seed, too, and since the greenhouses were heated she was very interested to know what could be achieved.

It was morning when Julia came to, still clutching her doll. She didn't even look about her in surprise, she didn't say anything. Hilary didn't take her into breakfast where the other children were, she guided her to the kitchen and put porridge in front of her. Julia stared at it. One of the cats, Brewster, loved porridge and when Julia didn't attack it with gusto as the other children generally did, he put one paw on the table to see if anyone was going to stop him. When nobody said anything – Hilary was watching carefully from the stove and kept pretending she had something to do – Brewster, who was a large white and ginger cat, got on to the table without much ado and began to lick the milk around Julia's porridge. There was brown sugar glistening on the top of it, covering the whiteness. Julia watched him.

'He's very fat,' she observed presently, as though such goings-on happened every day. Or maybe she was fascinated because she had no animals in her home.

Hilary, trying not to feel triumphant, sighed.

'He eats a great deal of porridge.'

'It's my porridge.'

'I'm sure he won't mind sharing it with you,' Hilary said and turned her back. When she glanced around both cat and child were attacking the porridge. She just hoped poor Brewster wouldn't get any germs from Julia. As a farm child she had seen such things happen. The old cowman she had known said that even rats didn't carry disease like people did. Animals, he said, are clean.

When the bowl was empty Brewster climbed on to Julia's lap, moving around half a dozen circles in order to settle himself.

'What is he doing?' she asked in a tone of not quite certain amazement.

'He will go to sleep now. He always sleeps after he eats.'

'What is that noise he makes?'

'It's called purring. Cats do it when they are full and happy.'

'Do people do it?'

'Not that I've heard.'

Julia carefully carried the cat on to the old sofa which stood under the kitchen window and was reserved for anybody who was tired or didn't feel well and then she and Brewster lay down. Brewster purred and Julia went to sleep and the doll fell out of her arms on to the material of the sofa. Hilary put it by her and got on with her kitchen duties.

Fifteen

Ned had imagined that prisons looked like the place which his father led him to. It took everything he had not to run away right from the beginning. Everything about it was grey and it was very big, sprawling all over the place as though it was taking up as much room as it could.

He had never seen so many boys. He had been allowed to make no friends at home. The village boys were beneath him and, although people came to stay, there were never any children. He hadn't thought about it up till now. Perhaps it was because of Julia being different. They were all wearing the same clothes as he was – how very odd, he thought and why would anybody do that? – except that the bigger boys were wearing long trousers and some kind of tweed jacket which made them look a bit like gamekeepers. His father took him inside.

A boy came to get him and after that he did not see his father again. Ned was taken up some long wide stairs and led into a room where his trunk was standing by a bed. He gawped. There were two lines of beds, at least ten on either side. He had never thought that he would have to sleep in a room with a lot of other boys.

He gazed down at the trunk.

'Don't worry,' the other boy said, 'you don't have to deal with anything. That's what the slags are for.'

Slags, he came to understand, were the maids. What a horrible way to refer to people who were there to look after you, Ned thought, and such things as this made it all harder to be here. The maids cleaned and they made and distributed the meals in the big wide hall where the noise was so loud that Ned thought he would never stand it.

The meals were inedible. At first he thought he had just come on a bad day but the porridge was lumpy and the dinner they had in the middle of the day was mostly gristle and hard carrots. For tea there was very often nothing but bread and butter and some kind of soup which had things floating in it. If you didn't eat quickly you missed second portions or other boys stole your food from your plate.

At night it was very cold, much colder than he thought September had ever been. The room where they slept was called a dormitory and here the boys his age, who were the lowest class, lay there in their beds and tried not to cry for their mothers. At least he didn't cry for his mother, there was always something to be thankful for. He couldn't remember her ever doing anything for him so why would he cry for her? He wouldn't cry for Julia. Somehow he had to get out of here.

At first he thought he would write to his father and beg to be taken home but you were not allowed to write letters like that. It was lucky that he did not write the letter before he saw that letters were only allowed to contain certain things and these would be put up on the blackboard so you had to copy them.

My dear Mother and Father,

I am well and enjoying everything here. We are having a very fine autumn. I hope you are well too.

Best regards, your son.

And here you put in your name. Even after that it was scrutinized before it was allowed to leave the premises.

He spent most of his time trying to escape being beaten. He did not wish to appear clever because the other boys looked down on that, but if you got your lessons wrong you were dragged out in front of the class and caned. Ned managed to avoid it. At night he brought to the front of his mind the summer days when Mr Blake had been there and he and Julia had spent their whole time on the beach. He could hear her laughing. He could not bear to think what was happening to her and there was no way in which he could find out.

'Is Ned here?' It was the first time that Julia had spoken since she had woken up after her sleep in the kitchen with Brewster. Hilary didn't think this ignorance boded well for what happened now.

'Ned has gone away to school.'

'Isn't this a school?'

'He has gone to another school.'

'Why?'

Hilary wished she knew and couldn't think of a sensible answer. Brewster had gone off. He would only let anybody cuddle him for a short time – typical male, Hilary thought, take what you want and leave.

'Ned will be learning Latin.' It was the only fairly sensible thing that Hilary could think to say.

'What is Latin?'

It was known as a dead language but Hilary couldn't say that and she didn't believe it. She thought Latin was a beautiful language.

'It's the church language we use.'

'Is it?'

'In the chapel.'

'What do you do with it?'

'We pray.'

'What is that?'

'It's when you put down the work you have and ask God for his help, ask him to listen if you have any problems you can't sort out. The prayers are sort of like chants. We do them four times a day and it makes us able to go forward better to achieve the things we need to.'

'Do you sing as well?'

'Oh yes, special songs.'

'Can I go and hear it?'

Hilary tried to think of a reason why not and couldn't.

'You would have to be very quiet.'

'I'm very good at being quiet. Will Ned be there?'

Hilary told her again that Ned had gone to another school and then she let the child accompany her into the chapel. The girl sat apparently rapt and made no noise. She had brought her doll and was clasping it to her but she listened to the singing and chanting and stayed quiet until it was time to go.

'I have heard the words before,' Julia volunteered.

'Perhaps you went to mass with your mother in your local church.'

'Oh, no, my mother goes nowhere like churches,' Julia said. 'She goes to hunt balls and to musical evenings and she gives a lot of parties. I have sat on the stairs and seen her gowns but very often my parents are not there. They go to visit other people a lot of the time. Will Ned be here tomorrow?'

Hilary had to say that Ned would not be there tomorrow, which set up the inevitable 'When would he be there' questions, and she gave up trying to explain because Julia did not understand. Even when Hilary put her to bed that night and attempted to read a story to her she asked over and over until she fell asleep with the doll clasped in her arms when Ned would come to her.

Hilary knew by now that no good could come of asking her sister to do anything. They cared only for the boy. They might have cared for this fairy child had they thought her normal, had she been normal, but she was not and therefore they just wanted to get rid of her so that they could carry on their lifestyle without concern.

When Julia woke up in the morning she made no noise and she didn't move. Hilary was aghast at thinking what on earth they were going to do with this child.

'We have got to do something,' Hilary said. She had left Julia in the kitchen, knowing that the child would not move. Hilary even wished that Brewster would come back; he had been the only thing to distract Julia so far.

'What would you suggest?'

They were in Maddy's office.

'She is being badly treated.'

'Most children are badly treated.'

'And is that supposed to help?' Hilary turned on her, glaring. And then she relented but she said, 'Why do people go on having children when they can't treat them well?'

'Because biology betters them.'

'What?'

'Lust, marriage, whatever you want to call it.'

'You want everybody to be like us?' Hilary was almost shouting and then she heard herself and subsided into a chair. 'I'm sorry.'

'Oh, don't be. If I could think how to help this I would. Maybe there is something I could do. What if I go to the school and ask if Ned could come here and see his sister?'

'Her parents would never allow it.'

'Then what are we to do?'

'I don't know! I don't know, Maddy.' Hilary was so frustrated and she felt helpless because this child was the nearest she would have to one of her own. She did not run but she got herself out of there as quickly as she could. She cared so much not just for this child but for every child who suffered, for everybody who had been turned out of the place she loved best so that she might never feel the cold North Sea under her feet again, so that she would never urge her pony forward into the waves as they broke on to the bubbled beach like pigeons' wings in full flight, white and grey and spreading out, and then going back as though in triumph.

Children had no triumph, nothing but adults urging them forward into things which did not suit them, which did not work, into futures where they did not matter. Julia sat in the kitchen saying nothing all that day and it wore Hilary out. Julia ate nothing and drank only a glass of water.

Later Hilary took Julia into their bedroom and talked to her until she slept. When Hilary finally went to bed Julia was still asleep there with her doll in her arms. Abigail found Hilary perched on her bed and she sat with her for a while as Hilary thought of the land and of the children and of all those things which might have been.

Abigail had been a child of the streets and that was how she knew when folk were distressed. When she'd first come there she had tried to sell the golden candlesticks off the altar and sometimes Hilary wished she had because there were hundreds of thousands of people who were dying because they had no food, no water, no medical help, no parents. They were often so ignorant that they visited upon their children the horrors of their past, thinking it was right, that somehow they would appease any god they had by sending their children into hell.

Julia cried out so much that night that Abigail got up and took the child into her bed and cuddled her close. Hilary was exhausted and Abigail sang to them the local songs and it seemed to quiet them. In the night she even told lies. When Julia came to and asked for perhaps the two hundredth time whether Ned would be there tomorrow, Abigail told her that he would be and she was not to fret.

When the girl slept Abigail called herself stupid but she had by now told so many lies for so many different reasons that she didn't care. She slept because she was still alive, despite memories of cold pavements and an empty belly and being alone on the street. Her triumph was that she was not dead. As a nun she could not blame God but she felt then as she had often felt: that having somebody to blame would be useful. So she did blame him and when she had given her eloquent tongue to as many foul words as she could think of, and imagined herself battering God's face until he bled good dark red blood, she fell asleep and her breathing was in tune with Julia's.

Sixteen

The walls of Ned's school were grey inside and outside, and because the summer had long since given over the skies were grey too. There was no real weather, Ned thought, it was just grey cloud and grey bricks and lessons and meals he couldn't eat and the monitors who made you eat soggy cauliflower which had tiny little flies in it. The monitors thought it funny that you had to eat the little flies.

Ned had worked out that if he went on being right in lessons he would be despised, so he didn't and was beaten often. He couldn't be himself and he didn't know how to be anybody else so he hovered in the middle and was nobody. The other boys thought it was good of him not to care but he did care and he did know the answers, but by then he had worked out that the only respect you could earn was by being good at sports.

Where sports ever got anybody he had no idea and he didn't like them but thankfully he turned out to be good at them. He ran very fast and he picked up rugby straight away, though he thought it was stupid. He hadn't known that, having never had anybody tell him that he moved much more quickly than other people, it didn't matter what he did. With so many talents it occurred to him that he might make use of them if he ever got out of this godforsaken hole.

Rugby was simple. All you had to do was outrun other people and put down the ball, whatever it was called, in a certain area and everybody cheered. How strange. He was good at gym too. How had that happened? He knew nothing of such things and yet he could get over anything with a flourish so that the master praised him. Did he care for praise? He thought the whole thing stupid but there again it kept him from being caned and it meant that he might sleep and even eat. He must learn to endure this life somehow and he must try not to think of his sister. She must not be having a worse time than he was, she could not.

He avoided the older boys because he knew that they did no good. He was lucky he was not slender and fair-haired because sometimes these boys were attacked in their beds by the older lads. He wasn't quite sure what happened but from the silence around him and the cries and sobs of the boys in the beds it wasn't good. Having dull brown hair and looking at no one was the way forward.

He began to think of Christmas as being very special. Perhaps Julia would be there. Perhaps his parents would notice him. Perhaps he would be able to get out of here, at least for a few days. Given freedom he would run, he knew it now. He could not come back here. He could never do this again and it would be his only way forward. He worked out exactly how many weeks and days it would be.

He came across a gang of boys in the playground and one boy was on the floor. He was brown-skinned and he was not looking up and they were shouting and spitting at him.

'What are you doing?'

'He's a nigger.'

Ned pushed them aside, got into the middle and pulled the slight boy to his feet. Then the biggest boy came to him and threatened him and before another instant went by Ned had punched him so hard in his face that the blood ran. He was caned of course, he had become used to it, but he was so glad that Mr Blake had taught him how to fight. He hadn't realized it would be so useful and the next day the leader, a boy several years older than Ned, came to him and he said,

'Awfully sorry, old boy. I didn't know he was a friend of yours.'

'He isn't,' Ned told him, 'but he was alone and you mistreated him. Does that make you a gentleman?'

'He doesn't matter.'

'Because he looks different? That's stupid. Everybody matters,' Ned told him.

The boy looked vaguely ashamed but he so obviously didn't care and went off. Ned watched him all the way across the quadrangle and he thought what the hell are we doing, that people behave as though anybody different doesn't matter. How frightened of life people must be that they try to destroy whatever they don't understand.

The dark-skinned boy began to follow Ned around. It wasn't that they were friends, it was just that he had worked out that nobody would hurt him if Ned was close by. So they sat together in class and at mealtimes and after that anybody who was bullied, and it happened a lot, began to trail around after Ned like he was some form of insurance.

Had he managed to retain a sense of humour it might have made him smile. He had no real friends and he didn't want any. All he wanted was to get back to Julia somehow. It was just as well he didn't write for there was no way he could get a letter out to her without someone noticing.

He was lucky also that he was tall, as tall as boys three or four years older than him. He had not understood before now what an advantage it would be. Mr Blake had insisted on a lot of exercise, such as running up a wet beach for miles, which had made him strong too. If any of the older boys took him on he thought he might manage at least a few punches but nobody offered.

Also the sports teachers didn't say anything but it was obvious that they approved of him and this helped. He was popular. It was weird. He mattered, he could reign there if he chose. He didn't choose but he was careful and every night when he went to bed he prayed to God that he and Julia would be together for Christmas.

In the end he did manage to get a letter to his mother. He wrote it in a little stationer's in the town and posted it off. It was two weeks before his mother replied. Letters coming in were not scrutinized and anyhow nobody could object to it and this is what his mother had written.

'My daring boy,' he had never been her darling boy until he had left, Ned thought bitterly, perhaps he should have gone sooner, 'your sister is well and happy. She has gone to a convent school which your Aunt Hilary runs in some awful little pit town in the middle of the Durham moors.' They were fells, not moors, he thought in disgust, didn't his mother know anything? Julia in a convent school? Was such a place as bad as here with nothing but dull lessons and duller meals?

Maybe the nuns there treated her badly. He had heard nasty stories about nuns who didn't like children, who hit them and locked them up in dark rooms and told them they were unworthy and that they were not good enough for God.

Somehow he must get to Julia. He was unhappy so she must be unhappy in such a place, and although he did not know what to do he was resolved to find a way.

Seventeen

Hilary had no idea what to do with Julia. If she went to normal lessons she would find she didn't understand anything, and she showed no inclination to leave the kitchen. It was like having a shadow. She clung to Hilary in a sense as she had clung to Ned, Hilary imagined. She could not bear to be alone. She was not the only one.

Hilary liked having people in the kitchen and although she had a lot of help there was certainly enough room for Julia and her doll and even Brewster, who kept down the mice and rather bigger vermin outside. Sometimes he brought in a rabbit which Hilary, being sensible, skinned and put into a pie.

'May I do that?'

Hilary had become so used to having Julia in the kitchen that she was rather surprised at the soft voice at her elbow as she chopped carrots and then she realized that the child was bored.

Julia had been here two weeks and still every day asked when Ned would come. She was starting to look better with good food and long sleep but she could go for hours without speaking, without moving. She would stare out of the kitchen window but Hilary was convinced that she did not see was what there. So it was odd that the child wanted to chop carrots. It was a very sharp knife but Hilary didn't want to turn down the first request

Julia had made so she said that if she put down the doll and was careful she might try.

It was hard work for a slight child but Hilary showed her exactly how to do it, how to hold on to the other end of the carrot and then chop straight down and it worked. She gave her the smaller carrots and after several false starts Julia managed it and seemed pleased with herself. She was very good at it, very soon. Hilary was impressed.

There were also Brussel sprouts to wash and to put a cross in at the tops. Julia watched carefully.

'Why do you do that? Is it something to do with God?'

That made Hilary laugh and she had to confess that she didn't know.

'The best way to eat Brussel sprouts is fried in butter with salt and pepper,' she said. 'What made you think it was something to do with God?'

'Because I saw you making that sign in the chapel.'

Julia began to recite the mass. Hilary was fascinated. They also discovered another of Julia's talents: Jay Gilbraith, who ran the village, had awarded them a piano. Maddy had thought it was a needless expense and told him so but he had insisted. He liked pianos, he had a grand piano in his house and he had paid for pianos in various churches, chapels and meeting places. Maddy thought that the piano took up a lot of room in the hall and children were endlessly banging into it when they rushed past, even though it stood against the wall.

Jay said that he thought music was the most important thing of all and he was going to introduce music into the class-rooms and encourage the children to play instruments. Maddy thought this impractical when there were so many things for the children to keep in their heads but he wouldn't listen to her and was searching for somebody to help. In the meantime his housekeeper, Miss Proud, played the piano at his house and she sang. Jay was keen on the idea of concerts and was always encouraging people to go to the house to listen. He needed to find somebody who could teach music, that was his next problem.

So anybody who wanted to could play the piano and, since it was in the big hall next to the kitchen, it was near enough that Julia found it. After she heard music for the first time in the chapel Julia could sit down and play anything. As she played people about her would sing and it was such a joy for so many children that it made a huge difference to have Julia there. Jay was rather smug about the whole thing and told Maddy what a brilliant idea it had been. She said nothing.

Hilary had never seen anything like it. Julia would play for hours if allowed, it seemed to be the one place she was happy other than the kitchen. She took her doll with her and Brewster had taken to following her too, and she would stay there. Things were really bad, Hilary reasoned, when you were grateful to a fat ginger moggie just for purring and being around.

It finally occurred to Julia that Ned was not coming. Every day she had looked for him and she had almost got used to the fact that he would not come.

'I would like to write to my brother,' she told Hilary. 'Do you know the name of the school where he is?'

Hilary was rather taken aback at this, she had not thought Julia had latched on. She knew that Julia could not read, write or add up so the whole question was laden down with how her niece had thought this through. However, Hilary was so pleased at Julia's progress that she offered to write for her if she would tell Hilary what she wanted to say.

That afternoon, when everybody else had gone and everything was washed up from the big meal in the middle of the day and there was not yet any fuss about supper, they sat down at the kitchen table with a large piece of paper and a pencil. Julia looked at it as though it had fangs.

'What do you want to put?' Hilary asked.

'That I want him to come here.'

'Julia, he may not be allowed.'

'What does "allowed" mean?'

'That he cannot just leave because he might want to.'

'But he has to come here because I can't do without him any more and you and Sister Abigail keep telling me that he will come so now I know that he won't.'

Hilary sighed. 'We meant well.'

'It wasn't true though.'

'You were very upset and we didn't know how to make it better other than by getting you to eat and sleep and you are much better.'

'I don't feel better. I feel like I'm breaking up into little pieces and it hurts. Could I go to him?'

'I don't think girls are allowed in boys' schools.'

'Why not?'

Hilary couldn't quite work that one out.

'I don't know.' Hilary was about to suggest that perhaps Julia might like to go home but she knew it for a stupid idea before she spoke.

'I would like to say "Please, Ned, come and get me and we can run away together. We could go to Mr Blake, wherever he is. Love, Julia."'

'I don't think I can put that.'

'Yes, you can. I want you to. He will come then. Mr Blake would help us to get away from here, I know he would.'

Hilary wanted to say sensible things like 'You have no money,' 'You have nowhere to go' or 'Do you even know where Mr Blake is and isn't he very poor?'

'I shall tell Ned that you are thinking about him and that you miss him and hope to see him for Christmas. He will come home for Christmas.'

'It's a very long time away, isn't it?'

'Why don't we put some squares on to a piece of paper and you can cross off each day as it comes so that you will know when Christmas is?'

Julia stared. Hilary gave it up.

Hilary wrote the note and put on the foundling school address and, since she knew the name of Ned's school, she was able to send it off. She couldn't think of what else to do.

Ned wrote back to his mother asking the name of the place where Julia's school was but received no reply. Was it because his mother didn't want him to know or had she merely decided that it was unimportant? Then a letter arrived from Julia in somebody's sophisticated handwriting, which he guessed was Aunt Hilary's. It gave him just a little bit of hope that things were not as bad for Julia as he had assumed.

Eighteen

Bill, the Fancy Man, or Mr Wilson as he was generally known in Consett, did not understand why he was so distressed about Ella. He had no child of his own, he had never been involved with any woman who had children nor given her one, so he was aghast at what had happened. Until then he had lived for himself and his wife.

Lydia had always been his main concern. He had loved her from the moment they met. He had thought there was an agony in her eyes which he had never seen in another person. He had always thought that when he married it would be to a woman he could not resist physically, that she might be somebody funny or kind, but to his astonishment Lydia was none of these things. She was like an animal caught in a trap, about to gnaw off its leg to escape and he couldn't bear it. He couldn't leave her. Her friends, such as she had at the time, called her Liddy, which he hated. To him she had the most beautiful name on earth but she was not beautiful. She was skinny and white-faced and afraid. She had so many faults that he hesitated to name them, it might take too long. She had been and seen too much and she had no resistance left.

She married him because he asked her; he was not deluded. She had nowhere to go, she had seemingly no one to run to. She did tell him that she had a mother and a child but she could not live with either of them and he could not bear to ask her why. He had to accept her the way she was, damaged, guilty, but she at least had cared sufficiently or been desperate enough to trust him so that she could live with him. He had met her mother once but she had not asked him to go again.

There was no point in questioning what she did. He got no answers. He had to accept that she sometimes went to see her child on a Saturday and that the child lived across the town but that was all. He gave her the money she needed for them, nobody spoke about it. More often than not she didn't go and he knew that it was because she couldn't bear it.

He didn't know why and he had to teach himself not to care because he wanted her there at the end of the day when he came home from work. He had never wanted anything as much as he wanted her there in his house, making his tea, rarely smiling and nothing to say, but there and just for him. He had never had anything or anybody for himself before now and he was like a man slaking hunger and thirst. He feasted his eyes on her.

She was almost impossible to live with. At first he tried to stop her from doing too much. Every day the house was clean, every day the step was whitened. She made wonderful meals – he had no objection to that – but she was so tired that very often she could barely make it through tea and he would carry her up the narrow stairs and into what was a very clean room and a very clean bed and a window so clean that the stars looked like large shining pebbles. Her very presence hurt him and often he angered her just by coming home, whereas he knew that if he did not come home she would panic and run outside.

He had to try not to disturb the hell that was her mind because if he did she would lose her temper and scream and come at him and hurt him. They were always small hurts – he was stocky and well built and she was a slight woman – but it hurt inside that he could not penetrate the shell of her mind, he could never ease from it the covering which protected it. She was like a silver snail, beautiful but ready to retreat back inside should danger approach.

Now they had gone beyond the bounds of what had been unconsciously agreed. He had lost his temper with her and in front of the child. He could not forgive himself, come to terms with or excuse what he had done. He had never hurt a woman in his life and now he was afraid that he might kill her.

He tried not to drink because he wasn't sure whether it helped, but it was like he was a man with a broken leg, the beer had become the stick on which he leaned and not having the drink was like having that stick cut from under him so that he could not stand, so that he was in pain. There was nothing to help the rawness and all that was left was going home to the house which was so clean he was afraid to move within it.

Ella had stopped that. He didn't know quite how she had but she had altered their household from the moment her bright shiny little self walked into it. He had loved her from the start, not just because she was Lydia's child but because she brought light into the darkness of their desperate lives.

She was a wonderful being and he had ruined it with his stupidity and his drink and his temper. He went to the office – he worked in and out of the office as a sort of go-between for the men and the boss at the ironworks – he liked his work. That was the other thing which kept him going, he had found something he was good at and he was appreciated and it had meant that he had enough money for Ella and her grandma and for himself and Lydia. He had liked being the man in the house for the first time in his life. He liked the sweet power of being able to provide. He longed to meet the grandma and the little girl once more but since Lydia could not bear it he lived with the ache of not knowing them.

So he told the boss quite freely that his little girl – she was his little girl in his mind, the sweetness of her was still there but the loss of her was so fresh that it was a pain deep inside him – that his little girl had got lost. He wouldn't say that he had caused her to run away, he just said she had got lost in the town somewhere and he was so worried. The boss, Mr Plews, they got on very well, said that yes of course he should take time. He could have two days, they would manage as best they could without him.

And so he went for the third time to the house where she had lived with her grandma. He was astonished at first that it was so tiny, so dark, so poor, as though he had never seen it before. Other people had moved in and the woman assured him that she had not seen his little girl.

He went next door and Gert had not seen her either. And so he went to the doctor and then to Mrs Henderson and her horrible musty house, smelling of stale biscuits and wet-bottomed old woman. He could also smell mice in the corners so he got out of there as swiftly as he could and after that he couldn't think what to do.

When he went home Lydia was scrubbing the kitchen floor. She tried to pretend that she was not anxious but neither of them ate and after that they sat silently over the fire without candles or lamp.

There was a fire burning in their bedroom though. It was a cool autumn night. He couldn't remember not having a fire in the bedroom unless it was summer. She went on with her housework, it kept her from whatever devils gnawed at her stomach.

Later they lay there in the dark on their backs and wondered where on earth Ella could be.

Ella had made no friends at the school. Everybody was nice to her but she had nobody to go off into a corner with and whisper secrets. She remembered Charlotte and how nice she had been to her but Charlotte was different. These children were hurt in all sorts of different ways and a lot of them had nothing to give.

In the end she went into the kitchen to ask for something and found Julia chopping carrots. She was amazed.

'Can I do that?' she asked Sister Hilary.

'I thought you were in lessons.'

'We finished, just now, and Sister Abigail said would I come in here and see if you had any goat's milk left for Alice.'

Hilary poured her a jug of milk and she said,

'Yes, if you like and Julia doesn't mind, you can come back here and help. We can always do with another pair of hands.'

Ella didn't usually boast but she knew she was skilled in the kitchen so she delivered the milk and came back to help. Sister Hilary was cheered at her efforts. She tried not to outdo Julia because Julia was strange and Ella thought she might do what her grandma had called 'taking umbrage', whatever that was. So, not wanting to upset Julia, she chopped vegetables together, leeks and carrots and onions for broth and then they watched Sister Hilary put it on the stove with lots of water and barley and then they had nothing more to do so they went outside.

It was a lovely October day and up there on the tops October is a beautiful month. Nobody knows why because there are few trees to give up their dying leaves. It was more, Ella thought, something like how the cold wind smelled like drying sheets and it nipped at your hands like a friend. The sheep stood and let their fleeces almost lift from their backs and smoke came from the chimneys where the housewives were cooking dinner for when the breadwinner came home.

Ella was getting more experienced at dealing with people and she knew that Julia was unusual, if that was the right word, so she didn't ask anything and Julia didn't ask anything. Ella had never had any kind of friend before so she took it for what it was and they sat together at meals. In time she found that Julia asked if she could sleep in the bed next to Ella and Ella knew that for this strange girl that was huge.

At night while the others slept Julia began to tell her about the place she came from, about the sea and the beach and the animals. It sounded to Ella like a fairytale. Julia told her about Mr Blake and how they'd had picnics on the beach and how Mr Blake had taught her to recite poetry. Ella was amazed. She could recite the mass but she had never learned much poetry beyond nursery rhymes. Also she discovered that Julia could just sit down and play the piano. She was allowed to use the piano at any time, she didn't do regular lessons, and although Ella liked being in the classroom she also liked to be with Julia. Nobody stopped her from sitting listening to the lovely sound of the piano. It was like Charlotte's house for a few moments. The rest of the time they haunted the kitchen. Sister Hilary could always find something for them to do.

It was the first week in December when Hilary received a letter from her sister. She did not look forward to these letters. Her sister never wrote but she created a problem.

*

Dear Hilary,

I am hoping you will be able to keep Julia with you over Christmas. I'm sure it will be very good for her to spend time with nuns and we are having adult parties here and it will be no place for someone young. I know that you have a great many other children in your care and so this will not come as a burden to you.

Yours affectionately,

Jossian

Hilary wanted to spit and say awful things like 'God damn' and of course since she couldn't she went seething into Sister Maddy's office, letter held out before her, and there she told Maddy about it.

'We have promised Julia that she will go home. Ned is going home. He wrote and told us so and they are so looking forward to being together. My sister is taking huge liberties here and she has no right.'

Maddy smiled suddenly. Hilary was not fond of that smile, it meant that she thought she knew better and, worse, she was usually right.

'We could have both children here.'

Hilary stopped her pacing, wafted the letter in the air like a kite and she said,

'We can't do that. My sister wants him home.'

'Your sister wants everything her way.'

'Of course she does. She has everything.'

'I doubt Ned would be persuaded to go home if he knew that Julia wasn't gong to be there.'

'Perhaps your sister wasn't going to tell him.'

'A mistake, I feel. From the little I know of him I would say that Ned has a great deal of intelligence and is a stubborn person. He would probably walk all the way here if he had to.'

'I wonder whether he has written to your sister about Christmas.'

'She probably lied and told him Julia would be there.'

'In that case you could write to Ned and tell him he can come here for Christmas if he chooses and write to your sister and tell her that both children will be welcome here if she and her husband will allow it.'

Hilary therefore wrote to Ned first to tell him that he was welcome at the foundling school for girls so long as he wrote to his father and received an answer that was positive. She didn't think that would put him off as long as Julia would be there. Then she wrote to her sister and said that Ned would prefer to be with his sister and, if Julia wasn't going home, he could go to the convent school and spend time with her there if Jessica and her husband would agree. Or they could have both children back with them, whichever seemed the better, but the children were anxious about it.

The result was a letter from her brother-in-law.

My dear Hilary

I think you have misunderstood our intentions. We asked you to keep Julia with you for Christmas because we thought she would be a great deal happier than if she came home. Ned is to come here.

This was decided long before he went away. We have friends who are bringing a boy of Ned's age to stay over the Christmas season and we are hoping that they will become firm friends. Please do not meddle.

Your affectionate brother,
Edmund Waverley

Hilary wanted to go to Northumberland and stamp all over him. Failing this, she did not see how she could tell Julia that she was to stay here and Ned was to go back to Northumberland. She had a letter from Ned within a week and it read:

Nothing would induce me to go home for Christmas when Julia is going to be with you. It is bad enough that they sent me to this ghastly place and made me stay here for a whole term. I am coming to you for Christmas so please make arrangements. If my parents do not let me have my way I shall come anyhow. Give my love to Julia. Ned.

Hilary was beginning to wish that she had been an only child and none of this had happened.

Nineteen

Ned knew that the foundling school for girls was not that far from Durham. Northumberland was a good deal further so somehow he had to leave here before his father came for him. After that there would be no help for it, he would have to go back home for Christmas and there was no way he could live without Julia any longer. It was torture. He told himself that he fully intended seeing the term out and talking to his father but he knew that his father would not allow him to go or help him to get there. So with several days left of term he simply ran away. He didn't decide to, he just walked out

He had to leave in the darkness, it was the only way. He had no money, they were allowed nothing. Perhaps the school was aware that children wanted to get out of there and would use any means they could to stop them so he went.

It was not that difficult – yes the doors were locked but the keys were left in them. It was almost amusing except not quite. He swore to himself that he would never go back and he would never go home, he was done with it all.

He knew in which general direction the foundling school was and it was only eleven miles but it would be a great deal further and out of reach if he went home. He had the feeling that his father would try to prevent him from seeing Julia and he could not endure it.

So he walked. He wished he did not look like an escapee, his school clothes gave him away. He turned his coat inside out so that it would not show and had to be content with that. He walked for several miles before a man with a horse and cart came along. When Ned asked him for a ride he merely nodded and so Ned got on and was carried away from the school. He began to feel better straight away – he had done it, he had broken loose, he was out.

He had not been sleeping, he had been too busy trying to make decisions. Suddenly tiredness crept on him and the rocking of the cart caused him to drift off. When the cart stopped he was jostled awake.

'This is as far as I go,' the carter said and so Ned got down and thanked the man and walked on.

The first place he came to was a small village called Sacriston and here he asked directions and was advised to go straight on to Lanchester and then up the hills and over the top and it was only a few miles further.

The road seemed endless and he went over on his ankle so that he was limping. By the time evening came he was so tired and cold that he longed for his bed in that awful school. There was no shelter and he could see no housing. In the end he just lay down and tried to sleep.

He couldn't get off, he was unused to such cold. He had told himself that the dormitory was cold but it was nothing like this. There was a wind which never gave up. He went on a little further, it was pitch dark by then but he could see what he thought must be a farm by the side of the road and a lot of buildings.

Surely he could shelter in one of them without anybody noticing. He crept nearer.

A dog barked. He hesitated. What if the dog was loose in the yard or what if it was tethered and sleeping outside? He must take a chance so he went on and the moon helpfully lit the sky. There was a dog, he got such a shock when he felt warm fur about his ankles. He nearly yelled out but it made him smile. The dog licked his freezing cold legs and then led the way into a barn. The door was slightly open and he and the dog went inside. This was obviously where the animals slept because he had barely got inside when another much smaller furry animal purred around his ankles. It was a large cat. Why did they welcome him, he wondered, and how was it that they were being so kind?

It was warmer in here and there was hay in the loft which he managed the ladder to. The dog and the cat followed him there by jumping over dislodged bales and lay down beside him like friends. What a shame people were not as nice as animals was his last thought before he collapsed into sleep.

When he awoke suddenly it was because there was noise. He had slept until daylight and people were up at the farm. He must get away. He scampered down the ladder and out of the door. The dog and cat went with him to the road and then they stood there, watching him out of sight.

It took him two hours to reach the little town and he knew it was the right place because it all looked so new. Everything looked good, nothing worn, nothing old that needed replacing, and the men were busy everywhere with new buildings.

Ned stopped a workman and asked him where the foundling school was and the man pointed to a building at the top of the village.

'They calls it the butterfly house,' the man said, 'goodness only knows why.'

Now that he was there Ned was worried. Perhaps his father had heard what he had done and was already there. But he could see no carriage, no horses, no sign of anybody, so he pressed forward. Ned found the door open and inside were a lot of people.

He could see a nun among them and he went towards her, thinking that it must be his aunt until he remembered Hilary was big, tall, wide and sturdy and this woman was tiny. She looked almost like a child in her habit but then she turned and he saw her face and she was perhaps the same age as his parents.

She came straight to him.

'Now then, my petal,' she said, 'what have we here? Are you Ned, mebbe?'

He was surprised. He had not thought that nuns were like this. She spoke with a thick Newcastle accent – he had heard it many times before as some of their servants came from Newcastle.

'I've come to see my sister.'

'We thought you might. What your father will say I have no idea. You'd better come along then,' the nun said, 'I'm Sister Abigail.'

She took him through a corridor and then Ned heard a shriek and the next moment Julia flung herself at him and laughed and cried and hugged him to her.

'Ned! Ned! I thought I would never see you again,' and then she cried properly.

The nun was practical. She said,

'Have you had owt to eat today?' When he said he hadn't she took him further into the house, Julia clinging to his arm and talking so much that he couldn't concentrate either on what he was seeing or what she was saying but it wasn't important. They could deal with all that later. He was here and Julia was here and it was the only thing which mattered. He felt a certain peace fall on him that he never had when he was away from her.

He was led into a big room which had lots of tables and wooden benches and here Sister Abigail sat them down. It was obviously not a mealtime or presumably, Ned thought, lots of other children would be sitting there. The nun went into another room and then she came back and here he saw his aunt Hilary. She looked gravely at him.

'Oh Ned, I was hoping this wouldn't happen.'

'You said I could.'

'Not yet – when the term ended and if your parents would allow it. Now I can see that you have run away.'

'I couldn't stand any more,' he said. 'I couldn't bear to be parted from my sister and I knew she was having just as bad a time – even though I'm sure you are very kind,' he added, quickly.

'Whatever will your father say?'

'He sent me to that awful place and then I found out that Julia wouldn't come home for Christmas and we wouldn't see each other. What was I supposed to do?'

'He will come for you, you know.'

'I'm not going back there, not ever, not to his house without my sister or to that awful school. I will stay here and work and you can surely find something for me to do.'

'I wish it was as simple as that. As soon as he finds out you are here he will haul you back home.'

Ned didn't reply to that, pretending that he didn't care.

Abigail brought out huge mugs of tea and they had soup. Ned had no idea what the soup was, he didn't care, but it was a lovely orange colour and had big pieces of what he thought was carrot and potato and onions in it and there was lots of bread and butter and cheese. Julia sat so close to him that he could only just manage to eat.

Ella felt bad. It had not occurred to her that somebody her age would run away from school, never mind that Ned, Julia's brother, would do such a thing. Children did not. He was very tall and she thought him scary, he looked at people with a kind of straight look which prevented her from meeting his eyes. Also, after Ned got there, Ella felt she had lost Julia. She felt more alone than she had since she ran away. Sister Hilary seemed to sense it and, since Julia followed Ned everywhere, Hilary took Ella into the kitchen a lot and also encouraged Ella to go to more lessons. That filled up the gaps, though not in Ella's heart.

Now that she had lost the only friend she had ever known the loneliness cut into her like a kitchen knife. She watched the twins going around so closely together. At one point Ned got cross with Julia and after a minute or two he yelled, not like the Fancy Man had yelled, but loud enough for a boy,

'You never leave me alone!' They were outside and Ned was supposed to be going to the farm along with several other boys. Girls had not been asked but Julia could not understand that.

'I want to go with you. I've been on my own here for ever so long. Didn't you come here to be with me?'

'Yes but not all of the time.'

Ella wanted to protest but she hid back in the shadows of the house. It was early in the morning, they had just had breakfast. Mr Nattrass had come to Ned with the invite to the farm and Ella could see from across the table where she was eating bread and jam that Julia was not included and how Ned's eyes shone. They came from a big farm so he probably wanted to go because of that but Ella felt awful for both of them when Julia began to sob and Ned wouldn't back down.

Mr Nattrass collected up the boys. Julia followed. Mr Nattrass told her that she could not go, she had to stay with the sisters, this was just for boys today.

'I haven't got enough help. You can come another day, we will sort something out,' Mr Nattrass said. 'Mr Gilbraith has more buildings going up and we can do more and soon.'

'I always go everywhere Ned goes.'

Ned was so obviously embarrassed by this and one of the boys laughed and dug another in the ribs and Ned's face went bright red. Ella could see that in part he wanted to stay there but now that he had seen that Julia was all right he wanted to do other things. Ella could see the longing in his face.

In the end Sister Maddy came and took Julia by the hand and even when Julia ran to Mr Nattrass, Mr Nattrass told her quite sternly that she could not go. Ned was mean to her and eventually Julia sort of broke up and sobbed until she couldn't stand. At that point, though she had longed to spend time with Julia without her horrible brother, Ella moved back. She didn't want to be involved in anybody's fights any more.

Sister Hilary came out of the kitchen and picked up Julia off the ground and carried her away while Julia turned and howled in against Sister Hilary's shoulder. Ella would have gone away but Sister Maddy called to her and Ella was so grateful that they had not forgotten about her.

Sister Maddy took Ella into her office and there she made her a present. It was a big writing book with stiff green card to hold it together and inside it had thick cream pages so that she could write stuff. Also Sister Maddy gave her a pen and ink and several coloured pencils and two ordinary pencils.

'These are for you. It's what is called a journal and you can write anything in it.'

Ella hesitated. She had asked Sister Maddy if she could have a book of her own to write in but it had never occurred to her that she would be given such a wonderful present. She stared.

'Do I have to give it back?'

'No, it's for you.'

'I don't have to share it?'

'No.'

'I can take it everywhere with me.'

'Of course and you can draw in it if you like.' And Sister Maddy showed her that every other page was blank.

'On those pages?'

'Not necessarily. It's completely yours. Nobody can take it away and you can draw on the lined pages and write on the blank ones if you prefer.'

The loneliness fell away. Ella went off to classes. Sister Abigail was teaching them arithmetic. Ella liked Sister Abigail – it was the sweetness of her voice, like she was about to break into song. Were sums like songs? Was one a part of the other? She didn't know, only that the song of Sister Abigail's voice made the numbers come alive.

Sister Hilary did not forget this incident and when she got Mr Nattrass on his own, something that had happened less and less since they all had so much to do, she said to him,

'I have been thinking that perhaps you should take some of the older girls to your farm to see how things are done.'

Mr Nattrass didn't look at her and he didn't say anything. Hilary couldn't help but feel disappointed somehow. She had thought that he would understand but perhaps because he was doing so much for the school already it was an ask too far.

'I know it feels like a lot but you have two women and a small child there. Women are just as much a part of farming as men and for Julia to be excluded seems to me hard.'

'The lad needed to get away for an hour or two.'

'Yes, but what about what she needs?'

'Lasses need other things.'

'I don't think they do,' Hilary said, looking straight at him so that Mr Nattrass took his gaze from the nearest wall and returned the look and they smiled at each other.

'Why don't you come to the farm?' he said. 'You never come any more.'

'I have a great deal to do.'

'We all have — a great deal to do. And we never go shooting any more.'

This was true and Hilary rued it. She thought that the shooting with him was a guilty pleasure and yet it provided food for the children and why shouldn't she enjoy it? She could not be a nun all the time so why not a little recreation which had such results?

'You shoot,' was all she could manage.

'Aye,' he said heavily. 'And Dobber's conversation is rubbish.'

It was unlike Mr Nattrass to make a joke and somehow it was all the better because he did not meet her eyes at that point. Hilary laughed and could even see a reluctant grin from him when they both acknowledged his wit.

'I didn't know you cared about my conversation,' she said lightly and that was when he looked at her. For the first time ever she felt uncomfortable in a sort of glowy way, it was the only way she could think to describe it. She found her cheeks warm and her lips pressed together as though not to acknowledge that Mr Nattrass was the closest thing she had ever had to a friend who was a man. He liked her. It might not have been much to most young women but it was a revelation to Hilary. Every time she saw him she felt better, sunshiny, wanted.

'I think your conversation sets the day on fire,' he said.

Hilary tried hard to work her way free of such talk before she stopped breathing altogether and that was when Mr Nattrass said, softly,

'Why don't you bring some of the lasses?'

'All right then, I will,' Hilary said and she got away from him and back to her kitchen where she felt safe.

'I fell right into that one,' she said to Maddy later.

'No, you didn't. You're both correct. It's a lot for him to take girls as well as boys and Mrs Plass and her friend are there to work and not to see to children but the girls should go. A lot of them don't know anything about farm work and I'm sure they would enjoy seeing the animals.'

Hilary agreed and she took Julia, Ella, Alice and Sarah with her. Julia beamed at being able to spend time with her brother but maybe she was learning because she didn't go and walk with him. She kept her hand in Hilary's.

Hilary was astonished at how she felt when she got there. The farm was bonny to her eyes like never before, though she couldn't work out why it looked even better than the home she had left. It was as welcoming as her own home had once been. In a way here she was going backwards but it was a good kind of backwards with a lovely man she'd been dreaming about. She had spent a lot of time here and it had never looked like this, but things had moved on and Mrs Plass, Irene and the tiny girl were established there so that they came to meet her and the others.

The house was perfectly clean and they were making bread and wonderful meals and were able to show the girls around and Hilary was jealous. There was no question about it, she thought, when she went back to the school, she was jealous. The beds were neat and clean and the fires were on to fill the rooms with warmth and light. She was right, it had needed a woman's touch and now it had that. Mr Nattrass had lived there alone after his mother had died and although Abigail and Hilary had cleaned it they had never been there to stay. The whole place was lit somehow by the people who talked and laughed and spent their days and nights in it. That day the smaller children ran around, screaming and laughing. It was the kind of house which needed that, Hilary thought; maybe every home did.

She had had nowhere to call home but firstly a convent and now a school. She wanted to be here, she wanted a home of her own with a husband and children and, lacking it, she wanted to sit down and cry. She wouldn't let herself of course but it was only a couple of days later when Maddy called her into the office, closed the door and asked softly,

'Whatever is the matter?'

Hilary shook her head and looked at the floor.

'Surely you can tell me.'

'I didn't think it showed.'

'I know you so well,' Maddy said with a slight smile and Hilary saw it and knew that she could be frank, perhaps it might help.

'I am ashamed of myself. I went to Mr Nattrass's farm and I wanted to be those women. I wanted the house and the man and a child, and then I came back here and saw how much there was to do and I wanted to be here. Now I don't know where

I want to be or what I want to do and I thought I was doing a decent amount of God's work and it had nothing to do with what I wanted.'

'Things sort themselves out if you just give them a little time.'

'I don't feel like that about it, I feel stupid.'

'There's no reason why you should. It's understandable that you should want a farm of your own, it's what you were brought up to believe. You've worked hard to cast off the memories which you found so hard to live with because you had such a happy childhood and it's all gone.'

Hilary looked up.

'It's been harder because of the twins. It's as though not only did my parents deny me a part of the farm but their parents seem to me to be treating them badly too. And that's not fair because I know that they are doing their best, however misguided it seems to me.'

'I think you should acknowledge to yourself that part of you will always want such a place for yours,' Maddy said.

'Mr Nattrass has asked me to go shooting with him.'

'Then go.'

'I feel guilty about it.'

'Oh, for goodness sake,' Maddy said, laughing, 'providing food here is one of the basics. Besides, I think it helps you to clear your head when you get beyond the village and into the fields. God is out there too.'

'But Mr Nattrass was so nice to me. What if I really like him?'

Maddy hesitated.

'Surely he's allowed to like you and you are allowed to like him. Why should you not?'

'I've never had a man as a friend before.'

'You have Jay – Mr Gilbraith.'

'He's your friend, Maddy, your rock.'

'I don't know what I would ever do without him,' Maddy said.

'And you're my rock. I would never get anything done if you weren't there to give me a push and then urge me over the stile.'

'Mr Nattrass has been a good friend to us all and if you can't think of it any other way think how his continued friendship benefits the school. He was one of the first people to give us his generosity right from the beginning. Doesn't that earn him our love as well as our gratitude?'

'I know. It's just that . . . I'm trying to avoid him. I like him a great deal.'

'He is a lovely man,' Maddy said.

Hilary nodded and went back to her kitchen but she did pop into the chapel later and put in a quick prayer that she might do the right thing.

Twenty

Four days after Ned had run away Edmund Waverley reached the school in Durham, having had an awkward letter from the headmaster saying that Ned had gone missing, and asked for an explanation. He was directed to the headmaster's office and that pale-faced man told him that Ned had disappeared. They had no idea where he was and had assumed he was homesick and wanted to go back to Northumberland.

'Perhaps he was tired,' Doctor Samuels said. 'It has been a very long term and he wanted to see his family. I thought he was with you.'

It had not occurred to Edmund that Ned would run away but he could see now that it should have done. Ned had gone to Hilary's blessed school. He vowed that when he got hold of his son he would give him the beating he so richly deserved. However, there was little to be done at this point other than make his way up to the godforsaken place where Hilary and the other nuns had their so-called school. He might even have to see Julia.

He had never been so angry. He had always known how intelligent his son was and he knew now that he had overindulged the boy to such an extent that Ned thought he had power here. It was ridiculous for a small boy to feel that way. Edmund blamed himself. He should have been a less tolerant father but then, because he felt for both children and hoped he was doing the right thing, it had been hard. Now all he could do was get himself out of the headmaster's study, having had to accept that his child had run away. He was humiliated.

Edmund was driven miles up to the new village where Hilary and the other nuns had set up their school. When he saw what it looked like he could not but think that it was a very good idea. But when he reached what he had been directed to as the butterfly house he grew even more angry.

He got down from the carriage, approaching the building from the front, and was instantly into a big wide hall. It was nothing like a convent or a school, that was the first thing he noticed, and there was no nun in sight. There were no children either and then a young, very good-looking woman came to him with a huge stupid sideways boat-shaped hat on her head and the long drab grey garment that some nuns wore. She was smiling her welcome but he did not return the smile.

'I'm Edmund Waverley. I understand that my son may be here.'

For a few moments his heart squeezed that perhaps something had happened to Ned on the road but the nun smiled a reassuring smile and invited him into her office. He followed her, sitting down when she urged him but saying immediately,

'He ran away.'

'So I understand.'

'It was good of you to take him in, you do have him here?'

'Indeed we do.'

'And my sister-in-law told him that his sister was here and so he ran away from school.'

'Yes, he did. He thought that his sister needed him.'

'That's very commendable but did you think it was the right thing to do when it was directly against what I and his mother wanted?'

'Sister Hilary said he was to ask permission from you and wait until the end of term but he found it so difficult being without Julia. He has taken no harm,' she assured him. She had lovely dark eyes – he could imagine a lot of men being taken in by them and being agreeable – but now that he had established Ned was here all he wanted was to get him away.

'I would be grateful if you would tell him that he is to come home with me.'

She hesitated. He didn't like that. She was a woman, even nuns had wiles, and he thought she was trying to use them here, but all she said was,

'You can tell him yourself, I shall send for him.' She went out and was not gone long. When she returned she was still smiling. 'He is at the farm with several other boys but I have sent word and he will come back. Julia is there too.'

'My daughter is to stay here, this was the agreement,' he said to her. 'You have been paid for it.'

She nodded but reluctantly and then she began to say something but changed her mind. She had no power here and it was best she should know it. These were his children. The smile was gone.

It was a long while before Ned appeared and to Edmund it seemed an even longer time than it was by the clock. He was not feeling well, his heart thumped, his temper had been lost and remained so, and he was more tired than he thought he had ever been. When Ned arrived, he met his father's eyes in a way that Edmund took as defiance and it made him even more angry. He resented the fact that his son had run away from an expensive school, had caused such problems and was confident in his look. Before he could say anything Ned began,

'Father, I would dearly love to stay here with my sister over the Christmas period. Please say that I may.'

'You left school without letting us know, you ran away from one of the best schools in the country. How dare you defy me like that? Have you any idea how stupid I looked, going there, after being written to by the headmaster because you had disappeared. Nobody had any idea where you were and I have spent the better part of a week trying to sort this out.'

Ned's gaze wobbled.

'I just wanted to see Julia. I missed her so very much and she missed me.'

'You are coming home with me.'

'Is Julia then to come home?'

'No.'

'But—'

'No. You will go outside and sit in the carriage.'

Ned hesitated.

'Please let her come back with us. She won't be a nuisance, I will look after her. You won't even know she's there. We hate being parted, you know that we do. Please Father. I know I shouldn't have run off like that, but you can't imagine what it's like being parted from her.'

His father didn't look directly into the boy's face, he could hear the quaver in the child's voice and almost see the diamond glint of tears in his eyes. Ned always assumed he could have anything he wanted, his father thought, he only had to employ the right tactics, and it would not do.

'Please let us be together, just for a few days. I will even go back to school, I swear it to you, only don't leave her here without me and make me go back to Northumberland without her.'

'You will do as you are bidden. You will go back to school when I say you will. Go outside and sit in the carriage.'

Ned stood as though rooted.

'If I have to tell you again it will go badly with you. I have been far too lenient a parent. You are a disgrace. Go to the carriage this instant.'

Ned went with a defeated look on his face. His father ignored him, didn't even look at him and no one spoke. This nun must know how wrong she had been, he only wished his sister-in-law could be present so that he could tell her what he thought of her. He had rarely been so angry. His doctor had told him to stay calm because when he didn't he could feel his heart thudding in his chest and sometimes he could see the room moving in front of him. He tried to calm himself but it was difficult in such circumstances.

He thanked the nun as politely as he could manage for her help and then he too got into the carriage and the carriage rolled away.

'This was partly my fault,' Hilary said, watching, for she had joined Maddy at the window. 'I should never have given Ned our address and encouraged him.'

'We did the best we could. Will you tell Julia?'

Julia didn't need to be told. Ned had left her abruptly when he was told that Sister Madeline wished to see him in her office. The twins' eyes met and they knew that they would be separated this Christmas. Julia went into the kitchen and there she curled up on the window seat with the cat and her doll and turned her whole body away as though she had given up on the world.

Twenty-One

Ella found it hard to understand what was going on. First Ned was there and then his father came and took him away. Julia didn't speak after that but neither did she cry for any length of time. Ella had hoped that she might find a friend but since that didn't seem to happen she didn't know what to do or whether she had any place here.

The day after Ned was taken away Sister Madeline asked if Ella would come into her office and when she did she was confronted by the Fancy Man.

He didn't look very fancy any more, Ella thought. He was thin and pale and tired and his cap was in his hands and his hair was all over the place and he looked lost. She stared at him. What on earth was he doing here?

'Ella, I am so relieved to have found you. I have searched everywhere, I was nearly demented. I asked the Father in the end and he said there was a foundling school and that you might have come here so I have walked here to collect you.'

Ella said nothing but her first instinct was to go nearer to Sister Maddy. She did not want to go back and live with her mother and this man even though he had been kind to her. Her mother had never yet been kind.

'Is this your father, Ella?' Sister Madeline said.

'No.' She wished she could hide in Sister Madeline's skirts but she just stood, stone in her throat, and shook her head.

'Ella—' he prompted.

'You aren't my father and you had no right to come here.' Somehow she managed the words, though she almost choked.

'I'm married to her mother,' he said.

'This is your stepfather then?' Sister Madeline said softly.

'After my grandma died I went to live with them but they fight. Do I have to go back there?'

Sister Madeline shook her head.

The Fancy Man looked at her and then beseechingly at Ella.

'I never thought you would run away,' he said.

He made her angry, saying such a thing, so she looked him straight in the eyes.

'What did you think then, that it was all right for you to go on fighting like that in front of me when my grandma was dead and I had nowhere else to go?'

'I have had such a job to trace you.'

'Well, I'm sorry for that but you can go back to where you came from. The nuns have given me a bed and food and safety and you and my mother don't seem to be able to offer me any more and certainly not safety.'

This was possibly the longest speech of Ella's life but she was so afraid that Sister Madeline would send her away. It was not that she liked being here, so many things made her afraid, but neither did she want to go back to that house where her mother was so harsh and this man was so scary.

'I'd like you to come back with me,' he said, looking down at the cap he held in his fingers.

'And does my mother want me there?'

He hesitated.

'She doesn't. She never wanted me,' Ella said. 'That's why I had to live with my grandma. My grandma was the only person who ever cared for me. Do I have to leave here, Sister?'

'No,' Sister Madeline said and Ella turned around and walked out of the room.

Bill Wilson watched her.

'I'm sorry. I thought I might be able to persuade her.'

'And that seemed like a good idea?'

'I was hoping so, I thought that maybe her mother did want her back though I doubted it. I wanted to try and get something right, just for once.'

Ella didn't know what to do. She watched the Fancy Man leave and there was something about his back and the way he carried himself she had never seen before. It was defeat.

He had failed to be a husband, he had failed to be a father to her because of how he treated her mother. Whatever else he was trying to do he needed to be good at something, she thought. He was the only man who had ever been kind to her but she could not watch him when her mother shrieked and cleaned and ignored her to the point where he closed his hands around her mother's throat. Sooner or later, Ella thought, he would murder her and she was not going to be there when it happened.

Not that she was happy here, it was just somewhere to eat and sleep. She had made no friends among the other girls. She couldn't think what to say. As she stood there, watching him out of sight, Julia appeared with the doll in her hands as always. Julia had ignored her since Ned had been there.

'Is that your dad?'

'Not my real dad.'

'Who then?'

'He married my mother.'

'You don't have a brother?'

'No.'

'They wouldn't let me go with Ned or have him stay with me.'

'I'm sorry.'

'I can't manage much without Ned.'

Nobody spoke for a long time after that but Julia didn't go off like she always did and Ella knew that she must be missing him an awful lot to think of somebody else, which she never normally did.

So after a little while she went and joined Julia on the window seat in the kitchen where the ginger cat usually lay.

'He's gone out,' Julia said. 'He pretends to catch mice and voles but really he just takes them off the other cats and comes in here as though he did it himself.'

That made Ella smile.

'Ned may come back,' Julia said. 'He is always – what is the word, Mr Blake used to tell it to me – resourceful, that's what he is, but we must wait only for a few days and after that we will take action.'

'Take action?' Ella said, horrified.

'Well, I don't suppose he will stay there when I'm not there but if he doesn't come here then I think I will go and find Mr Blake. He always knows what to do about everything.'

Ella stared.

'What run away? Again?'

Julia laughed.

'You've already done it so you are nobody to talk,' and after that they giggled together. Ella had never giggled together with anyone and she thought that it was such a lovely thing to do.

Ella had always loved Christmas with her grandma. Her mother sometimes turned up on Boxing Day but on Christmas Day it had always just been the two of them, going to church when Grandma had been fit and coming home and having a chicken for dinner, a huge luxury. Her grandma always knitted her a new hat, scarf and gloves in red, which was her favourite colour, and she would buy her sweets and usually some kind of game which they could play as the short afternoon faded. They would sit over the fire and eat Grandma's Christmas cake, which Grandma put rum into. She would feed it for several weeks before Christmas Day. Also she made plum puddings and Ella got to stir the puddings and make a wish. If she could make a wish this Christmas it would be to be magicked back there, to those days when she had been happy.

Now Christmas was getting in the way here and it seemed to have nothing to do with anything she had met before. There was lots of carol singing in the nuns' chapel and although the songs were the same as she'd heard before they made her want to cry, especially 'In the Bleak Midwinter'. It had been her grandma's favourite because she said it reminded her of childhood when they nearly always had snow. Ella longed for snow so that it might feel the same but it was just cold and wet and windy and unpleasant so that nobody wanted to go outside. Sister Hilary and Mr Nattrass went gathering holly and mistletoe and came back bright-cheeked and looking happy. There was a fir tree put up, evergreen for life – the wood of peace, so Sister Hilary told them.

Ella and Julia helped in the kitchen and the smells were good but Julia had little to say and Ella was restless. They just wanted it to be over and done with. It had nothing to offer them any more.

Twenty-Two

Ned went home with his father. Nobody spoke all the way. The only thing Ned envisaged was Julia holding on to her doll, eyes full of tears because she knew what would happen. Why could they not be together? Why did nobody understand and why was it so important that she should be sent away and he be sent to school and then home without her? What was the point of it all?

When they got home his mother was not outside to meet them, nor did she come to them. All his father said to him was,

'We have asked friends to stay for Christmas. As a treat for you we asked them to bring their boy who is about the same age as you. We thought it might make up for Julia not being here. None of our friends knows what you have done so we will say no more about it, but I want you to promise me that you will do the best you can while the festive season is here so that we and they can enjoy what is meant to be the happiest time of the year.'

'Of course, Father,' Ned said, not raising his eyes.

His father looked perplexed, as well he might, but Ned had nothing more to give him. Ned kept his eyes downcast, he felt as though this was all he could do. He had not known until that moment how angry he was and he certainly couldn't let his father see it.

His father talked of other things. He was to dress and go downstairs and talk to the boy who had been asked there for his benefit. Ned tried hard not to think of Julia and how they were apart. He wondered what her Christmas would be like and realized it would be the first Christmas they had ever spent apart. However would they get through it? He knew that for the moment there was nothing more he could do and, since he had agreed to obey his father, he did as he was asked, washed, dressed and went downstairs.

Harry Naples came from a tiny hamlet called Hauxley Bay, not that far from where the Waverleys lived. His parents and Ned's parents met several times a year at various events and sometimes went to stay in Alnwick when there were dinner parties and dances. They had only the one child and he was very precious to them.

They kept on telling him this so that Harry got tired of hearing it and bored with his lonely life. His parents had an estate which looked out across the sea. There was nothing but the place itself, the tiny village which he was not often allowed to go to, where the fishermen and their families lived, and after that just land and dunes. Harry had a tutor who expected a good deal from him and Harry had learned to dislike this learned old man and had become fed up a long time ago. So he had approached his father in the stables one day – it was the best place to get him, he loved the horses and went to see them every day,

'Do you think I might go away to school?' Harry asked when they had been round all the horses, his father fussing and admiring and Harry murmuring how well they looked.

His father frowned in surprise and turned from Baywater's silky mane.

'Go away?' He finally turned to look at his son and was still frowning and then he said,

'Oh Harry, I went away to school and it was an awful place, having to sleep with lots of other boys in a huge dormitory, the walls were grey, the masters beat us, I learned nothing and I was very homesick. I don't think you would like it.'

'But I have no friends here.'

'You aren't happy?'

Harry was astonished that his father had not noticed but then his father rarely noticed anything beyond the horses and his books. He employed good men to look after the place, so he said, but Harry thought his father must be very clever to look as though he was doing nothing and yet the place ran so smoothly.

'Not really,' Harry admitted as though it was somehow his fault.

'Oh dear. And Mr Finchale is such a good tutor.'

'He's old.'

His father smiled. Harry wouldn't have said he was afraid of his father, indeed his father would be horrified to think anybody thought of him like that. He called himself mild-mannered but it was just because everybody had such respect for him that they would not have crossed him.

'I know he is a very learned man but I need people my own age,' Harry said.

'There isn't anyone near enough to be a friend for you and we thought this best, considering the wretched childhoods we had.'

Harry knew very well that his mother had grown up in some awful freezing parsonage and his father had spent even the holidays in school because his grandparents seemed always to be away, or abroad, as his father termed it, and he had never seen them.

'There are so many awful things happening in the world that we swore when we had a child we would cherish him and so it has been with you.'

Harry had not failed to see his mother's gaze follow more fortunate matrons who took their little brood to church. 'We didn't think that you would need more company so soon, you are only eight.

'I tell you what. We have been asked to go and stay with friends for Christmas and they have a son. We weren't keen on the idea, not really wanting to spend such a precious time of year in other people's homes, but since you ask I think we might go. Edward is about your age. I haven't replied yet but, if you think it is something you might care for, I shall approach your mother about it.'

Harry thought it was strange the way his father would approach his mother, as he called it, rather than just saying over breakfast,

'By the way, dear . . .' or whatever married people said to one another over breakfast.

Everything in their house was so formal, so organized, sometimes Harry thought he would die of ennui.

'Your mother is always complaining that we have no company and perhaps we will invite them back here for Easter.'

His father beamed at him and Harry went away, pleased. He almost wished he had mentioned it sooner but he did know that his parents were grateful to have a child. There were whispers that before she had him his mother had lost three children in childbirth, which made him all the more important. Being a solitary child was so stifling. All that responsibility. All his parents' hopes and dreams. Dear God, it was hard.

Everywhere he went he had to take a servant with him. When he had learned to ride they hovered as though he might kill himself and now, given any opportunity, he would go off on his own, swearing the stable boy to secrecy and having to bribe him because the lad feared for his job should any harm come to Master Harry.

'Deny you have seen me,' Harry would say and then he would wheel his pony about and set off. His pony was called Domino and could go as fast as the wind. Like him, the pony loved to be on the beach when the tide was halfway down and they would gallop and gallop until they were both worn out. Then Harry would lead his pony up to the sand dunes not far from the house and there they would sit and watch the tide come in or go out. He always kept fruit on him and Domino loved apples and pears and would stand there chomping while Harry watched the tide do what it wanted, it had nothing to do with him. He liked that.

He tried not to leave it too late when he went back and would say that he had not ridden far and his parents learned to accept that he was only on the beach. But he found his studies hard work. The tutor was not a harsh man but he was not a teacher and could not convey what he knew, though he knew a great deal, including several languages, two of them dead ones – Latin and Greek – as well as French, Italian and, for goodness' sake, Arabic, as though Harry would need that. But then maybe one day he would travel far and wide and need such things, and the travelling appealed to him and so he tried harder.

The tutor also knew about geography and history, was keen on mathematics and, most importantly, he discouraged the reading of fiction which was one of Harry's distractions. Fiction was his escape from reality and he thought that story books were a lot more interesting than the way that he was living now.

He hung on to the idea of Christmas. Perhaps Christmas would help and he lay in bed at night and imagined that perhaps he and Edward could go away to school together and how that might be very good. He might make friends and since he knew he was quite clever, even his tutor admitted it, he could do well and be applauded and best of all he would get away from here.

Ned tried to behave as though everything was normal but he could think of nothing to say and, although this boy tried hard, all Ned wished was for Julia to be there. In the darkness he went out of doors to be by himself but he could hear Harry Naples following him.

He waited for Harry to speak but Harry just went and stood beside him, as though sensing that his new friend was upset. When he did finally voice it Ned was grateful.

'I was so much looking forward to meeting you, I don't have any friends, but I can see that something is upsetting you. I can go back inside if you like but if you want to talk about it I would be glad to listen.'

'I wanted to spend time with my sister. She is in the middle of nowhere in a place the nuns have there. She isn't allowed to come home.'

'Why ever not?' Harry said.

'My parents are ashamed of her. She's different, you see.'

'Ill?'

'No.'

'Mad?'

'I suppose so.'

Harry shrugged.

'I'm surprised all children aren't mad.' Ned was astonished at the remark. Up to now he had not thought anything of this boy who was supposed to be his immediate friend, but just then he saw that the other boy had the same problem he had: he was being made to do what adults wanted and for no good reason.

'Do you have a brother or a sister?'

'None. That's why it seemed good to my parents to bring me with them. I very often spend Christmas at home with my parents and the servants. I have a tutor, I'm never allowed any friends and this seemed an opportunity.'

'It's an opportunity to run away,' Ned told him.

Harry stared and then his eyes gleamed.

'What an excellent idea,' he said.

'And this time I shall be cunning,' Ned told him. 'I shall steal money and take clothes and I can creep out into the darkness and go so far away that I can never be found.'

'I'd like to go too.'

Ned stared at him.

'You want to?'

'I hate it all but I have no money.'

'My father keeps a safe in his study. I think there are probably a lot of things in it which might be valuable.'

'Isn't it locked?'

'Yes, but the back of it is nothing special. A decent axe could get through it in no time.'

Ned wasn't really surprised that the safe gave up its contents without a struggle late that night. He couldn't understand why people went to all that trouble with the front of it and left it virtually unprotected at the back. He concluded that they must be very stupid.

He put in his hands and scooped out everything that was there and emptied the lot into two small pieces of luggage, which was all the boys decided to take with them. It was mostly money and heavy but Ned tore up the papers that were also inside it and fed them to the almost dead fire. He had not known that being vindictive would feel this good.

They left before it was daylight, making their way towards Newcastle.

Twenty-Three

Mrs Plass wasn't well. Hilary deputized other women to go over to the farm and help but when the report came that Mrs Plass was worse she sent Mr Gray, the local doctor, to see her, and followed it up with a visit herself. There was a great deal of work to be done there looking after the boys, but with Mrs Plass, who was the organizer, in her bed, things did not get done as quickly as Hilary would like. Consequently she ended up going there twice a week and leaving other people to run the kitchen as best they might without her.

Between the farm, the school, the kitchen and her sister's children, Hilary was exhausted. Maddy offered to have somebody take over the kitchen but Hilary found it hard to delegate. The kitchen was the place she loved best, though it was losing some of its charm now, especially when she couldn't be there all the time to make sure that the meals were right and the cleaning was done as meticulously as she liked. She knew that she was extra fussy but food and cleanliness were her biggest worries; she didn't want anybody getting anything nasty because of her kitchen.

Mr Gray, the doctor, said that Mrs Plass needed bedrest, which put her out of helping altogether – indeed she needed to have someone to look after her. Her cousin was doing her best but

Hilary could not bear that a day should go by without her being there making sure that things ran as well as they ought to.

The little girl, Mrs Plass's daughter, also needed looking after. And Mr Nattrass did not seem happy any more. Hilary felt guilty that Mrs Plass and her friend living here had been her idea and it was causing a lot of problems. She knew very well that new ideas being put into action did cause problems but it seemed that she could not manage without extra help.

Mr Nattrass had been doing so well, getting on with organizing the boys and the farming. By now several of them were working on other farms in the district but more new boys had come and they did not all take to country ways. The last four had come from Middlesbrough. One of them had run when he saw a cow and cried when a hen came near him.

It made Hilary laugh when Mr Nattrass told her all about it. It was a lovely day up there, nowhere better she thought, and once again she was really enjoying the farm and its outlook across the fell. She tried to hide the smile because he was so serious. She was also aware that she had not taken up his offers of going shooting, though it was the thing she liked doing best. She had wanted to but there had been too much to do and now she felt guilty, although when she would ever have found the time for it she had no idea.

She was aware that he always found time to come and talk to her, no matter how busy they were, and she liked his conversation better than anybody else's. It didn't matter that it was just about pigeons or the weather or how the fields were, she just wanted to be where he was. She had to admit to herself that she was longing to be there more and more and she was very surprised at herself that the foundling school kitchen was losing some of its charm. She never had time to linger and yet he would follow her about, making conversation, and she found herself neglecting everything else.

She decided that she must stop coming, he could manage well without her and she was glad of the day when Mrs Plass announced she was much better and was able to get out of bed. Hilary went back to the school and asked Maddy to send a new girl whose parents had moved to the village. The girl was now fifteen and had been wonderful in the kitchen for the last two weeks.

Maddy was slightly worried about this.

'We send a fifteen-year-old girl among all those boys?'

'She wouldn't be staying there, just helping out for a week or two until Mrs Plass is completely better.'

Maddy, however, decided to send Jemima Smith who was about to marry and settle down but had not left yet. Jemima was almost thirty so there would be no issues there, the two nuns thought. Hilary was glad to have solved the problems at least for the time being but she found herself thinking of the farm and what it might be like to have her own household. It didn't have to be anything grand like her sister's but something just for her to have all to herself. It seemed now as though she spent her life waiting on others. That was what nuns did, she knew it, but it had never been as hard as it was now.

The day after this Mr Nattrass came to the foundling school. He wandered about outside, Hilary could see him from the kitchen window, pacing up and down, and for the first time that she could remember he didn't have the dogs with him.

Eventually he came inside. Hilary had just finished with the midday meal. He looked flushed, he looked unhappy; she had been right, there was something the matter with him. She wished she could have found the courage to ask him but her instincts forbade her. Also she had spent time lying in bed worrying about him. She called herself hopeless.

Mr Nattrass looked carefully around him as they met in the hall.

'Have you got five minutes, Sister, I would like to talk to you?'

'Has something gone wrong at the farm?' Hilary said, thinking of how pale Mrs Plass had looked when Hilary left.

He shook his head and led the way outside. It was not a day for standing around, there was a howling gale sweeping across the fell. She wanted to ask him if they could go back in but he looked like a man who wouldn't move anywhere until he had told her what the problem was.

'I've tried not to do this,' he said, which was not, Hilary thought, a promising start. Her worst fears were about to be realized: he had asked Mrs Plass to marry him and they would need more help. He stopped there.

'Mr Nattrass, I'm frozen,' she said.

He ignored this. He had been looking down at the ground. What there was to catch his eye there Hilary had no idea. He stood for so long saying nothing that she wanted to prompt him but couldn't. Eventually he took a big breath and, looking her straight in the eyes, he said,

'I want you to marry me.'

Hilary stared. His face had now gone white and he wasn't looking at her any more. Hilary went on staring.

'I know you probably think I'm stupid and that asking a nun to marry me is the most ridiculous thing in the world but I am aware that nuns like you can leave, at least I hope so. I don't know how to read you. I know nothing about you but that you come from a very good Northumbrian family, far above anything I have ever or could ever manage. I've never loved anybody but my parents and the animals so I don't know how this happened. It's just that I can't manage without you, I can't think of anything except you. Sister Hilary, you have stolen my heart.'

He tried to smile here because his voice broke.

'I love you very very much. I never thought it would happen and I've met a lot of women and I think sometimes they might have had me had I asked but I just couldn't see them by the fire with me in the evenings. I couldn't see us with children and peace and a home. I do have a very nice place, as you know, but nothing like what you were used to. I have no brains for anything but farming and I know how clever and well-read you are and . . .'

He stopped there and he was turning his cap round and round in his slender fingers. Hilary had often thought what exquisite hands he had and sometimes she had imagined them cupping her face before he kissed her.

'Mr Nattrass, I don't know what to say. I can't think what to do. I'm just so amazed.'

'I thought you might be. Take your time,' he said and then he turned abruptly and walked away.

Twenty-Four

The following morning after the two boys had left with the contents of the safe Edmund Waverley went into his library. He pottered about at the desk, thinking of what a successful dinner they had had the night before. Ned was home now and Edmund knew that Julia was safe with the nuns so he could afford to relax. He thought back to Ned meeting the other boy. They seemed to talk and smile straight away. He had thought that the Naples boy would help. He was a quiet, studious chap, nothing like Ned at all, had never given his parents a moment's trouble. Indeed Edmund was thinking that he might employ another tutor for Ned so that he could stay at home; it had obviously worked so well for Harry Naples.

A more advanced tutor than Mr Blake would know languages and more of science and the world in general. Edmund smiled to himself over this. It would be a sop to Ned to compensate him for having had to spend Christmas without his sister and perhaps in time they might be able to send for Julia and she could come to stay in short bursts. There was no problem which could not be solved, Edmund thought now.

The dinner had been perfect, the conversation had been of the kind he very much liked, all about his county of which he was very proud, the new buildings he planned to replace the cottages with, which were only just adequate, and his favourite horses. After dinner the men had had port and cigars and sat around the table in an aura of well-being, he thought. They were all successful and Edmund was now one of them because of his astute moves as a younger man and his dear wife's position in society.

He thought Jessica had never looked more beautiful. He had assured her that all would go well and she had taken her place at the head of the table opposite him and the necklace which made up part of the Darling diamonds winked exquisitely in the candlelight. He had rarely been so proud.

He saw to the papers on his desk and then realized there was one in the safe which he needed, an old title on a property he was hoping to make into a school for the local children. There was already a school and it was adequate but, having not had an education himself, he was determined that the local girls as well as boys should have what he had missed and what he was so diligently trying to give Ned.

Edmund went across to where the safe stood against the wall and opened it. There he found nothing, nothing but a big hole in the back. The safe was empty. He thought he was seeing things, he looked hard into it as though his eyes betrayed him. Then he got up, pulled it away from the wall and went around to the back. There was nothing but the big piece of whatever metal it was which he had thought kept his valuables secure. There was nothing to say how it had been opened. Edmund had never thought that someone might do such a thing. Had somebody broken in in the night? Why would anybody take the papers, they were of no use to anyone.

While he was standing there, Mr Naples, Harry's father, came in, not knocking, not pausing, pale-faced, his eyes huge and dismayed behind his round spectacles.

'I can't find my son.'

Then the truth dawned in Edmund's mind like the first ray of light in the early morning blazing above the sea across the skyline. He knew where his money was now and, pausing only for a second, he went across to the dead fire and there he saw a little pile of not quite burnt papers. The writing made sense though there were only a few markings.

Edmund did not look at Mr Naples, nor did he know what to say. He had heard before that people's hearts sank but he had not previously realized that that was exactly how it felt. He expected to hear the clunk as his heart reached his shoes and then he felt sick. He felt so very sick that he had to run out of the room and down the hall and outside and there he retched against the wall and choked and retched again until he couldn't breathe. His breathing was now labouring so much that the inhalations were becoming shallower and shallower and his chest hurt. With a kind of resignation his body slid down the outside wall and finally, thankfully, there was nothing but blackness.

He awoke to his wife's calm voice, telling him that he would be all right, It had been nothing but a fainting fit. He managed to sit up and there were servants all around, two of them helping him into a sitting position. His wife was looking anxiously into his eyes. He was back in the library where no doubt they had carried him and on the big sofa where he only sat when he was deep in a book, it was his favourite place right beside the window which looked down across the lawns and he was fine, his breath was normal and his heart was no longer thudding.

'How do you feel?'

He knew exactly how he felt, more angry than he could remember ever feeling before. He shook off their help and stood up and ordered the servants from the library.

'We have been robbed,' she said. 'That was the shock you had.'

'Not exactly robbed,' he said.

'But everything has gone from the safe.'

Edmund looked at Mr and Mrs Naples and he told his wife to close the door and then he sat down and looked directly at them all and he said,

'Ned has taken the contents of the safe.'

Mr Naples gazed at him.

'Your son has taken your money?'

'I believe he has.'

'And Harry?'

'I think he may have persuaded Harry to go off with him.'

Mr and Mrs Naples looked at one another and then Mrs Naples began to smile in disbelief.

'It's not possible,' she said. 'This is ridiculous, Harry would never be so influenced. He just wouldn't, he's the most obedient child in the world.'

Jessica was staring as though she had never heard such a thing and possibly she hadn't.

'This is all Hilary's fault, filling the children's heads with such nonsense.'

'I don't understand,' Mr Naples said. 'Do you think your son has stolen from you and that he might somehow have injured our son?'

Edmund recovered himself, inwardly calling himself names for having reacted like that. He had not been well lately and this was not Ned's fault, awful boy that he was. In a stupid way he was quite proud of Ned for being so outgoing and he was not going to have the Naples family think even worse of him than they would now.

'Ned would never hurt anybody. I should have known he would think of something and I dare say he has persuaded Harry to go off with him. I ought to have known,' and Edmund almost smiled.

Mr Naples shook his head.

'I don't believe it,' he said. 'Harry will turn up – even if they have done something stupid he will come back in a couple of hours, I know my son very well. But the papers?' Mr Naples seemed nonplussed.

'That's just a childish tantrum. I have copies of the papers both here and with my solicitor and Ned is just angry with me. I almost understand why.'

His wife had gone pale.

'I do think you should lie down, dear, the shock has been too much.'

'No, it's just that – I don't want our guests to think that Ned is some evil creature. He's headstrong and wilful but there is nothing bad about him really. I haven't been well for some time.'

His wife waited patiently.

'You haven't seemed good,' and she came over and took his hand. 'You must learn to be more careful. We will have to look after you.'

'You really think that they have run away?' Mrs Naples was so obviously horrified that Edmund tried to smile encouragingly at her.

'This is the second time recently Ned has run off.'

'You aren't angry?' Mrs Naples said.

'I'm angry with myself for not taking more notice. Ned didn't used to be like this. I think I have underestimated my son and also his attachment to his sister.'

'We did what we thought was right,' his wife said, looking at him with tear-filled, anxious eyes.

'I know we did but perhaps one must admit when one has been wrong.'

'We haven't been wrong.'

'I hope not. They may come back but I think they will have to be found,' Edmund said and he sighed.

Twenty-Five

'What are we to do with these coins? Some of them are sovereigns. We will look really stupid trying to buy anything with them,' Harry said, rather alarmed that things were working out and that they were now quite a long way from Ned's home. It felt odd.

'A lot of them are worth less than that and if we can walk as far as Alnwick there will be shops that will exchange such things.'

'How do you know that?'

Ned shrugged.

'Somebody will. Everybody must make profit and we will have left before we can be picked out.'

'To go where?'

'Newcastle. There will be a train to Newcastle from there.'

'Why Newcastle?'

'Because it's big enough for us to get lost in.' Ned glanced at Harry, who was looking down. 'You can go back and say it was nothing to do with you. Or that I made you come with me.'

'How could I do that?'

'I'm very good at punching people. I could punch you in the mouth and then you could go home.'

Harry stood for a few moments and then shook his head.

'I'm not going back there. I'm so tired of sitting in rooms

reading and not being allowed to talk to anybody my own age and my tutor is a fool.'

'Mine was lovely.'

'You were lucky. Mine is ancient and smells of books.'

That made Ned laugh.

'How far is Alnwick?' Harry said.

'Just a few miles. We can do it easily but we need to keep off the road in case our fathers come after us. I don't think they will.'

'Why not?'

'Because my father is stupid enough to think I will have gone to the foundling school where Julia is. But I've learned my lesson there.'

The two boys, laden down with money, were able to take trains. Nobody asked them anything and Ned produced the appropriate money so they got to Newcastle easily and he was rather proud of how they had managed this.

Nobody took any notice of them. Reaching Newcastle was wonderful to Ned's eyes. He did not know what to do next, he only knew that with money you could do anything. They decided to have something to eat before finding a comfortable hotel. Harry looked at the streets with great awe.

'I've never been anywhere like this,' he said. 'The buildings are wonderful.'

Eldon Square, with its three terraces facing a central garden with grass and seats and flowers, with cast-iron balconies for decoration, seemed very elegant to Harry's eyes and the streets were all stone and well-built and there was a theatre. They found somewhere modest to eat in one of the smaller streets and then, as they were about to turn down a dark street, somebody bumped into them, knocking them both over. There followed a fight during which the two lads were outnumbered and all their money stolen.

Just a few minutes later they were lying there penniless and rather bruised. Ned could not believe what had happened to him. All that money was gone and here they were stuck in a town where they knew nobody and had nothing. Whatever would they do next?

Harry was battered and frightened. He had never seen any form of aggression before now. His nose was bleeding and his clothes were torn. The shock made him stay completely still, he could not get up, he had been kicked and thumped. He ached all over. His jacket was torn completely at the shoulder so that one arm showed through but what bothered him worst of all was the jeering of the other lads, half a dozen of them, not caring, not aware of how much they could injure other people.

'How did they know we had all that money?' he asked Ned when he could speak.

'I should think they followed us or they saw me counting out money in the eating place,' Ned said.

Ned was also sitting in the dirt and, even worse, it now began to rain. People just walked on by. This was scary too, as though such things happened every day, and Harry could believe that they did. Nobody stopped to find out whether you were all right, nobody cared about you. The city and its inhabitants went about their business with little regard and he soon came to understand why. As the boys roamed the streets, trying to think what to do next, he saw how poor most people were and, as they walked further and further away from the centre of the town with its fine buildings and big shops, he saw that the majority of people here had nothing. He gawped at first, he had not known that people lived in such ways. Children sat on the edge of the pavements, having nowhere to go. The rain came down more and more heavily. Some people ran under bridges, others seemed past caring and didn't move. The streets were filthy and the filth turned to mud.

It rained for three days and at the end of the three days Harry was thinking longingly of his comfortable home which looked to him like luxury now. He thought of the lessons he had hated so much, of the dappled pony which his father had bought especially for him, of the way that he was able to go to the beach by himself, but most of all he thought of his soft bed and how the dining table was rich in big plates of good food three times a day and how his parents had looked after him so carefully all his life. He even thought fondly of his lessons and his elderly tutor.

He had had to do nothing, everything had been done for him. He knew himself now for an ungrateful wretch and longed for the chance to go home.

Ned was not plagued with such fantasies. Nothing would induce him to go back, he would somehow manage, though his empty stomach, his soaking clothes and his body, aching from lack of sleep on cold wet pavements and roads, filled his mind with comfortless thoughts and made him wonder what he would do now.

Most of all he thought how disappointed his father would be, having seen what he had done. The money was all gone and he had burned his father's papers, which he now knew had been a stupid and pointless thing to do. His father was too aware of such matters to have just one copy of important documents. Ned felt disappointed in himself. What had he been trying to achieve? The anger against his father and mother was dissipating now that he could see how hard other people's lives were. Although he still missed Julia and wished they were together, he could hear his father saying 'It was all for the best' as he so often did. Ned missed his parents now almost as much as he missed Julia and was sorry for what he had done but he thought of all those times when he and Julia were kept apart. It was the most important thing of all. They needed one another more than anything and it was Julia that he really missed as ever. Was he going to spend the rest of his life like this, longing for her, worried for her and not able to urge from his mind the awful nursery with the empty grate and the dark trees banging off the windows, the empty shelves where books should live and most of all the tiny girl in the big bed who seemed to have no future. Somehow they must be together again forever.

Twenty-Six

The two men tried to eat and couldn't. They didn't know what to do. They drank some whisky and water, they sat about by the fire, but all they could talk about was how could this possibly have happened. Edmund felt so guilty; this was all Ned's fault and therefore his.

'Has he always been a difficult child?' Mr Naples asked and Edmund thought that no, Ned had not been difficult. He had been a biddable child but that was when the twins were small and Julia had lived upstairs and Ned had lived in his own room and they had been mostly kept apart. Edmund did not understand what had changed except that for some reason they wanted to be together always and it was unrealistic.

Those years now seemed to him such a wonderful time, there had been no problems. By then his wife had come to terms with the fact that Julia was different and they had tried to accommodate that difference, while still giving Ned the ordinary childhood they felt was his due. But ever since they had tried to split up the twins when Ned was due to go to school it had gone so wrong.

Edmund found himself telling Mr Naples and having Mr Naples say,

'I think you have been particularly clear-headed in this matter.

You must not blame yourself. A lot of people would have got rid of the other child to some sort of asylum.'

'I couldn't do it. We tried to make things right but my wife felt so guilty. Every time she caught sight of Julia she felt a failure so we tried to restrict the child and Ned was aware of it and became more and more aware. I thought that sending him to school would be advantageous and, since Hilary was living at the school in the new town, we thought that a good idea for Julia.'

Mr Naples said nothing for a few moments as he took in this new information and then he looked clearly across at his friend and he said,

'That's exactly what I would have done. You mustn't blame yourself. Whatever could you have done that would have been different and right?'

The sympathy was almost as hard to bear as if Mr Naples had thought he was wrong.

Early in the morning they set off again and reached the Durham fell tops by mid-morning. Edmund hurried into the school, he knew exactly where to go, and headed straight into Sister Madeline's office without pausing.

She was sitting behind her desk and looked astonished.

'Is Ned here?'

Mr Naples appeared behind him.

'Is my son here?'

They both thought they were right and this nightmare would end but the nun stood up gazing at them with such astonishment that their hearts really did hit their boots.

'No, I . . . No, Ned is not here. Had he been I would have let you know.'

'And Harry?'

'No, we have had no new children.'

'Julia is here then?'

'Yes, of course.'

The two men, suddenly exhausted, sat down.

'Do you want me to call for Julia?' asked the nun.

'Yes, please,' Edmund managed.

When she came in Julia seemed so small and white-faced. She was clutching to her a doll which her father remembered. She was not Ned, she was not clever, she was not to blame.

'Is Ned here now?' she said, in a faint, hopeless voice, looking behind him, as though Ned would appear any second and put paid to her anxiety.

'We thought he might have come to see you.'

Julia stared at her father but came no closer.

'But you told us we couldn't see one another. Why should he come here after that?'

'Because he is disobedient,' Edmund said before he could stop himself and then he saw the child's eyes get bigger and bigger and she clutched more firmly to her the ragged doll which he thought she had had since being a baby. Somehow that smote him the more because she had been given that doll in her cradle and he knew now every time she had seen him she had clutched it to her as though afraid of what might happen. Edmund wished and wished that she had been normal. He could have loved her.

'He's run away?' Julia said as though it could happen and he saw it now. Yes, Ned would always leave but how could Edmund say it to her? But then she knew.

'He might come for me and that's why you thought he was here?' she sounded hopeful. 'Always he comes for me.'

Nobody said anything. She appealed to the nun.

'Sister Maddy, do you think he will come for me?'

'I'm sure he will,' the sister said, and the child hid against the nun's skirts.

'I thought I might talk to Hilary,' Edmund said on the way out.

'I don't think she knows anything which might help.'

'She caused this problem.'

Sister Madeline looked directly at him and it was not a gaze he could endure without flinching.

'That is grievously unfair,' she said and, keeping Julia very close, she turned and walked out of the room.

Hilary was in the kitchen but when Maddy went in she turned from her cooking. Julia had by then let go and was softly playing the piano in the hall, as she always did when she was upset or unsure.

'Ned is missing,' Maddy said.

'And what a surprise.'

'He has taken with him the other boy who was staying for Christmas.'

'Ned could charm the birds from the trees. And who is to say that the other boy didn't wish himself elsewhere?'

'According to Ned's father they went off with the contents of his safe.'

'Oh dear,' Hilary said. 'What about Julia? Her father didn't take her home?'

'If he had it would have solved so many problems,' Maddy said, 'but I couldn't send her since she didn't want to go and had he insisted I would have fought him in any way I knew. I'm not having any more children dragged out of here.'

*

'I'm leaving tonight,' Julia told Ella. 'Do you still want to come with me? I can go on my own but it would be nice if you came too. Don't feel that you have to.'

Ella had heard all about Ned and that he had left the parental home and she didn't want to stay there without Julia.

'I'll come too,' Ella said.

'We have no money and we certainly couldn't steal any, not from the nuns.'

'I'm sure they wouldn't begrudge us some food.'

The following morning Hilary found her larder depleted and then she knew that she had been easily deceived. Why had she imagined that Julia would stay there knowing that Ned was on the loose? Perhaps Hilary hadn't wanted to know, she felt so resentful towards her sister and her brother-in-law and perhaps she was not as upset as she might have been.

'And Ella?' Maddy said when Hilary reported this.

'You said they were close.'

'Well, at least we will know they aren't at the parents' home in Northumberland. We won't make that mistake.'

Twenty-Seven

Bill didn't want to go back and tell his wife that he had found Ella but that Ella had decided not to come with him. Alas, his wife was standing by the door when he got back from the foundling school, ready to question him.

'Wherever have you been?' she said and he was upset suddenly. Here he was failing again at something else.

'Why, were you worried about me?' He said it lightly because he was feeling so awful and it was all he could manage.

He knew that Lydia would never say she was worried, even if she had been. Sometimes he thought she had never cared for him, it was just that he had been able to keep her and her mother and her child. But then if that was the case why did she not want her own child and why was she not upset that Ella had gone missing?

'I went to look for the bairn.'

She gazed at him. He dared say that she hadn't looked at him so straight in years.

'All this time?'

'I did say. You don't listen.'

'I stopped listening to you a long time ago, Bill.' She sounded weary and why wouldn't she, she never stopped cleaning the damned house.

'I found her in a school that the nuns run up on the tops but she won't come back here because she knows that you don't want her.'

Lydia drew away from the door and started once again on her endless cleaning. Bill was so used to it now that he didn't notice what she was doing half the time.

'I never wanted her,' his wife said in a low tone.

'She's your bairn. How in the name of God could you not want her? And she's the loveliest little soul I have ever met.'

His wife didn't face him, she was almost turned away by now, but she had stopped whatever it was that she was doing and her hands put whatever she was holding on to the table as though she couldn't go on. It was a cloth, sometimes he thought she would take a cloth with her to heaven when she died. He shook his head and looked harder at her before saying,

'She is your bairn?' and he was even more anxious about this now. What had gone on that he didn't know about and why hadn't she told him whatever it was that pushed her away from Ella? Lydia didn't say anything for so long that he couldn't bear it but neither could he leave or go forward.

'Isn't she?' he prompted.

And finally his wife said in a very low voice,

'No.'

He stared, his feet holding the floor like they were glued. Part of him didn't want to hear any more but he couldn't help himself.

'She wasn't yours?'

'No.'

Then something sort of snapped in her, he could tell by the way that her body almost slumped, as if her defences had given up. She didn't move but he felt she had somehow collapsed.

'I was left with her, had to look after her. She was my sister's child. Some man forced my sister and she had Ella and then my sister died when she had the bairn, we couldn't find any help. The man denied that it was his, would have nothing more to do with it and we had no money. I took her home to the man who was looking after me, we were never married properly, I just told people we were. He didn't want her there and he left me.'

'Why couldn't you tell me this?'

'Because it's shameful. Because I felt as if it was all my fault, that somehow if I had looked after my sister better none of it would ever have happened.' Lydia was no longer looking at him, but at the floor that she scrubbed every day as though she could scrub away her past. 'I can't bear Ella. She looks just like my sister. I called Ella after her. My mother didn't know. We had long since left home and gone to work in Newcastle, cleaning in other people's houses, and we hadn't seen her in such a long time it was easy to hide the truth from her. My mother thought I had brought disgrace on the family so I didn't say anything. I couldn't ever tell her because she adored my sister. I told her that my sister had died of a fever. Ella was the baby, the young child, so I let her think that the baby was mine. Ella hadn't wanted a baby, so there was nobody but me with her and then she died and there was blood everywhere. It was like a lake and the floor was all slippery with it.'

Bill strode across the floor and tried to take hold of her but she escaped from his arms like a moth flitting away towards destruction into the firelight or a fish on the beach flapping for lack of air and unable to breathe and somehow almost grateful for it.

She managed,

'When I met you I needed you to keep us. We had nothing

and my mother was ill even then and I couldn't get any work because I was disgraced. Everybody knew that I had a bairn and no husband. I was so grateful that you took me in and then married me, I couldn't believe anybody would do that. So I lied and told you my husband had died and my mother wanted Ella with her because she was lonely now after my father died. You marrying me meant I could come back here and at least see my mother and give Ella to her.'

'And that was all, I took you in? You didn't care for me?'

She hesitated and then she turned to him and went on looking straight at him such as he could not remember her having done before and she had never offered him conversation like this.

'To be honest with you, Bill, I liked you very well for a man. I had had enough of men by that time, all I wanted was a house of my own so that I could be there. I'd never had anywhere, my mother didn't really like me, but you, you gave me a house and I wanted it to be the best house in the world.'

'It is.'

'I have to keep it that way.'

'It's the best house in the world because you are in it,' he said but she turned away once again, shaking her head.

'I must never learn to love anybody, neither you nor Ella, because every time I love somebody I lose them. I lost my man and my sister and after that I swore I would never get myself in deep like that again so I have my clean floors and my clean sheets and the smell of soap. I want it to stay clean. I have nightmares that somebody has come in and taken my house and I can't ever come back here again and have it for mine. All I wanted was somewhere to be. I dream all the time, nearly every night, that I'm flung out and the place is in a horrible mess and I can't get rid of it, no matter how I try, so I lose it and have no money and nobody to care about me and there never was anybody until you and I can't bear that I might love you because you'll leave me.'

He had always regarded her as perfect like a marble statue, as wanting perfection to meet her perfect self and nothing must interfere. She stood there like she was going to break into small pieces, shrinking into herself until he couldn't bear her defeated stance.

He took hold of her and this time she let him. He grabbed her and held her and then she put her arms around his neck. He liked that so much that he hoped she would never move away. He sat down on a kitchen chair by the range and held her there in his arms.

'Why didn't you tell me all this?' he said in a low soft voice and she said, in muffled tones from close against his shirt,

'Because I cared about you, I wanted to keep you. I didn't want anything to spoil that and I could see what a ruin I was making of it. Last time when you choked me I just wished you had finished the job and I didn't have to go on any further.

'My sister was so very young and so very beautiful just like the bairn. I lied to my mother because my sister was the younger child and my mother adored her. I couldn't let her think my sister had had a child and no wedding. Ella came to me in such distress. I loved my sister so much but this child – she gave up her life for this shitting screaming child and I hated it. I had to give everything for it, I had to pay for a dirty woman to feed it because she had milk. I had to give up my house and go on the street because my man left me so I prostituted myself to keep the child. I went on the streets and lifted my skirts for disgusting smelly old men. I had to. I couldn't go back to my mother with nothing. I had to wait until I could learn to live with the lies because I didn't want her to know what had happened. We lived in some horrible tiny hole and Ella had to go everywhere with me. She doesn't remember any of it, just that she thinks I'm her mother.'

Lydia stopped speaking and within seconds her breathing was quiet and even, and that was when he knew she had gone to sleep, she was exhausted. Then he carried her upstairs and put her carefully into bed just as she was and he lay and looked at her for a long time while she slept.

Twenty-Eight

Ella didn't want to go back in the direction of Consett but according to what they knew it was the right way to Northumberland.

'We will go to Mr Blake, who lives in Rothbury,' Julia said.

'Is that a long way?'

'I fear it is,' Julia said. 'I remember him talking about how far it was from where we lived so it must be much further from here.'

'There was a saint who walked to Rome. It can't be that far.'

'I'm sure he didn't have any parents going after him,' Julia said.

'Mine would certainly never go after me,' Ella said. 'It was Saint Wilfrid. He went twice.'

'So Rothbury is nothing,' Julia said.

But it wasn't nothing, it was a very long way and the weather turned wet. On the third day they had not eaten or drunk and although they were lighter of burden for this neither of them mentioned going back, they were determined to go on. Julia talked a good deal of Mr Blake and even recited 'The Eve of St Agnes', which Ella really liked.

Ella began to think that they would never get there. They begged bread and water from various houses they came to and were refused once but nobody offered any kind of help.

Julia kept buoying herself up with the idea that Mr Blake would be at home and he was bound to help her. She thought about how ungrateful the nuns would think she was and it was true, but she knew also that they would understand. They would worry about her but she could not have said anything, she felt sure they would have stopped her from leaving. She could think of little but Ned and how short a time they had had together before their father appeared. It was two days but seemed only a few hours. She hated how once people had gone from you you couldn't hold them or see them or take any sort of comfort.

Even the images of Ned were not set so much in her mind that she could recall them very well, but she could recall that perfect summer. She brought it back to her every time before she slept at night. She thought of it as the last summer. Perhaps it was the last summer and she and Ned would never meet again. Maybe that was why God had made it such a pleasure. It had been the best time of her life. Mr Blake and she and Ned walking, running or just talking while the tide went in and out and in and out. She had loved each moment. Every single word that Mr Blake uttered she remembered, and he had read a lot of poetry to them. She could recite it all off by heart.

She had been the same with the piano but she'd never been allowed into the music room after the first time her mother caught her playing. Julia could hear something and reproduce it straight away but Ned was supposed to learn to play and he couldn't, even when he was given music to show him which notes to play. Her mother told her that if she went into the music room again she would be very angry. It was nothing to do with her, learning was the important thing, not this being able to recall a tune. After that her mother brought down the piano lid almost on her hands but Julia drew them away swiftly to avoid it. She was told if she played the piano again she would be in a great deal of trouble. She must stay at the top of the house.

The notes of music remained in Julia's head. She thought about the summer, sunrises and sunsets. The sun rose above the sea and went down all over the place, leaving red and gold flames in the sky, falling on the farm and its buildings like a cloak as the sky darkened. Hilary referred to their home as the farm so Julia thought of it like that, though she knew her parents thought of it as large and something called an estate and very important.

She thought that the idea of the farm was much more friendly and had often got Hilary to talk about what the place had been like when she was a little girl. Julia knew that Hilary had loved it as much as she had but that Hilary had lost it too.

Hilary had told her how she had walked her dogs on the sands there and ridden her pony into the waves. How when the tide was full the birds came to feast and the gulls and ducks bobbed against the waves, and when the tide was halfway down the beach the cormorants spread out their wings on rocks and looked across at one another. There were herons, so large and grey and white – as Hilary said, they waited for the fish the way your servant would wait at the fishmonger (if you were lucky) for the fishing boats to come in. And when they did the fish lay there slick and silver and you could buy lobsters and crabs.

Hilary's spaniels would run in and out of the waves and pull at great chunks of seaweed and carry them along to where the sand was soft at the top of the beach. Hilary had said how she loved the way that the tide constantly moved and changed every day and Julia thought how comforting to know that it would and that it was also always there in a way, it didn't go out of sight and worry you.

And Hilary had loved best the castle which Julia had known only at a distance. It was Dunstanburgh, Hilary told her, and it looked like seahorses with its special towers that almost seemed to float in the sky. Julia hadn't heard of seahorses but she understood when Hilary told her what they were like and, though Hilary said it didn't happen, she could imagine seahorses on the beach along with the curlews and gulls.

Julia knew that Mr Blake was the person to go to now, that if she could spend time with him he might be able to help her find Ned. When it was dark and she and Ella lay down in the cold to sleep all the pictures were presented before her and she was almost happy.

It took them a week to reach Rothbury and when they got there Ella wasn't happy with the place. It was a small village of pretty houses. She had never seen anything like it before. There was nothing pretty about the area she had lived in in Consett.

The tiny house which Julia said was the Blake family home looked attractive from the outside. There was a garden of sorts though overgrown. The door was answered by a tall young woman, very thin, wearing a grey dress that had seen a good deal of use. She looked blankly at them.

'I am Julia Waverley, I have come to see Mr Blake.'

The young woman went on staring and behind her Julia could see several curious faces.

'Let me through,' a woman said and she edged the girl aside.

'Julia Waverley, Mama,' the tall girl said.

A tiny scraggy woman with grey hair in a bun at the nape of her neck stood in the doorway.

'Who?'

'I am looking for Mr Blake.'

'My husband has been dead many a year. What is your need?'

'Mr Blake was Ned's tutor, I am trying to find him.'

Comprehension lit the woman's face.

'Oh, I see. You're the little lass at the house that he talked about. What on earth are you doing here, child?'

'I'm trying to find my brother.'

'And what makes you think he's here?'

'I need to see Mr Blake.'

'I think you'd better come in.'

Ella was the person most surprised. This place was so unlike where her mother and Mr Wilson lived that she gawped. It was very dark, the windows were tiny and almost covered in ivy. Ella betted there were huge spiders in there. Luckily you couldn't see them.

A tiny fire sat in the kitchen grate and several children, all older than she was, but not really grown-ups, hovered there. One much bigger was stirring something over the tiny fire. It was porridge.

Julia went around, looking for Mr Blake but also for Ned. She felt so certain he was here, somewhere in the gloom. Any moment now and they would both appear. Ella watched her. How had Julia been so sure about this? Especially when it became obvious there was no one in this tiny house other than this skinny hungry family.

The children who were occupying the seat nearest the fire vacated it when their mother shifted them to make way for Julia and Ella. The house was horribly cold as though it had not been heated for years. Ella and Julia had enough room there to sit together. The children were dividing their gazes between the pot on the fire and the newcomers. Now they stood in the centre of the room as if they had no place to go.

Ella sat down from politeness' sake but Julia went on staring around the room.

'My son got a post in Newcastle,' Mrs Blake said.

Ella could not believe that they had walked so far and all for nothing. How could Julia have thought it? She felt stupid at having believed her. Julia gazed at Mrs Blake as if she was lying or as if she thought they were out the back or up the stairs and Mrs Blake didn't mean it.

'Whatever are you doing here?' Mrs Blake asked.

'We have run away,' Ella said when Julia let the silence go on and on as though she had not understood.

'Whatever for?'

Ella was beginning to wonder herself. Up at the foundling school they had food and a bed and lessons and people who were kind. She was wishing herself there but in fact she had nowhere else to wish herself to be, unless it was back with her grandma. Ella had thought things were so bad when she only got to see her mother on Saturdays, but now she longed for that time. It was the very best that things had ever been, living in that tiny house before her grandma became so ill. She had liked school and been happy there. Now she knew how unhappy people could be. This house almost smelled of unhappiness, want and poverty.

She watched as the children sat down on two wooden benches at the table and the older girl spooned porridge into bowls. Ella could see the girl had set bowls for them too so that nobody got more than two big spoonfuls of porridge. She would have refused but she was so very hungry. Ella knew that Julia would not eat the porridge because she was so distracted by the fact that Ned and Mr Blake were not there. Ella understood Julia well enough by now to know that this meant that Julia was ready to move on. And so Ella left half her porridge and could see the children looking hard at both bowls.

Julia was already asking directions for the way to Newcastle and to the place where Mr Blake was living. Ella was astonished. Why did she not give up and they could go back? What could Mr Blake do about the situation which would remedy it? And then she saw that Julia was obsessed with her brother. Ella had thought they were fairly usual but she saw now that it was not so. Julia must find him, it was her quest, he was her whole reason for being alive.

Ella did not feel as though she could go back by herself, it was such a long way. But then how far was Newcastle from here and why go there when they had no idea where Ned might be?

From what Mrs Blake was saying it would take them another week to get to Newcastle and then what? She was scared now. Nowhere was safe and they could not stay here for any length of time but she wished and wished that Mrs Blake had a bed for them just to rest for a little while and could give them something more to eat. She was imagining the joy of eating at the foundling school when Julia thanked Mr Blake's mother and then they were out on the street again.

Julia set off immediately. Ella couldn't move, she was so upset. Julia saw she was walking alone and stared back at her.

'Are you coming?'

'What if we can't find him?'

'We got his address from his mother, didn't we? Come up, hurry up. We won't get there any quicker if you don't get a move on.'

Ella doubted the wisdom of the whole thing. What if Mr Blake hadn't seen Ned? What if they should starve on the streets of Newcastle? She knew that it was a big place and more people starved in big places because nobody would know anybody to help them.

However, there was no point in saying anything. It was as far back as it was there, Ella thought, she might as well keep on going and at least there were two of them. Julia didn't seem to think or to doubt herself, she just kept on heading as best she could to where she thought she wanted to go. Ella hadn't listened to the directions, hadn't thought she needed to, Julia obviously remembered every word, and so they kept on going until it was dark and nobody spoke.

It was the worst kind of monotony and the further on they went the further it seemed to be to Ella. She wished and wished that she had not started this, even if it meant letting Julia go on her own. She wasn't sure she liked Julia any more. Julia had nothing to say, just kept on walking as though unaware of anything around her, and although Ella might be hungry and tired she was more worried about not being able to find Mr Blake, or Mr Blake not knowing where Ned was. What would they do then?

The address in Newcastle was in Jesmond, which neither of them had heard of before, and it was a very long walk from coming into the big town and getting through it and then somehow beyond it to the other side. Ella was soon bewildered and had no idea where they were going so in the end she just followed Julia. She had never seen such high buildings in such long wide streets and there were people everywhere. She was amazed they didn't tread on one another, there were so many, all of whom seemed intent on going somewhere.

There were a lot of children their age and younger on the streets, wearing rags and looking even worse than Mrs Blake's brood.

When they reached Jesmond, so the sign told them, there were lots of trees and big bay-windowed houses in long terraces. It looked so clean and prosperous. It was almost dark by then, they had spent all day in this place, and Ella thought her feet would not carry her much further. It was then they found the house which they had been given the address of. It stood in its own grounds not far from Jesmond Dene, a big park which they had come past and about a mile from the town centre. Ella was cowed but Julia marched up to the front door and, when the maid with a white apron and black dress and a frilly cap on her head appeared, asked for Mr Blake.

'He isn't with us any more,' the maid said and closed the heavy door with a thump.

Julia banged on the door again. The maid opened it again.

'We have to find him. You must know where he went.'

'He's been let go, he wasn't good at his job and I have no idea where he went. Back home to his ma presumably,' and she put out her tongue at them before closing the door even more firmly this time.

Ella wanted to cry. She was hungry and thirsty and very tired. The tears somehow worked in her throat and mouth and eyes all at once so that she had to swallow very hard not to burst out into huge sobs.

Where Mr Blake was now they had no idea. It seemed silly to hang around but they were out of food and water. They discovered a drinking fountain nearby but there was no food and

Ella was now convinced that they would starve here. They went back to the park and after that they lay down under a big tree and both fell asleep, exhausted.

It was not the kind of park such as you imagined great swathes of grass were, Ella thought. There were a lot of people sleeping there. She was astonished that so many had no homes. From time to time there was shouting and a short sharp scream which Julia said was an owl but Ella couldn't sleep for long even though she had never been so tired.

The following day they got up in search of food and walked back into the city centre. Ella was resigned to having to steal something. Worst of all they came past a bakery and she could not help stopping outside and gazing in through the window. It was some kind of eating place, the smells were wonderful and through the windows she could see ladies wearing hats, sitting at little round tables with cups and saucers and plates and tiered cake stands featuring various delicacies. There was the smell of coffee wafting through the door as people went in and out.

Julia would have moved on but since they did not know where they were going it seemed a huge waste of energy. Ella sat down on the pavement and, after a while of gazing pointlessly through the window, Julia did the same.

'What shall we do now?'

'I don't know,' Julia admitted.

As they sat there, however, they saw two nuns, just like the ones at the foundling school with their long grey gowns and their weird boat-shaped hats. Without saying anything the two girls got up and followed these women as they wove their way through the streets.

Julia would have asked them if they had seen Ned but Ella

stopped her. They might be going somewhere like a foundling school or to a place where people got help so they should just follow. They did.

To Ella's disappointment they did not go into a church or anything that looked like the butterfly house, which was the main building of the foundling school. Instead they went to a very big house. By now the streets had grown narrower and narrower. The sign on the end of the street had said it was Bath Lane. The windows of the place were small and although Julia grasped hold of the door handle it did not turn, somehow being locked from inside after the nuns went in.

'We should have asked them to help us,' Ella said, fruitlessly.

'That was what I wanted to do in the first place, but oh, no, you were too clever for that. Now look.'

They stood about, not knowing what to do. Nobody else came out or went in for about an hour and then a tall young man appeared and he said to them,

'Were you waiting to get in?'

How had he known, Ella wondered, did it look that obvious? Or did people often wait to get in? Then the door opened somehow, magically it seemed to Ella, and he let them go inside with him. Ella was suspicious but Julia followed him without a word.

Inside it was just like the butterfly house in some ways. There were lots of children everywhere and Ella could see the two nuns among them. It was a huge hall and there were rows of children at long wooden tables and they were eating. The smell wasn't as good as the smell of the coffee house but it was still acceptable for people as hungry as Ella and Julia.

The children were obviously poor but they were being looked after here and the noise was tremendous. The hall was big and the ceiling was very high and there were women waiting on the people sitting down.

The young man showed Ella and Julia where to sit but Julia could not wait.

'I'm looking for my brother, Ned Waverley,' she said.

'Why don't you have something to eat?' the young man said. 'Then we can talk about it.'

'I have to know.'

'Later. Sit down.' He said the words briskly and was obviously used to being obeyed, holding Julia's gaze until she did as he told her. Ella did the same and they were soon given a large chunk of bread and soup of some kind, Ella didn't really care what it was, she scooped it down. Julia sat disconsolate for a few moments, watching as the young man weaved his way among the tables, speaking to the women and sometimes to the children, and then he disappeared into another room.

It was obviously a kitchen. Huge pans kept being brought out and more soup given to the children. Julia did not wait. She ate what was she was given and then got up.

'Where are you going?' one young woman asked her.

'I have to find my brother.'

'Sit there for now. Lots of folk are looking for others.'

'He might be here.'

'If he is we will find him. Are you from Newcastle?'

'No, we have come a long way. We lived near the sea but we have been sent away from home and we ran away from school and now I can't find him.'

To Ella's dismay Julia's voice quivered. She had held herself together when the pursuit seemed to her worthwhile, but now perhaps she had come to the end of her energy. The young woman ushered them upstairs and there were a lot of beds, every inch of the room had a bed in it except where you needed space to get in and out. She gave them each a pillow and then they did what they had been wanting to do for almost two weeks. They found somewhere warm and dry and Julia was too tired to cry for long. She fell asleep almost instantly and Ella did the same.

Twenty-Nine

Mr Nattrass came to the school. Hilary knew that she must give him an answer to his question of whether she would marry him but she couldn't and she was trying not to think about it. She felt guilty. It was not fair on him not to know but she did nothing and she did not look at him. She could not make a decision, she felt as though she was being torn in half.

His arrival at the school just then ought to have been nothing special – he came there two or three times a week, taking the boys away and bringing them back – but each time she saw him it all became harder. Hilary tried to keep in mind what she was attempting to do – expanding the project again to include more girls – but she knew that she was getting ahead of herself and without more people they probably couldn't do it.

Hilary was worried that something had gone wrong but she was busy and so she did not approach him until he had been there most of the morning. When they finally spoke she asked after Mrs Plass and things in general and he said that it was going even better than usual. He didn't look at her either but there was tension between them now and it did not make either of them happy, Hilary could see, but it was beyond her powers to talk to him about marriage.

Since she had not been involved recently, Hilary felt slightly miffed that her presence had not been missed. She had never taken up his invitation to go shooting with him, and that day she would have given almost anything to have been involved. She could have laughed at herself. It having been her idea in the first place, she should have been overjoyed to see it grow and evolve and be successful. Instead of which she felt left out, like a small child in a playground watching the other girls playing skippy without her.

They talked about the extension of the barns and she said to him again that she wished there could be more space for girls but it wasn't practical at present. That was when he said, after taking a deep breath,

'There is one way in which it could be made practical.'

And she innocently said,

'What's that?' She thought he was going to suggest building nearby and there was no reason they shouldn't have another big building just in front of the house so that it was protected from strong winds and driving rain. They could have a dormitory and workrooms but they would need more money. Always the problem was money and, although Mr Gilbraith was usually willing to put in more money, Hilary knew that he also had a lot of outgoings now that the village was completely finished except for those buildings some people thought the most important of all: the church and the hospital. The lovely church not far from the school was not yet done and it had been very costly, the Methodists had built a hut near the bottom of the hill. The small hospital was overflowing and Mr Gilbraith had just built an institute where the men could go and play billiards and read and have a pint of beer. So there couldn't be much money left, she thought.

'I would put up another building if you would come and run

that side of it for me,' Mr Nattrass said. This was quite simple, as though he had given up on the concept of marriage, as though he had taken her silence for lack of consent. Hilary wanted to be pleased but she wasn't. She felt so discontented now, it was hard.

She stared at him.

'That's not very practical, I can't keep going between the two.' She didn't say also that Maddy needed her advice and counsel because it would have sounded bad but it was true. Maddy needed her there most of the time.

'You wouldn't have to if we got married,' he said and then he looked so far away that she could only just see the sunset on his cheeks. There the problem was, out in the open, and somehow it helped even though she didn't know what to say.

For several moments she thought that she had misheard him. She couldn't think of a single word to say and that was not like her. The single sentence went round and round in her head until she was as embarrassed as he was and wished she had not gone out there to see him. She felt certain there were a hundred different things to do in the kitchen.

She badly wanted to laugh as the situation sounded so ludicrous but he would be very offended had she done such a thing and, besides, it was hardly funny. She thought honestly that in a lot of ways she had stayed from the farm almost on purpose. It was partly because she wanted to be there so badly and, in a sense, to oust the two Mrs Plass and her friend from what had become possibly the most important building in her life, especially the kitchen there. It was not a big kitchen, being long and narrow. It was in fact the smallest room in the farmhouse but she had come to love it dearly.

She knew how the rain fell on the window and how the sun sometimes seemed to pause outside by the buildings which almost filled the view from the kitchen window. She liked how from there you could see most of the workings of the farm itself, the boys going in and out, and hear their laughter. Sometimes she'd had them in there in tears because they didn't understand something, or because they'd been hurt slightly with a bloody knee or a knocked head.

She was so truly jealous of the two women that she felt like she had a single child and was holding it to her as closely as she could. Now she was ashamed and aghast. Now that she could have what she longed for she wanted to run away back to the kitchen which had been hers for almost four years and to hide there like a child who is afraid to move into a bigger class.

Mr Nattrass found his voice.

'Nobody is like you.' It sounded like gravel, emotional as though he was only just managing his words. 'I miss you. Having told you how I care for you I think that is why you barely come to the farm any more. I feel like I've spoiled our friendship because I care for you so very much. If I could help it, I would. I'm not sure I like caring so much for somebody else. I never did. Until you came here, after my dad and then my mam died, I contented myself with the animals and my fireside and the dogs. You've spoiled it for me.' He tried to laugh, but couldn't, and turned even further away lest his face should betray what his mouth had already spilled.

'Nobody does things like you and it's not just the ideas and how you look in the kitchen, it's not about that sort of thing. I never thought I would love a woman, especially a big bossy nun like you. My heaven is in the fields with you, holding a shotgun and bringing down a pigeon that I can barely see. I admire all those things about you which I never thought to admire in anybody.'

Hilary was completely lost. She took several breaths and even then she couldn't look at him or at anything else.

'I know that you are a nun but I also know that you don't have to be. That you can leave if you would want to. I've always liked you so much better than any other woman I ever met. You remind me of my mother, she was such a countrywoman. I miss her company and those two women,' he nodded his head in the general direction of the farm, 'they aren't my kind, good as they may be.'

He stopped here again so that Hilary could have intervened, had she had any voice at all.

'I've never asked any other woman to marry me, I never thought of it until you got here, but I miss you so I'm asking you again now. I like going shooting with you, I'd like to sit over the fire in the evenings with you. I really like you, Sister Hilary, you mean everything to me. Will you at least think about it again?' And then, without even looking at her, he set off at a brisk pace and disappeared beyond the school.

Hilary went back to her kitchen and burned the scones she was baking for tea.

Thirty

The following day after breakfast Ella and Julia were ushered into a big office and there behind the first desk was the young man and, coming out from behind the second, was a young woman, smiling at them.

'Now,' she said, sitting them down on hard wooden chairs, 'I'm called Ruth and I will try to help you.'

'I'm trying to find my brother. He ran away,' Julia said and out came the whole story, only one part of which the young woman asked about.

'You were at Sister Madeline's school?'

'Yes,' Ella said, amazed that this young woman knew about it.

'You left to find Julia's brother and then you went to Rothbury and now here and you still don't know where he is. Do you think he might have gone home?'

'No, he wouldn't do that,' Julia said. 'They won't let us be together, you see, and we have to be.'

The young woman asked Ella about why she had ended up at the school and Ella haltingly told her that her parents had not been able to keep her.

'Then we will tell Sister Madeline that you are here, she must be so worried about you, and you will be able to go back to the foundling school. We will arrange some transport.'

Ella wanted to say that she didn't want to go anywhere without Julia but that would sound desperate and pathetic, and besides, Julia had been so difficult lately it did not matter that she was the only friend Ella had ever had. She could not help thinking that Charlotte would have made a better friend. Julia was so caught up with her brother. Being twins must be even harder than just being one person but it also meant that you were so selfish you didn't think about anybody else and Julia was definitely not giving Ella any room in her head at all.

But somehow, in the midst of these feelings, Ella remembered how lonely she had felt after she had first run away. With her grandmother dead and her mother not wanting her, she had been inclined to cling to anybody her own age who seemed to make her important to them, no matter how hard that friendship might turn out to be.

Julia was a very difficult person to like, so different she was and it was not just her being a twin. She was obsessed with things and ranted on and on about them until Ella wanted to stop her ears, but the loneliness came upon her even now.

Julia said,

'I must try to find our tutor, Mr Blake, I felt sure he would help us but when we got there his mother told us he was here. Ned will have gone to him, I'm sure of it.'

Ruth smiled.

'You are in some luck, at least for now,' she said. 'Mr Blake is working with us and has just left on an errand. He won't be very long so you can stay and see him.'

'But if he isn't here then Ned won't have found him,' Julia said. 'So we can't stay, we have to go out and look for him.'

The young man said, 'I think the best thing for us to do is write to your parents, Julia, and tell them where you are—'

'You can't do that. I'm not going back, not ever, not without Ned.'

'They must know where you are. They will be frantic with worry. They should come and get you and in the meantime we will try to find Ned and when we locate him you could be together at home.'

'It won't happen like that,' Julia said. 'They'll do the same again. Every time we are together they pull us apart.'

'You were both away at school. Privileged children have a good home and get to go to a good school.'

'It wasn't a good home and I hated the school and so did Ned. If you won't help us I'm leaving,' Julia said, getting up.

'We can't let you out there roaming the streets when there are hundreds of children who need help,' the young man said. 'It would be our responsibility now if something happened to you. Give us a little time.'

'And I shall write to your parents, Julia,' Ruth said. 'And to the foundling school and then people will be able to come and collect you.'

'You can't keep me here,' Julia said.

'I'm staying,' Ella said. 'I've had enough and I'm worn out. I wish I was with Sister Hilary now.'

The young woman smiled at her.

'An awful lot of people have said the same thing.'

'You know her?'

'She is one of the kindest people I ever met.'

Julia said no more, she had never been as tired in her whole life.

Thirty-One

Ned and Harry lasted a week before they ended up at the convent. It was the only thing Ned could think of. His aunt Hilary ran her foundling school and he realized that the nuns here might do the same thing. It also occurred to him that if there were such a place it would be stuffed with homeless orphans.

It was, however, the only thing he could think of and Harry was not going to argue. They were exhausted, having been unable to sleep because of the cold and the rain, so when they found the dark building which apparently had no entrance they were in despair. Harry was silent and almost weeping and Ned, while wanting to scorn him, felt like doing the same.

Eventually they found the way in and banged hard on the thick oak door, but nothing happened. Nobody went in or out. Ned was beginning to think that the nuns did not live in such a place. Darkness fell and he saw lights in another part of the building and banged again on the door.

This time it was opened by a little fat woman in the reassuring habit which Ned was so grateful for that he too could have wept.

'I have come from Sister Hilary and the foundling school,' he said in a voice which quavered just a little but got them entrance.

Inside it was dry while not particularly warm. After a long time in a hall which was inadequately lit they were urged along a corridor and taken into what looked to Ned like an office. Behind the desk there sat a woman who would have frightened him had he allowed himself. Harry fell back two steps slightly to the side so that he was behind Ned.

She was large – not fat, just very big – and had a booming voice. Or did she choose to make her voice boom?

'Now then,' she said, 'what do you mean by coming here?'

'I had to get in, Sister,' Ned said, trying to better her by familiarity. 'We need somewhere to stay and something to eat.'

'We have run away,' Harry added.

Ned turned and glared at him. That was the least helpful thing he could have said.

'From home?'

'I want to be with my twin sister, Julia. They won't allow us to be together but we couldn't go to Julia's school because we would end up back where we started.'

The woman was speechless, Ned thought.

'We had some money, we thought we could manage, but we were robbed.'

The sister needed to hear where they had come from and all about how they knew the foundling school for girls on the hill top in Durham County and about their parents. Harry was crying by then because she quelled them with her look and he was already saying that he was very sorry. Ned thought him a poor creature to give way like that. When the story was over the nun sat back in her chair and surveyed them severely.

'You thought the streets of Newcastle would suit you very well and have discovered that they won't? Well, I think we might be able to give you some aid,' she said. But instead of offering beds and food, which was what Ned had been relying on, she merely sent them to sit in a room where there was no fire and no light but a single candle. There they waited in the cold for what felt like a very long time so that even Ned began to doubt that help would arrive.

In the end they each sat down on a very hard chair and tried to sleep. It was then that the door opened and a young man holding a candlestick came into the room.

Ned was awake at once.

'Mr Blake!' he said.

Mr Blake's first name was Thomas. He was his father's only son and had so many sisters that his parents despaired. They lived in Rothbury, where his father had been a carpenter and made a reasonable living. The trouble was that he had died when Thomas was fourteen years old. Thomas had had some education because of his uncle's generosity and his mother wanted better for him than to follow in his father's footsteps so he had not been taught carpentry. He thought later that it would have been better if he had. Yes, he was good at school but he was obliged to leave when his father died. His mother found him a job as assistant master in a local school and after that he had worked at various places and always hated it, except for the last summer when he had been left with the Waverley children.

He then took a post in Newcastle but there the eldest daughter took a fancy to him, although it could not be said about the other way round. He was dismissed without a reference and left with his wages. These he had to send to his mother but he could not go home to Rothbury. They had so little money that his family would starve if he did not do something.

His mother was not a strong-minded woman and when he had suggested that his older sisters might go out to work she was horrified at how low this would bring them. The result being that his family was forever on the verge of starvation in a tiny house. Tom felt he was a snail carrying them all on his back and he was beginning to despair.

He longed to tell his mother that they were carpenter's children, they had no status and in a small place like Rothbury it didn't matter. What did matter was that they could pay rent and feed the family. But when he began to explain this to his mother she burst into tears and told him that he had no heart, that his father would be ashamed if he knew that he treated his mother and his dear sisters that way.

The despair overtook him. After he was turned off, he tried and failed to get any kind of work in Newcastle. His clothes were shabby and he knew that when people looked desperate they gave off a particular smell. He thought people could smell that desperation on him so he did not flourish and was obliged to spend just a little and frugally so that at least he had something to eat once a day.

He could walk home, it would take some time, but the idea of the tiny cottage, his useless sisters and his wailing mother who knew little of economy did not encourage him to go back to Rothbury where they would all starve because there was nothing for him to do.

Just as things seemed unable to get any blacker he fell ill and the next thing he knew a young woman with bright red hair was standing over him. As she came slowly into focus he saw that she was looking at him with some concern from cornflower-blue eyes.

'Are you all right?' she said. She was plainly dressed but he did not associate plainness with poverty; he had learned the difference long since. She wore a grey hat which was stylish without ornament except for silk ribbons, and a cloak and leather gloves which were well made.

Tom was embarrassed and got up as quickly as he could but she cautioned him.

'Sit down a while.'

'No, I – I really must get on.'

'Have you eaten today?'

His pride bettered him.

'I thank you for your concern but indeed I have,' and he tried to walk away. That was it.

The pavement rushed up to meet him like an impatient friend and this time when he came round he saw two pairs of eyes gazing down at him and the young man was frowning.

'Come on,' he said, 'let's have you up and out of here.'

This time Tom couldn't get up without help and they slowly walked him across the street and into a building he had not seen. He noticed nothing when he was in it other than that he was being taken along a corridor and into a big kitchen. He wondered whether they were evil people who would sell him into some kind of slavery and then wanted to laugh. They sat him down and soon after that a large pot of tea thick with sugar and milk was put in front of him.

There was also bread and jam and, when he had eaten this, the young man who was still with him, though the young woman had disappeared, asked him about himself.

At first Tom didn't like to say anything. He was unused to telling strangers of his business but, since there was little to be gained by not telling the man, he found himself spilling out much more than he should, being angry that his father had died, angry that he was finding it impossible to keep his family. Each time he stopped the young man asked a polite question so that the story went on. When it was done Tom sat there, ashamed, looking at the floor and almost feeling better and then rather sick. His view swayed.

'I think you need to rest,' the young man said.

'I can't stay here.'

'I'm afraid you will have to. There is no way you can go any further as far as I can see.'

'I mean, I can't put on to you. You don't know me and I don't know you.'

'That's easily remedied later.' And so he was led next door to a room with several beds in it. The room was dark and Tom could hear breathing and even someone snoring. But there was a clean bed ready for him so, when the young man left him, he took off his boots and his coat and fell thankfully into it.

His dreams were troubled at first and then they ceased and nothing around him mattered. There were comings and goings but his mind knew that they were nothing to do with him, snorings and snufflings and quiet conversations but they were all beyond his ability to stay awake.

It was as if his eyelids refused to lift, they urged him beyond it all to a place where he felt so peaceful. He even worried that perhaps he had died and his life was over and, considering his responsibilities, maybe it was just as well. He went into a happy dreamless place and let it go on and on.

He had no idea how long he had been there when he finally opened his eyes. He turned over. There were other people in beds, all of them taken, like some kind of boarding school for adults, or almost adults. He could not tell much about the people in them, just that it was a male dormitory and therefore must be very respectable.

He was just thinking that perhaps he should get up and

investigate the daylight which almost beckoned beyond the curtains when he heard a noise beside him. The young man who had led him there was standing by the bed and he said what Tom thought were possibly the best words of his whole life.

'What about something to eat?' he asked softly.

Tom put on his boots and coat and followed him back into the long corridor and then into a large room where the smell of food was so enticing that he wanted to cry for lack.

There he sat down and women waited on him with large sandwiches of bread and cheese, a kind of hot stew with beans and onions and big pots of tea. When he had eaten the young man took him through into a room which was an office and there he introduced himself and his wife.

'I'm Nathan Armstrong and this is Ruth.'

They seemed very young to be married but Tom was too polite to enquire into other people's business. There were two big desks, a number of easy chairs, three or four hard chairs, bookcases and papers and a very large fire. They asked him to sit down and Nate enquired into whether he might like to stay there and teach, since it was his profession and they would be glad to have his help.

Tom stared into the other young man's face.

'But you don't know me.'

Nate shrugged.

'I'm good at working out who people are and you seem genuine to me and I feel that you are a good teacher.'

'I can't think how you decided that.'

'I've done a lot of it over the past months. We have both become good at judging people. We've made several mistakes. We employed one man who in the end had to tell us he couldn't read or write, we got in another who claimed he was a doctor and nearly killed one of the children, and then we learned to pick out the good people and we think you might be one of them.'

'I don't think I have much to give.'

'Tom, that's not going to help,' Ruth said. 'We are going to trust you for a week and see how you get on. In that time you will have only a bed and your meals and some fresh clothing, a bath, shaving and a haircut. Then we will assess whether you are what we want. If you aren't we will try to find you somewhere else to work, but I think Nate is right and that you might do well here.'

'How many children do you have?'

'It varies. Some come and stay the night and don't like it, especially in the summer when they have fresh air and can pick pockets or find work. Some children are brought in from the streets half dead and stay for weeks.'

'It's a huge task.'

'An impossible one. We do what we can but most of all we make sure that the children have food and somewhere to rest and then we try to enable them to make the best they can of themselves. Most of that is teaching. You can find work a lot more easily if you are fit to work in the first place and then you might raise yourself with your education. If you can read and write or even add up and be clean and neat you can do a great number of things. Though most are menial tasks there's nothing wrong with that. We have to teach the children independence but also that if they get stuck they can come back.

'We aren't the only people doing this. There is the convent to which we are attached and there are various other groups in the city. We just keep on trying.'

Tom was astonished at the energy and vision of these people and so glad and relieved to have found them. They made him feel as though he too could achieve a great deal, and he wanted to help in every way that he could. He saw that he had eventually come home – this was what he wanted to do for the rest of his life and he would try his very hardest. He thought that his father and uncle would have been proud of what he was trying to achieve. And in time he would try to bring his family to Newcastle. He felt sure that his sisters could work and help too, and as long as they had shelter and good food and decent clothing it would be a huge step forward.

The big office which Ruth and Nate had shared until now became a three desk office. There they could be private and share their troubles and joys, and very often late in the evenings they discussed matters over tea and the fire.

Tom looked on Ruth as another sister, though she was as unlike his own sisters as she could be. His new relationship with her was the best he had had with a woman so far and he was glad that it was so positive.

Nate and Ruth had their own room but other than that they were always about, always useful, and set Tom such a good example that he wished and hoped he might find somebody like that for himself.

He had never thought himself a good teacher but he could teach children of all ages so he must be fairly useful and Nate, who never said anything untrue, told him that he was inspired by Tom's teaching. Tom, who had never felt inspiring before, was glad and he gave more and more to the children because of it, gaining more and more in his turn.

When not tired or hungry the children were keen to learn and Tom also learned from them about Newcastle and about the circumstances they had come from. Some of them were from foreign lands and spoke other languages, their fathers having in the most been seafaring men, who had brought them here to a new land. Once Tom could get them to stand up and talk it made such a difference and everyone could learn so much.

All kinds of people had come in here from the ships which docked in Newcastle. Men in turbans and women in clothes which covered them from head to foot, including their faces but for their eyes. People from warmer climes had to be given warm clothing.

There were folk from Scandinavia who spoke what sounded to Tom like an almost local dialect. They were so similar to the people born and raised here that it was hard to distinguish who had been born here and who had not.

The children were often left to fend for themselves but when they didn't have to they blossomed. Tom liked when this happened. Many who spoke little English seemed to grasp what he was trying to teach, or perhaps it was just that they liked the pictures he drew and the sound of his voice and how he would sing to them.

Music was for everybody and Tom had been in the choir at the church when he was young and even now had a decent voice. He encouraged them all to sing with him and he taught them simple tunes so that they could join in. He bought a cheap violin and enjoyed playing it; it had been such a long time since he had been able to indulge any of the past pleasures he had known when a young boy. He loved to give them coloured pencils and paper so that they could draw whatever they wanted and simple books which Ruth devised with pictures of the letters of the alphabet. Every day he felt as though he was finding more and more to tell them and show them and they heard the enthusiasm in his voice and he was glad of it.

The children drew pictures of ships and of sea and of the lands where they had been born and of their lost families. Some of it was hard to make out, but he thought it helped him to understand them and he hoped they might learn to understand a little of his life as he told them where he had been born and brought up. He soon learned to love many of the children and almost thought, as never before, that God's grace was all around them and had given him the chance to do some good.

The jewel now in Tom's crown in his first days at the safe house was the way he heard a scream of joy behind him before Julia flung herself at him.

He was so pleased to see her that he held her in his arms and told her how glad he was and asked how she had got there. She explained that she and Ella had gone looking for him because they had been so certain that they would be safe with him. They thought that surely he would be able to take them to Ned or to find Ned and bring him to them.

Tom was obliged to say that he had no knowledge of Ned but that he would do his best. In the meantime he was just so glad to see her and to meet Ella.

Thirty-Two

After a month it was suggested to Tom by Nate, who wasn't very good at people not doing what he wanted them to, that he might bring one or more of his sisters to them and they would find them work. Tom found it hard to believe that he and Nate were thinking alike but it was now his dearest wish.

'I know your mother doesn't approve but she isn't in any position to object. In the meantime I will give you your earnings for the next month, trust that you will come back, and you can give your mother money and bring either one or two of your sisters back with you. We will find them something to do, even if it's scrubbing floors. They may not like it but it's a lot better than starving in Rothbury.'

Tom's mother was horrified to discover that he had lost his post.

'Whatever did you do to make such a thing happen?' She, like many mothers, assumed that it was her son's fault. He could not tell her the truth, so, like many a son, he lied and said that his education had been inadequate, as it had for Ned Waverley's further education. That because he had too little Latin and Greek he had been turned off, but that he had found another post teaching in an orphanage.

Mrs Blake was not pleased that he had felt obliged to take such a post, she thought it brought shame on the family. She was not particularly grateful for the money he gave her either, he thought, striving for patience. She was aghast at the idea that her two eldest daughters would go to Newcastle and end up as something like kitchen maids.

'I couldn't possibly allow it. What on earth would people think?'

The girls, who would do anything rather than contradict their mother, said nothing, simply hovering reluctantly, but Tom wasn't having it. He remembered how Nate went on and he turned to them and said,

'Get your things together. We are leaving in half an hour.'

'Tom, you can't take them away from me and from the rest of the family,' his mother said, sobbing and holding on to his arm.

'We need money,' was all he said in response.

He was trying not to dislike her – she was his mother after all – but he could not help ruing her lack of practicality. Who did she think she was? Did she imagine that pride would buy food, warmth and clothing?

Tom was relieved that Nate hadn't suggested he should bring his mother and the rest of the family to Newcastle. He would be happy to get out of there. His mother had never been much of a housekeeper, claiming she came from better things and ought to have had at least one servant. She kept getting in front of him so that he could not leave, and in the end he gently pushed her aside and saw Meg and Polly out of the door.

He had the feeling that all three of them gave deep sighs once they got out on to the road and when they reached the nearest railway station Polly, the youngest one, said, 'I hope you don't think I'm going to put up with you telling me what to do when we get there.'

'Don't talk to him, Poll, he isn't worth it,' the other one, Meg, said.

Since they were skinny and almost in rags, he just ignored them, they were not going to see their family starve no matter what they had to do, he swore to himself.

'Mother promised us we should never have to go out to work,' Polly said with a lift of her chin which enraged him.

He couldn't help retorting,

'It has been a long time since Father died and I cannot go on keeping us all. This is an opportunity for you to help me. We have to act differently, we will all have to work,' he said, thinking of how lazy they had learned to be. Well, that was over.

Getting off the train they walked to the safe house and were given food and beds and then expected to help out in the kitchen and there were objections from both girls. Tom ignored them. They were peeling potatoes when he left.

There was a new girl in the kitchen, who he had not seen before, and although he had to go and talk to Nate he hovered there uncertainly. She was dark-skinned and dark-eyed and she looked up carefully at him. He couldn't help smiling at her and to his delight she smiled back at him. He began to think of how he could spend more time there, getting to know her. He did not miss how her gaze followed him as he left the kitchen for the rest of the house. But, reluctant as he was to go, Nate was waiting for him.

Nate called him into the office and explained to him that Reverend Mother had two boys at the convent who claimed to know him. Tom said nothing to Harry's name but when he heard Ned's name he groaned.

'You do know them?'

'The little wretch. I understand how he feels, that he is parted from his sister, but for him to run away and like this, their parents must be worried sick. I don't know the other lad but Ned is gifted and clever and could persuade anybody into anything.'

'Shall I come with you?'

'No, thanks, I'll go and bring them back here. When Ned discovers that Julia is with us he won't be able to stop himself from running through the streets.'

Tom was unwise enough to tell Julia that Ned was in the city. He thought that she deserved to know, but he had forgotten how impetuous both twins were.

'Can you take me to him?'

'I am about to go and collect him and bring him back here.'

'I'll come with you,' she said, and didn't even think about Ella.

'No, you must stay here with Ella—'

'But Mr Blake—'

'No, you must stay here. I shan't be long.'

Julia watched him as he left the building and would have run after him, so eager was she to see her twin, but Ella took her by the arm and pleaded with her that she should stay. Julia was torn and impatient. She felt like half a person when Ned was not there and longed for his presence. She watched as Mr Blake went out of the door and then she sat down in the hall to wait.

'Aren't you going to come and have something to eat?' Ella said, it being almost midday.

Julia shook her head so Ella shrugged and went off by herself. Julia sat there and watched the door.

Mr Blake found Ned and Harry and they were so pleased to see him.

Ned's first enquiry was of his sister and then he was impatient to get to the safe house. Harry said very little, just that he wanted to go home.

'You won't send us back to our parents?' was the only thing Ned could think of and the reason why he hesitated as they walked.

Tom said he couldn't answer that, he was just making sure that the twins were united and that all four children were well looked after.

Thirty-Three

Harry's father, having had a letter from Nathan Armstrong who ran a safe house in Newcastle, was appalled at first and then relieved. He was reading his letters at the breakfast table when his wife came in. She was always later than he and he thought she could see that there was news.

'Harry?'

'He's been found and he is alive and well.'

She stumbled into her place. Her hands were shaking and as she sat down she put them over her eyes in relief. The maid, Maria, who was seeing to the breakfast thankfully withdrew but they would all soon be told that Harry was fine and Mr Naples knew that everyone in the family was concerned, everybody cared.

Mr Naples explained that Harry was at some kind of orphanage in Newcastle and that they would keep him there until his father collected him.

'You are certain he is well?' said Mrs Naples, who could not believe her good luck.

'Mr Armstrong says there is nothing wrong with him.'

Mrs Naples saw her husband's angry face and then she said softly,

'Oh dear, do try to be kind.'

'I have had enough. We are good parents, he had no reason to treat us like this. It will be the last time he leaves this place before my funeral,' Mr Naples said and, unable to get his breakfast down, he went and ordered the carriage.

Mrs Naples sat over the breakfast dishes until everything was cold. Maria, who usually saw to such things, had not come back. She was being tactful, Mrs Naples knew, but when she ventured into the hall Maria was standing by the kitchen door.

'Shall I clear, Ma'am?' she said.

'Please. You are a dear good girl.'

'We were so worried, all of us.'

'I know. I know.'

Mrs Naples couldn't do anything, she didn't even have the usual meeting with Mrs Chivers, the cook, about what they were to eat that day. She didn't think anybody would be eating.

Ned had to go in search of Harry who appeared to be hiding from him and Ned was not really surprised. He felt so guilty over the whole thing and was not inclined to run away again as his efforts had been futile. He felt as though the adults had won the battle. He finally found Harry in a tiny little room at the back of the property where he was sitting with a book on his knee, though Ned doubted whether he was reading it.

Ned found a hard chair beside him and sat down. Harry didn't look up.

'I'm ever so sorry,' Ned said. 'I didn't think I was going to get you into such a mess.'

And then Harry surprised him. He looked Ned straight in the eyes and gave a rueful smile.

'Don't say that. I never had a friend before and now I've got you and we live nearby and I think running away like that was the most exciting thing I ever did.'

Ned managed a smile.

'I didn't think of it like that.'

'Maybe my parents will understand.'

'Maybe they will never let you out again,' Ned said, sighing.

His father came to collect Harry the next day. Neither spoke on the way home. Harry couldn't think of a thing to say, he was so glad to be going there, he didn't know that he could ever say sorry sufficient times. When they arrived nobody said anything but they all looked. Harry escaped to his bedroom.

Later that day Harry was called into his father's study. He couldn't think of a single word to say. His father had always been kind to him but maybe this time he had gone too far. His father, however, he soon saw, was much too clever to say anything crass. He didn't get up, he didn't even shout at him, all he said in a very soft tone was,

'I have never been so ashamed of you, so disappointed.'

His father didn't look at him. Harry couldn't bear it.

'I'm so sorry, Father,' he said and his voice was hoarse. He wished himself anywhere but here.

'Have you any idea how sick with worry we have been? You ran away as though we had been terrible parents, as though we didn't care about you, as though you were not our only child and we had something else to aim for, somebody else to care for.

'We took you to see the Waverleys, we thought you might have something in common with Ned Waverley. We didn't think that you would run away with him, we didn't know you. We thought we were doing the right thing, we even thought that if you got on with Ned we might send you to his school next term so that you would know someone when you got there. We had such plans for you. You are our only son, our only child, and you have always been everything to us.'

Harry wanted to run away again so that he didn't have to stand any more of this but he couldn't budge an inch.

'We know better now. We know that you have to be watched, that you cannot be trusted to do the right thing. From now on you will go nowhere by yourself, not even to the beach. Do you understand me?'

Harry could only nod, having never been threatened like this before. He felt awful and he felt awful because he could see that his father was upset, not just angry and disappointed but so very upset that it hurt Harry that he had done this to his father. As for his mother, he dared not even look at her and even the maids avoided his gaze.

'Now you may go to your room. For the time being you will take your meals in your room and your tutor will go to you there. When I regain what has been lost of my usually level demeanour I might let you out of there but always with someone to watch you. You may go.'

After Harry had gone Mr Naples put both hands over his face in despair. His wife found him there and took him into her arms and said how sorry she was that things were so hard but that they would get better. Harry would improve and in the end he would make them proud of him. The anger and the relief clashed together but that evening Mr Naples went downstairs as if there was nothing wrong and he and his wife sat over dinner.

They didn't eat much, they didn't say much, and before they

were finished eating his wife was clutching at his hand. In the end they sat over the drawing room fire and wondered where they had gone wrong so that their beloved child could treat them in such a way.

Maria cried in the kitchen. She set off Mrs Chivers, who threw her apron over her face to hide her tears.

Later, by the kitchen fire, Maria, Mrs Chivers and the general maid, Pauline, sat drinking gin and water after their evening's work was over. They didn't usually do such a thing, though they could have. Mr Naples, having no butler and not caring what his servants ate and drank, was good to them and they were loyal to him, but this was different. However, they all slept better now that the boy was home.

Thirty-Four

Having told her tale Lydia then went back to what she had been doing. She desperately wanted to hide in her too-clean house but she soon saw that things could not go back to how they had been before she'd told Bill the truth. Everything had changed and her hiding place no longer worked. Bill was silent and they both tried to go on as usual. He got away to his work and she hoped it would all go back to where it was before Ella had come there but it wouldn't.

The little girl had changed everything, she had made a huge difference to their lives. Lydia had not understood how much her husband cared for Ella. Or was it jealousy – that having secured him for herself she could not abide the idea that he could care as much for anybody else? Now, by his silence and the empty look on his face, she could see how he too had altered. Perhaps it had not occurred to him that he could care for a child who was not his own, or perhaps he had just not seen that he could care for such a lovely little person as Ella had turned out to be.

That made Lydia want to cry and pretend it wasn't so and that she didn't care and that even though Bill had found her Ella was a good deal better off where she was and the nuns would look after her and give her what she needed.

In the second week she saw that she must face the problem,

try to come to terms with what had happened and what had been said. They must go forward because it was the only way. Maybe in the end she would be able to acknowledge that it had been a long time since her sister died and she had been left alone with a tiny child and a mother she had thought she must lie to.

Bill came home at the same time and went to work just as if nothing was any different. Lydia could see that he was trying to pretend to her that nothing had changed, though in that he was failing dismally. In the middle of that week he came home to find the kitchen in a mess and his wife huddled over the fire. She had intended differently but the absence of the little girl who had in so many ways become theirs and altered their lives could no longer be borne. She could not go on like this and she knew that he could see it.

'I haven't managed anything,' she whispered.

He took her into his arms and told her that it didn't matter but she was happy only when they took on the mess together. Then he made egg and chips. It was the one thing he knew how to make, besides porridge, and she smiled at him and ate. After that she lay down on the settee and slept until it was time to go to bed.

The following day it got worse. She couldn't get out of bed. She began to sleep all night and then all day. Bill did what he could in the house. He managed to get fish and chips for the Friday, he came home and put the fire on so that they had hot water. He bought bread, butter and jam and somehow he managed.

Then after another few days Lydia began to wake up during the day and to take on other tasks. She no longer went on about how dirty everything was and it was the worst that he could remember seeing it, she could see by the way that he looked around him in slight dismay. He was finding it difficult to concentrate at work and had to work harder just to keep up, he said.

Then came the day when Lydia found that she was no longer tired, she was no longer feeling so awful and so blank as she had done for so many years. Bill came home and found the fire on even though she was asleep on the settee because she had sat down and watched the fire and gone to sleep in peace for the first time. She woke up when she heard him come in but all she did was smile and tell him she had made a chocolate cake so they had chocolate cake for tea and very good it was too.

He did not tell her that he had had a letter from Sister Madeline at the foundling school and that Ella had gone missing. Just when things were starting to go well, all his plans were shattered. He couldn't tell her so he tried to carry on as usual, but he was so worn out that he lay down on the settee after tea and then went to bed early. When he woke up it was morning and time to go to work. He was beginning to think that everything was a nightmare. Forward one step, back six. He was so tired that he wished very much he didn't have to go.

When he came back that evening the fire was on and Lydia had cooked a meal. That week the house was cleaner and she was brighter – he was the one who kept falling asleep – and then she said the dreadful magic words.

'I thought that maybe we could go and see Ella this weekend. I think I might manage it, just for a little while. Do you think she might want to see me?'

Bill couldn't think of anything to say. He wanted to cry. He hadn't cried since he was a small child and some huge thing in his tiny life had gone wrong, but the urge now was so hard that he had to make an excuse and go down the yard and sit on the hard wooden seat of the toilet, holding his breath so that the tears would not make themselves felt on his cheeks and run down his chin. Where on earth had Ella gone and why? He had tried to pretend that she liked being at the school, he had held to him the illusion that she was safe and wanted and would not take any harm. Now he did not know what was happening.

He went back inside and told Lydia that he thought he might have to work at the weekend but they would go to see Ella soon. At the weekend he managed to get a lift most of the way to the school and then he walked the last few miles.

Eventually he made it into the school and this time he found the lovely nun that he had liked at the door; she had seen him coming. She apologized to him.

'Oh, Sister, this isn't your fault. You and the other nuns were so good to her. God knows what might have happened to her if you hadn't been there. It was me, I made the mistakes.'

They sat down and the nun told him about Julia and Ned and how the twins had run away to be together but that she had not thought Ella would go with Julia. They were getting on so well together and she thought Ella had just wanted an adventure. She didn't know where they could have gone, she did not understand where Ned and his friend had gone, she was just praying that they would be all right.

Bill made his slow way home and when he got there was obliged to tell Lydia what had happened and it was worse than he had thought. She blamed him for lying, she blamed him for not telling her what he had been doing, and then she blamed herself as much as she had ever done for what had gone wrong.

On Sunday she did not get out of bed. On the Monday he went to work and when he came home it was as if nothing was any different. The house was spotless, the meal was perfect. He felt sick.

Thirty-Five

Ned and Julia had been split up and slept in dormitories – it was girls in one and boys in another. When Ned objected loudly and swore he was taken into an office and there a tall young man who had introduced himself as Mr Armstrong had looked at him in a way Ned hoped nobody would ever look at him ever again. This man didn't play by the rules, Ned could see. Adults usually sat behind a desk and you stood in front, but Mr Armstrong stood in front of the desk leaning back just slightly as if he owned the world, only inches away from Ned, and he seemed extremely tall so that Ned had to look up to see his face.

'Why are you shouting?' Mr Armstrong said, his voice soft and yet menacing.

'I want to be with Julia.'

'I have written to your father and he is coming for you and Julia. He wants you both at home with him but he cannot come for a day or two, he has business concerns to attend to—'

Business concerns, Ned thought that was very strange, what business did his father have other than the estate. It made him doubt that his father did want them there and made him wonder if his father had plans to send him off to another awful school and keep Julia there by herself.

'We don't want to go home, our father will not let us be together there which is why we ran away.'

'You ran to starve and sleep on the streets then? That is your alternative?'

Ned couldn't think of an answer for that so he said,

'Mr Blake could take us home, he knows where we live.'

'Mr Blake is far too important to be left with such a task. He is teaching the children here.'

'He taught us. He knows us. He would like to take us home.'

Mr Armstrong stood further back against the front of his desk and went on looking at Ned in a way that made him nervous as he had never been before. Mr Armstrong's voice was quiet and even and had something of a flatness about it which really frightened Ned.

'Your father will come and get you both. Until then you will have to contain yourself.'

Ned was about to say that he would do nothing of the sort and then he stopped. He was almost scared enough to run away. This tall man had icy black eyes, nobody in his right mind would defy him.

'I just want to be with Julia,' Ned said softly.

'You cannot sleep near her and you might have different classes. It's only for a few days.'

'My father will make me go back to some new awful school and Julia will be left and everything we have done to be together will have been in vain.'

'Nothing is ever in vain,' said Mr Armstrong, with slightly less harshness than before. 'Part of growing up is realizing that you cannot always have what you want and that sometimes if you do get what you want it isn't the right thing. I know that sounds silly now, but try not to want this too hard because it might be costly for you.

'You are in danger of being selfish and caring for nobody beyond your sister and you can't do that, Ned. Lots of people care for you, you must understand that, despite what has happened. Now, you will give your father a few days so that he can come and get you and then you will go back home with him. There you will see your mother and you will learn to behave as though you were not the centre of the universe, which at present you seem unable to manage.'

Ned was rather lost at all this. He wasn't used to sarcasm and this was so cuttingly delivered that he felt he would remember forever Mr Armstrong's low but hard tone. He was ashamed of himself.

He knew there was no point in saying that his mother didn't like them, that his parents wouldn't care but to part them. He wasn't going to get anywhere here so he just shut up and nodded.

He could not run any further. He had seen how badly so many children of his age were treated in this city. He had tried to dismiss it but it was in a way the same thing as trying to help the dark-skinned boy at school. He was privileged and must endeavour not to take advantage because so many children had no homes and no food and no shelter.

Ella felt awful. She was alone now as never before and she would not trail around after Julia as Julia trailed around after her brother. Ruth found her wandering about the halls and took her into the office and gave her tea and biscuits. Ruth explained that she would take Ella back to the foundling school. Ella said nothing.

'Don't you want to go?'

'I want somewhere to be me,' was all Ella could manage.

'I know. I have had a letter from Sister Madeline and she says that your stepfather has been to the school and your parents are wanting you back badly.'

'My mother is just pretending. She doesn't really want me and I'm not going back where they fight. What if he kills her and then me?'

Ruth seemed to have no answer to this for a few moments and then she said,

'You must allow that things can change. Your stepfather seems most concerned about you. I'm afraid that you can't stay here, I don't think it would be right. It's a very long way from your home and, if your parents want to see you as they seem to, it would be much better for them to visit you while you are in Sister Madeline's care. Do you understand? Would you be willing to go back under those circumstances?'

'Will they want me back after I ran away?'

'Sister Madeline has assured me that you will be welcomed. They were so worried about you but they understand why you ran away. You want someone to yourself. We all do.'

'You have.'

'When I was your age I had nobody. Life has a way of treating us well when we have had a bad time and I'm sure that things will get better for you. Would you let me take you home? I used to live there and I haven't been back in a long time. You can show me around, I'm sure it must have changed a great deal.'

Ella nodded and then agreed. She was feeling a little bit better but very apprehensive. What if she ran away every time things were bad? She had done it twice now. What if things never got better and she got into the habit of running? Might there come a time when she could not stop?

She did see Julia before the twins left and Julia definitely did not want to go and was in tears. It was all about Ned. It always was about Ned and probably always would be, Ella thought, and she was a little jealous that, though the twins had problems, they had one another. She felt more lonely now than she ever had in her life. She didn't know what she wanted. She didn't want to stay here, nor did she really want to go back to the foundling school. And she certainly didn't want to go back to where she would be afraid at every moment of what would happen at the so-clean house in Consett.

From that moment onward Ella worried and could eat nothing, so it came as something of a relief when she and Ruth got on a train bound for Durham. She wished the journey would go on and on. She knew little of trains except that she liked the movement of them and spent her time watching the country-side as it rushed past like it had somewhere to go. She herself had nowhere to go in some senses. She wondered if she had gypsy ancestry and would not manage to stay anywhere, then she thought back to how happy she had been when her grandma was alive and realized that it was not true. What she needed was to show and be shown love and she was sure that everybody felt like that.

Reaching the school was a lot better than she thought it would be. She saw the thin figure of Sister Abigail who waved and instantly ran towards her, clasping Ella in a warm hug as she said,

'You little tyke. I've never been half so glad to see anybody. Wait until Sister Maddy and Sister Hilary see you.'

Ella was not sure this boded well but Abigail took her into the kitchen where Sister Hilary hailed her as long lost and now found, like the lamb. Sister Maddy welcomed her back and beamed when she saw Ruth and they also hugged. Ella thought she could get used to hugging.

It was strange being there without Julia so she found Brewster on the kitchen window ledge and took him into her arms and heard him purring.

She had been back three days when Sister Maddy talked to her again about her parents. She told her that she must write and say that Ella was back at the school and they were not to worry. Ella wished that she did not have to face something else that was new. She didn't want to see them.

'But they have to know that you are here with us again. I know how concerned they are.'

'Just him,' Ella said, eyes filling with tears.

'I must tell them at any rate.'

Ella didn't sleep that night, though she had been sleeping well before Sister Maddy had told her that her parents should know she was back. She had been trying to keep them out of her mind. She could see now that in some ways she had run away to punish them, as though they could help being who they were. And then she thought that grown-ups should do better – wasn't that part of what being grown-up was all about?

She wondered how the Fancy Man was. He had been kind to her but that was before he tried to kill her mother. She could not go back, she could never go back. She had a week of peace and then he came to the school. She was outside so she saw him first.

She wanted him to be the nice man who had made her porridge but he wasn't any more so she didn't say anything until he got right to her.

'Ella.'

'Mr Wilson.'

'You can call me Bill.'

'I'm not ever going to call you anything,' Ella said and she strode away into the school.

'Ella, please.' He had come after her and other children were looking at her. Ella stopped and didn't say anything to him, she just waited. He stood with his cap in his hands and a look on his face that Ella didn't think she had seen before. 'You ran away.'

'It seems to be the only thing I'm any good at,' Ella managed.

'You're good at a lot of things. Would you come back just for a day or two? Your mam really wants to see you.'

'She never wants to see anybody. She never cared about anything but that . . . that house.'

'Ella, look, she made me swear I wouldn't say anything to you but I think you ought to know. Come back outside, it's a nice day.'

Ella hovered but there were lots of people around and she thought he couldn't make her go anywhere with him. When she wanted she could come back in here and he would have to go away. So she went with him, but very slowly, until they were just a little way from the school, beside where all the streets of houses started up and where the hill began to wind its way down towards the bottom of the valley and the stream and the hospital at the bottom.

It was busy. Women were going shopping and, since it was Saturday, they had children with them. Nobody took any notice of Ella. The Fancy Man could have been her dad just talking to her but of course he wasn't. She didn't want him to talk to her so when he stopped and looked at her and started up she tried not to hear him but it was so hard and when he told her that her mam was not her mam she stared.

Her mam was not her mam. Maybe somebody nice was her mam. Maybe her real mam would come and take her away and she would have a lovely house near a park with swings and there would be cake to eat and she would have a husband who didn't put his hands around her throat to choke her. But then why had she not come for her before now?

And then the Fancy Man explained that her mam was her auntie Lydia and her birth mam had died. Her auntie had had to look after her and it was so hard. In the end Ella was listening to him. They had sat down on a wall and nobody was taking any notice and the whole world had changed.

'So that's why she doesn't like me,' Ella said. 'I'm not hers.'

Gradually, as he didn't say anything and Ella didn't say any more, she saw that the world was crashing. The Fancy Man was crying. Ella was horrified. Men didn't do things like that. He wasn't making a very good job of it. A lass crying might yell and sob and have a snotty nose but all that happened was that his face went very white instead of red, which she thought it always did when people cried, and he put his head down about as far as he could get it so that nobody would see, then he put the back of his hand up to his face and when he took it down it had a very faint sheen on it as though it had rained only on him.

And then he looked in the other direction and there was very little to see, just the way that the hill wound down from the top.

'She doesn't want me,' Ella said.

'She daren't. She'll go on scrubbing that bloody floor until she dies.'

'You mustn't say "bloody",' Ella told him, 'it's a swear word.'

'I don't like being there when you aren't,' he said, 'it's like somebody turned the lights out. I'm so sick of the floor.' And then he started to laugh and then he sniffed and then he blew his nose on a great big white hanky.

'At least you get a clean hanky every day,' Ella said and then laughed and after that he managed to smile at her and she at him.

Thirty-Six

Maddy knew there was something wrong with Hilary because the dishes leaving the kitchen were either overdone, underdone or just plain awful and the women who helped her would come out of there in tears, which had never happened before. Always people loved working with Hilary, she was kind, gentle and always forgiving, but that apparently had gone.

In the end Maddy ventured into Hilary's domain and asked for a few words and what Hilary said confirmed that something was wrong.

'I haven't time at the moment,' she said, hovering over the stove as a pan steamed up into her face, which meant she thought she could get away with not looking at Maddy – certainly a sign that something was adrift, Maddy surmised.

Maddy went back to her office but when she judged that the midday meal was over and everything had been cleared away she appeared again in the kitchen. Hilary left instantly and went outside.

Maddy went to her office and took a cup and put several mouthfuls of whisky into it and followed Hilary. She could feel cold drops on her face and wondered why the rain always began the minute she stepped out of doors. If she could have taken away from the Almighty the way that the weather always seemed against her, she would have done.

Hilary was standing at some distance from the school with her back to it, as though that would make a difference. Hilary took the cup, probably thinking it was tea, and then smelled the whisky and frowned.

'What is this for?'

'You need it.'

'I do not. I never drink spirits.'

'You do now. Come into the office—'

'I would rather not.'

'I want to talk to you and I'm not getting drenched, come on,' and Maddy waited for Hilary to lead the way. 'Sit down,' she ordered once they were inside the office and the door had been shut. Hilary tried to hand her back the cup but Maddy said,

'You're going nowhere until you've got that down you.'

'It's awful stuff, I've never liked it.'

'You need medicine.'

They both finally sat down and Maddy listened to Hilary's sighing.

'You've lost weight,' Maddy said, 'you've lost all your colour. Are you ill?'

'Of course not.'

'You would have said?'

'If it was anything that mattered.'

'But something does matter and you aren't leaving here until you tell me about it.'

Hilary half grinned and Maddy could see why. It was the idea that somebody as small as Maddy could physically stop her from doing anything. But she accepted the polite threat and when the whisky was drunk she put down the cup on Maddy's desk and said,

'Single malt, very nice.'

'You would know?'

'We are almost into Scotland,' Hilary said, as though Maddy had come from some deplorable southern hell. 'My father used to get through quite a bit of that. I always associate the smell of it with him so that's one lovely aspect of it. Every time I get near decent whisky I remember him so well.'

'You miss him?'

'I miss both of them and things have gone so badly. If things had been better it wouldn't have been nearly so hard.'

Hilary looked down at her hands which were now folded in her lap, as though this semblance of an obedient nun would get them somewhere.

'Mr Nattrass has asked me to marry him.'

Maddy nodded and then was silent for a few moments before she said,

'I thought he might.'

'You did?' Hilary stared at her.

'He makes excuses to come here all the time. He has made himself so useful because of you—'

'I don't think that's quite right.'

'All right, so he is a generous man with his time and his farm and his animals, but it is because of you. I think he's loved you since the moment he set eyes on you.'

Hilary paused as though about to deny this and then she sat pondering and frowning and in the end she said,

'Oh, Maddy, I do wish he hadn't and I've put off and put off answering him so that he's assumed I just won't have him and I feel so awful about it.'

And then it was like a huge bubble had popped inside her, Maddy could see. All the problems had come together and now Hilary slouched in her chair as though very tired.

'Do you want to marry him?'

'Yes, of course I do, and no, of course I don't,' and Hilary burst into tears.

Thirty-Seven

It was three days before the twins' father arrived and it was a very long three days for them. They didn't see one another until he got there and that was only when they were put into the carriage. He didn't talk to them or reason with them. He didn't even ask them why they had run away or how they were.

At first Ned didn't look at him, he was so resentful and he felt that his father was the person he despised most in the world. After a while, though, he heard his father sigh and sit back. When Ned felt sure that his father was staring out of the window he glanced at him and it was almost as if he didn't recognize him.

He looked thinner and older. He didn't look like somebody who was in charge. For the first time ever he didn't look like anybody's father and, rather than being glad about this, which Ned thought he would once have been, he felt as though something had been taken from him without which he couldn't manage and that was very strange. Was this the reason why he had not come for them straight away? Was he ill? Ned couldn't understand this. His father could not possibly be ill, he was just his father, he was always there and yet his father kept closing his eyes as though he was very tired and as though he wished he was anywhere else, this when Ned had taken the feeling of wanting to be elsewhere for his own. His father said very little and Ned wished he would be angry or say that they were bad children or that he wished they would stop running away but he didn't, he just sat there and stared out of the window like it was the only thing he could do.

Julia was also silent but then what was there to say? They had tried so hard to be together and now they were but it wouldn't last, none of it ever did, Ned thought.

After a long and rather weary journey they reached their home. They were both worn out by then and all they wanted was to sleep and eat.

The following morning Ned got up, ready to go and apologize to his father and say that he would behave better. He had thought about it a good deal when he awoke and he had decided that it was the only thing to be done. Something had to change and he must be the one to try and achieve it. It would show his father that he was becoming less selfish and more responsible. He felt rather pleased with himself and was determined to sort it out straight away. He had thought a lot about what Mr Armstrong had said and, having scoffed at it in his mind to begin with, he now saw that Mr Armstrong was right.

He would tell his father that if he wanted him to go back to school he would go, but when he had knocked on the library door several times and there'd been no response he entered the room softly, finding it was empty.

He ventured to the drawing room, expecting to find his mother who was almost always there, but she was not. In the end he went to the kitchen. Cook always knew everything.

'I can't find either of my parents.'

'Your father took bad after he came back and not surprising, you and Miss Julia behaving that way,' and Cook clashed a pan lid so hard that Ned jumped. She looked at him and relented.

'Your mother is upstairs looking after your father. He has not been well lately.'

'He seemed all right when he came to find us.' This was not true of course, Ned remembered how he saw his father differently for the first time when he had come to collect them and Ned wished so much that it had been just the same as always. It had not occurred to him that things at home would change. Things here must stay as they were, not alter like that while he was absent. You couldn't run away from home and then discover that it was not the home you had run from. That wasn't playing the game, that wasn't fair.

'Well, he isn't. He's been taking funny turns for a while now. The last thing he needed was to have to travel around the countryside after you.'

Ned left the kitchen to find Julia standing beside the door.

'Father's ill,' he told her. He could see straight away that she didn't understand that.

'Is Mr Blake coming?' she said.

Ned didn't have the courage to climb the stairs and ask after his father but the day wore on and in some ways it was a good deal worse than the days before it had been when he was hungry, lost and without Julia. His sister ate and drank and slept. Ned did none of these things and that night, with Julia sleeping beside him, he lay awake as the hours crawled past.

Ned hoped that his father would be better in the morning. He longed for what was normal, his mother giving a party, his father dining with friends. The house had never felt as silent. It had been bliss when his parents were away and this should have felt the same, he thought, but it wasn't. It felt empty and horrible.

He wished his father was in his library as usual. There was a side of him which wanted his father to insist he went back to school, he needed something to kick against and now there was nothing to kick against. Ned had got what he wanted, he and Julia were together, but the circumstances made it wretched. It was as if everything had been his fault. He had only tried to be in Julia's presence. Was that so very much to ask?

Later that day he caught his mother as she was about to ascend the stairs. She looked blankly at him as though she hadn't remembered he was there.

'Mother, is Father ill?'

She stayed her steps and looked at him. He couldn't quite make out the look and then she said,

'I'm so glad you came back.'

She had never said such a thing in her life.

'I'm sorry we ran away. I didn't understand what a beastly way it was to behave.'

He could see tears in her eyes.

'Where is Julia?' she asked.

'In the kitchen, eating something that isn't white,' he said bitterly. How Julia could eat now he had no idea. 'How is my father? May I see him?'

'Tomorrow, I think would be better,' she said and she went on up the stairs.

The doctor came and stayed the night. Ned ended up sitting on the stairs. He couldn't hear anything and it was quite dark. Julia had gone to bed. The night went on and on until Ned was almost crying.

He ran off when he heard footsteps on the landing. From a distance he saw the doctor and the man's black bag as he finished speaking to Ned's mother and then he came down the stairs. Ned ran out to see the doctor about to get on his horse and Ned tugged at his sleeve so that the doctor turned around. He was smiling just slightly. Ned hadn't seen the man in years. They were rarely ill.

'Ned, my man. How are you?'

'Is my father very ill?'

The doctor hesitated.

'I'm afraid he is.'

'Did we do it?'

The doctor frowned and, ignoring the stable boy who was holding his horse, he took Ned a little way off and then he said with a smile and lightened eyes so that they crinkled,

'How could you do that?'

'We ran away.'

'Did you? How very spirited of you. I ran away once, I got as far as the paddock. I was very small and when I saw that my mother wasn't coming after me I went back.' Then he saw Ned's face and he said, 'It has nothing to do with you running away, Ned, how could it have? Your father hasn't been well for some time. His heart has bothered him.'

'I didn't know.'

'Why would you? He has been to see me several times. Try not to be too concerned,' and he placed a kind touch upon Ned's shoulder and went back to his horse.

The doctor did not come again the following day. Ned took that as a good sign. He didn't know what to do. He had nobody to talk to and, although at one time he had been happy to spend all his days with Julia, now he found that her company was not as entertaining as it used to be. He thought about Harry and wished he could somehow be magicked there.

He even imagined himself and Harry at school together. Once

you had a friend with you it must be so much better. Harry had been good fun while they were away before he got really hungry. You could call Julia a lot of things but fun wasn't one of them any more.

The following night, however, when he was restless he heard the doctor's voice outside. It was cold. He listened to his sister's even breathing for a moment or two and then he put on his clothes and ventured across the landing.

He could hear the sound of his mother crying and the doctor with his sweet comforting voice and then they went into his father's bedroom and closed the door. Ned lay down and waited until dawn broke and nobody came out of the room. Later, at about six o'clock, he went into the kitchen. Cook ignored him. She saw him and sniffed and then she said,

'It's early for you to be about, Master Ned.'

'Is my father dying?'

'Nothing of the sort,' she said, sniffing hard and kneading dough, almost punching it to get the air from it. The other two maids who helped to run the kitchen were not looking at him. One had to rush out for something, the other concentrated on the washing-up, though it seemed to him to be nothing but early morning teacups.

Julia didn't wake until eight, late for her. Typical, Ned thought. When he wanted her to be there she wasn't. She went off to the dining room and was soon devouring brown toast and an omelette, as happy as though nothing had happened. That was the problem, to her everything was right, she was at home and Ned was with her. She smiled at him across the table.

'Let's go to the beach,' she said.

'It's pouring with rain.'

'Do you think Mr Blake will come today?'

Her obsession with Mr Blake was starting to drive Ned nuts. He said every day that Mr Blake was in Newcastle at the safe house and had no reason to come to see them and she said, as she always said,

'But he's our tutor. He must come. He will come later, won't he?'

Ned left the dining room and then he heard his mother's voice in the hall.

'Would you like to go up and see your father?'

Ned hurried to her side.

'More than anything in the world,' he said and she smiled just a little and touched his face, something she had never done before. Ned was encouraged. His father must be better since he wanted to see him, or could it be that it was his mother who wanted him to see his father?

Upstairs he paused on the threshold of his father's room and then opened the door as quietly as he could. A nurse was there. He hadn't seen her before but then perhaps she had been flitting in and out without him noticing her.

The room was not dark but the curtains were half across the big wide windows as though the light intruded and was not allowed in any further.

He hovered by the door as the nurse went out. He could not believe that his father was alone in bed there. He felt weird but all he said was,

'Father?'

'Ned,' his father said, as though in relief, moving his head to the side and seeing Ned as best he could without getting up. Ned felt strange and embarrassed to see his father like that. His father always sat behind his desk and was capable and oddly annoying and a decent combatant. 'Come a little nearer. I haven't been well the last few days so I couldn't really be there for you and Julia. How are you getting on?'

Ned couldn't remember how he was getting on, he was so appalled. The bedroom was huge. He had been in there before, had it always been as large as this? What should he do? What could he possibly say?

'Are you not well, Father?' was all he managed.

'Oh, it's nothing, I'm just tired. It does me good to see you. And is Julia well?'

It was as if his father hadn't noticed them in months, Ned thought. How odd, how very discouraging, when he had brought them home just a few days before. His father was lying down and Ned could see only his face. It looked thin and pale but maybe that was just the lack of light. The doctor, however, had been there again so his father must be very ill.

'We are so very sorry that we ran away. We didn't mean anything.'

'I know that.' Ned couldn't see his father's face very well but he heard the jest in his voice. 'You wanted to be together and I didn't think sufficiently about it. Very foolish of me. I wanted things to be as I wanted them. I thought the school would be good for you and that Julia would benefit from being with the nuns, though I'm not sure with hindsight that any of it was particularly beneficial. Never mind, we do what we can, what we think is right at the time.'

Ned could see his father's face properly by now as he had ventured nearer the bed. For the first time ever his father looked old and, worse than that, he looked white and exhausted. Ned was frightened. His father was his father, he couldn't be ill. He couldn't be lying there being so agreeable. That would be awful, it would put Ned in the wrong, a place he wasn't used to being and didn't think he wanted to go. It would make him like an adult and he wasn't and didn't want to be for a very long time yet.

When he was grown-up he would have to behave well and spend long hours working things out and seeing to the men on the estate and having to get married to somebody who wouldn't want Julia to live with them and it would be awful.

Julia would never marry anybody, how could she, but he would have to marry. Men were supposed to carry things on. Ned was a bit hazy about how this worked but he had seen cats copulating and having kittens and, although it seemed extremely odd, he had the feeling that people did something similarly disgusting. He would be called upon to do it to some woman and Julia would have to sleep alone and be alone and not get in the way and his wife might not like her and . . .

There Ned got lost off. All he could see was his father's slightly smiling, thin and wrinkled face and he hated it all. He was aware for the first time how people grew older, how children grew up, how things moved on, and it frightened him.

'I thought I had lost you,' his father said softly.

Was that it? Was his father not to blame him, not to ask him why he had behaved so badly, why he had run off like that over and over? He tried to think of the reasonable things to say but they no longer seemed reasonable, they just seemed stupid. All he managed was,

'I'm sorry we broke into the safe.'

His father laughed. It sounded sharp and brittle, Ned thought, like glass breaking into small shards, rough and throaty and almost forced. It was horrible.

'Oh Ned,' his father said, 'all I cared about was whether you were all right. The money in the safe was just what I had about me, not real money. I am not so stupid that I would leave any money which mattered in a safe which anybody other than an idiot could have broken into. I thought it was very resourceful of you and, though I was angry at the time, all I could think was that I would never see you again because I had behaved so stupidly.

'It was your mother I was thinking about. She has never been strong and she concerned me. And the papers are replicated, there are copies with my solicitor. You may think I am a chump and not much of a gentleman since I came to it late in life, and perhaps rightly so, but I am not a bad businessman. Otherwise I could never have asked a woman like your mother to marry me, she being so far above me.'

Part of Ned was bewildered, completely lost, all he had assumed had been turned upside down, as though a new world had dawned while he was away. Had his father not been a gentleman? He had always seemed the gentleman to Ned. He felt sure that it was not so much to do with where you came from but how you treated other people, and his father was known to be a good master and a kind man. There was also a contradictory part of Ned which was proud of the Darling heritage. Ned was aware that the Darlings had lived on this land for a very long time, and he was also aware that his father had had the money to marry into this family.

Ned had no idea where it had come from but some good people made money in business, at least he thought they did, and wasn't that one way of getting people together: that one had something the other needed and vice versa? His father was a gentleman, he knew it instinctively. And his mother was certainly a lady and, although his father might not have had a long lineage, he and Julia now were benefitting from house and money and what a fine arrangement it had seemed, he felt sure.

That was good and so surprising that Ned felt bad. Who was

he to judge his father at this point? And he understood at least partly that his parents had done their best, even though to him it had looked as though they had not because they had tried to keep him and his sister apart. They did not understand the way that twins were. He thought that perhaps they never would.

'I wanted you to go to school so that you could be prepared to do whatever you wanted with your life,' his father said. 'I want you to do well at school and go to Oxford or Cambridge and then you can have the whole world for your own.'

Ned wanted to say that he didn't care about any of that, he couldn't go and leave Julia, he never could, and could she go with him? He didn't think so. Surely they would be able to stay here together. It was all they really had ever wanted. It was their home, the place they loved best.

While he stood there his father's eyes dimmed and then he fell asleep. Ned waited for him to wake up again but he didn't and so in the end he crept from the room. He didn't go anywhere near his mother, he didn't even go to Julia. He went and lay down in the cold in his bedroom, numbed.

Thirty-Eight

Hilary had got to the point where she hated receiving letters. Somehow it was always bad news. But she recognized her sister's handwriting and she knew that it was important. Jessica would not write letters to her for the sake of it. The message was brief and bore no date, there was no formality about it and the paper was blotted with ink and bore traces of what she assumed were tears.

Dear Hilary,

Can you please come to me? My husband is so very ill and the doctor thinks he will not live long.

Jessica

Hilary went to Maddy, as she always did with correspondence or any problem which needed consulting about and talking over. Maddy always knew when things were badly wrong, though Hilary felt that Maddy would have known by now whenever she went in flapping a piece of paper.

She had thought she was in control of her emotions but when she got inside the room she wanted to cry. Instead she sat down heavily in a chair. Maddy immediately went over and closed the door, so quickly that Hilary barely had time to collect herself.

Maddy sat down beside her and took her hand.

'What is it?' she said.

'It's my brother-in-law. Jessica says he is dying.' She gave the letter into Maddy's hands and Maddy read it quickly and then she said,

'You must go at once. I will make arrangements and I will ask Abigail to pack your things.'

Hilary thought of all the things she should have been doing but within an hour she was on her way. She did not want to be there and at such a bad time. Her brother-in-law had never liked her and the feeling was mutual. She thought he was a jumped-up ignoramus who had married her sister for the estate. And then she conceded that perhaps that wasn't true, they did have a very good marriage; Jessica had gained his money and he had gained her status and they had looked like a couple right from the beginning.

It was jealousy on her part that made her dislike him, Hilary confessed to herself. He was good-looking, amiable and intelligent enough to have amassed a fortune by himself, his father having been a nobody. Jessica had adored him from the beginning.

After Julia was born it was all damaged somehow. She was imperfect, pity the imperfect child. They had tried to hide her, to pretend, they had kept up appearances, as it was called. They had made things so bad that the children had run away and, even now that they were both back there, trouble still dogged the family.

Hilary usually read her Bible or sang psalms in her head when things were difficult but she could concentrate on nothing. She just wished the journey away, it seemed endless.

When finally she reached the house her sister came outside and ran to her in a way in which Hilary couldn't remember her doing before, in spite of the servants and anybody else who might have seen her.

'He's dead, Hilary, he's dead,' and she broke down. Hilary walked her back to the house and then, in the privacy of the drawing room, she took Jessica into her arms and tried to comfort her.

'Have you told the children?'

Jessica shook her head.

'I didn't know how to, what to say. I haven't seen them. I think I might have been hiding from them, how awful.'

Her sister was in shock, Hilary surmised. She offered to tell them and Jessica nodded gratefully. When Hilary went in search of the twins, however, all she found were cold empty rooms.

She finally ended up in the kitchen and enquired of them and thereafter found them in the dining room.

'Oh, Sister Hilary,' Julia exclaimed and ran to her, rather as her mother had done. Ned merely sat where he was at the table with half a slice of bread and butter in his fingers. He looked down at it.

Then he threw her a searing look.

'He's dead, isn't he?' Ned said it with such flatness that Hilary was horrified. Poor boy.

'Yes.'

'I thought he must be.' Ned was still playing with the piece of bread while Julia clutched at Hilary's skirts.

She held Julia in her arms, close against her, aware that Julia did not understand concepts like death – but then did anybody?

'We did it,' Ned said, still messing with the bread and butter so that Hilary wanted to take it from him. 'We killed him by the way that we behaved.'

'Stuff and nonsense,' Hilary said, pulling the little girl on to her lap as she sat down at the table. 'Your father had a bad heart but he wouldn't listen to the doctors, he wouldn't slow down, your mother says, and she couldn't stop him. It was his life to live as he chose.'

'His heart failed?'

'It did.'

'Not because of us?'

'Certainly not. Men's hearts do not fail because they have disobedient children. Eat your dinner.'

She held Julia on her lap so that Julia did eat and Ned moved as close as he could get without actually sitting on her. She moved an old sofa near the fire and there they sat until Julia fell asleep.

'I knew he was very ill,' Ned said. 'I went up and saw him. I'm glad I did, too. He was kind to me.'

He moved even closer and Hilary saw for the first time in ages that Ned was just a small boy in so many ways. She put an arm around him and kissed the top of his head.

'They've gone to sleep.' Hilary was back with her sister.

'Thank you Hilary, I'm so glad you came, I didn't know what to do.'

'Do you want me to make the arrangements for the funeral?'

'If you don't mind, and write a note to the solicitor.'

Hilary did. She did not imagine there would be any problems. Ned was the heir and presumably his mother would take care of things until he was twenty-one. The estate was prosperous

– Hilary allowed that her brother-in-law had been a very clever man so everything was intact, even better than it had been when he arrived there. She felt sure that he had had good men to see to everything so there was no reason why things shouldn't carry on as they had been.

The undertaker came to see Jessica and Hilary sat in to give her sister support. Jessica seemed completely lost and was so thin that Hilary thought she could almost see through her.

The solicitor seemed reluctant to come to the house but replied to Hilary's letter, saying that he would be there for the funeral and afterwards would read the will. In the meantime a young relative of the same name would be turning up at the house and it would be good if he could be greeted with politeness.

Hilary didn't know what to make of this, so didn't mention it to Jessica, not wanting her sister to worry over whether she would know him, whether she ought to have done.

On the morning of the funeral a young man did turn up in a carriage but Hilary, happening to look out of the windows, didn't know who he was. Perhaps he was part of her brother-in-law's extended family, she imagined, though she knew nothing of them and didn't like to ask Jessica, who had enough on her plate. Her brother-in-law's parents had long since died and he had neither brother nor sister.

She expected the young man to come to the house but he didn't and she had such a lot to do that she thought nothing more of it. He was probably a relative they had not seen for years, merely paying his respects as so many were. People were so widely flung these days that many barely knew their families. Perhaps they were hoping that Edmund had left them something. People did gather for such reasons, Hilary was well aware.

A lot of people would be at the funeral and there would have to be two different meals, one for the family and friends and one for the estate workers. Though it would be difficult to arrange, at least it gave her something to do.

She would leave when it was all over. She felt sure that Abigail and Maddy were missing her and she liked being missed and was eager to go back. She liked having her own life and had never been as glad that she had moved away. And now she had another reason to be glad. She only had to think of Mr Nattrass for her whole body to sing. She knew now that she would marry him and she thought that perhaps having seen Jessica's loss she too had something to lose. She wanted to marry him and be there for him, to sit over the fire with him and have his children. She wanted to marry before it was too late. She had done her best at being a nun, perhaps she would make a good farmer's wife. She felt certain now that she would and she determined to tell him so as soon as she got the opportunity, if he would still have her.

Her brother-in-law, she thought, had been well liked. He had been more than fair to his workers and tenants, and popular, she dared say, with his many friends. She could be alone in not having liked him but that was because he had taken a great deal of what she had thought of as hers. It had not been real, it never would have been hers, but he had taken it as his and that had been that.

She could have stayed on. She remembered him summoning her for an interview after her parents had died and it was nothing more nor less, in the library, where he had sat behind the big desk which had been there for as long as Hilary could remember. He urged her to take a seat in the room where she had sat on her father's lap and talked with him and read to him and had him read to her. She had been very close to her father and perhaps that was why she so disliked Edmund – he was the usurper.

'This is your home, Hilary, I understand that very well, and you are entitled to live here with us.'

Her mother and father were dead, and there had not been long between them for the dying. She thought it was often so for couples who loved one another.

Hilary had been a nun for several years by then in Newcastle and, when she came back for her parents' funerals, she disliked everything that had been done.

She was shocked when her father's will was read and she had been left nothing. She had hoped at least for a contribution towards the convent, but then he had given a good amount of money over to her when she first went to become a nun, presumably the money she would have been entitled to had she ever found a man who would have her, a man she could have endured spending her life with.

Nobody had ever offered for her. She was too big, she was not a dainty feminine type like her sister. When she did dance she towered over her partners and neither liked it. She could not bring herself to simper and be polite and listen to them droning on about themselves while never asking anything about her. Besides which, everybody knew that the place needed a huge input of cash so Hilary didn't stand a chance even of being married for her money since she had none.

She had thought she saw relief in Edmund's face when she said that it was very kind of him but she thought she would stay where she was. She suggested that if he would like to give money to the convent in the future she would be very grateful for it.

That was all. In the event he never had given anything to the convent. His life was full of hunting, shooting and parties, and he spent vast amounts on gifts for his wife, which Hilary got to hear all about when Jessica wrote to her. First the dresses she bought, then trips to Paris and Rome, a grey horse she had much admired . . . All she had to do was name something and it was hers.

Hilary had not envied them. It seemed such a small insular way to behave and she thought worse of it still when she went to the little fell-top village. She was amazed at how selfish and self-absorbed they were. To be fair Julia had shattered that illusion – life had never been the same for them after they had what was called an idiot child. Now Hilary thought again of this while she attended Edmund's funeral.

Jessica had not wanted the children at the funeral, mostly, Hilary thought, because she didn't want to hear any of Julia's loud questions. The child was confused by her father's death; it was possibly the first death she could remember. She kept asking when her father would be back and, since they had no idea how she would react to the coffin and the church, Jessica, having so often neglected to take her children anywhere near a church, kept them well away.

Hilary spotted the young man who had come in the smart carriage. She noticed he was very well dressed. It was obvious that he knew no one and stood alone by the drawing room window, drinking tea. Hilary went across to him.

'Good afternoon,' she said.

He turned from the view, in some surprise, she thought.

'Oh. Good afternoon, Sister.'

'I am Hilary Darling. This was my home.'

'I am Frederick – Waverley.'

'It was very good of you to come to the funeral, Mr Waverley.'

'I had to come to the church and show my respect. I've never been here before.' He glanced around him in some apprehension but there was another part to his look which Hilary did not understand. Hilary thought that she could smell a rat, wasn't that what they called it? Not the young man himself, but some situation which was now arising and which she had had no notion of before this very moment.

'And what do you think of the place?'

'Well, it's . . . it's very cold and bleak,' he said, smiling just a little.

'You live in the south?'

'Mainly in London, though I do have a house in Kent.'

'I've never been to Kent,' Hilary said, 'though I know it is called the garden of England.'

'It is very beautiful. We grow a lot of fruit there.'

The implication to Hilary was that Northumberland was not beautiful. She tried not to bridle.

'So you have come a very long way.'

'I stayed with friends and made my way here more easily than I might have done. Not to come to the funeral seemed very remiss.'

'You knew my brother-in-law well?'

He looked down at the lovely oak floor.

'My mother died when I was very small. I was brought up by my aunt. She died about three years ago. I miss her very much. Mr Waverley was my last remaining relative.'

Hilary gave it up; he was volunteering nothing. Also, she could see Jessica looking across so she moved away and started to mingle with other guests. When they met amid the throng Jessica said,

'Who was that young man you spoke to?'

'Some kind of family, I think,' Hilary said, adding nothing which might worry her sister, who was already having too bad a day.

Jessica hesitated as she always did when she was about to say something which she thought mattered.

'I ought to go and hear the will read, even though I doubt there will be any surprises. Mr Flowers said it wasn't necessary and I should spare myself as best I could.'

Hilary knew that Jessica was waiting for Hilary to say that she would go in her stead, so before the end of the afternoon she was seated at the long table in the main dining room. Mr Flowers was already there and stared at her entrance. Hilary knew she could be an imposing figure in her grey habit with her boatly white topknot, as she privately called it.

Mr Flowers was standing at the head of the table. The young man from the funeral was sitting about halfway down the table so Hilary went and sat exactly opposite to him. He avoided looking at her.

Mr Flowers began to read the will. Hilary tried to arm herself but it didn't make any difference and in her heart she had known that it would not. There were various small bequests to friends, servants and people on the estate, but everything that mattered had been left to the young man who sat opposite. He was Edward's only child from his first marriage, she saw now.

Jessica was to have twenty pounds a year. There was no mention of the children. The young man did not react. Hilary's heart did something very nasty. She thought she heard it clunk on to the expensive Turkey rug beneath her stout shoes. The young man got to his feet and left seconds after Mr Flowers stopped speaking and before Hilary could collect her shattered thoughts and say anything. Mr Flowers, not looking at her, began to pack his papers.

'That is an iniquitous will. It cannot be right,' she said, bewildered.

He coughed.

'There was nothing wrong with the will. It was legally drawn up. Mr Waverley asked me to do it some time ago.'

'So,' Hilary said, 'were you going to tell me that the widow has been left twenty pounds a year or were you hoping to duck out of it? Was that why you discouraged her from being here, because you were afraid she might make some sort of fuss when her husband had just been buried?'

He eyed her.

'Sister—'

'Hilary. I am Hilary Darling.'

'I do know that.' She had known him since she had been a small child.

'I am appalled.' Hilary could hear her voice quivering just when she had needed it to be stout and true.

'I'm sure you are. There is nothing to be done. It was what Mr Waverley wanted.'

'I never liked him,' Hilary said, 'but I didn't realize that he was unfeeling and cared nothing for his wife and children.'

'It was a very usual will. Most men give everything to their first-born son. It saves confusion.'

'You knew that Edmund had been married before?'

'I would have been worse than indiscreet had I said so to anyone. He was very young and she was an heiress, which is how he was able to marry your sister and buy this place.'

Hilary had always believed that Edmund was a clever man and had made his money. Apparently not so. And she resented Mr Flowers' implication, though it was certainly true – the whole thing had been a bargain and Edmund Waverley had in fact bought the Darling estate. It made her want to be sick.

'Why did this young man not come to the house openly and introduce himself instead of lurking about like a mongrel?'

'I expect he was not given to hanging himself out to dry.'

'Did his father see him often?'

'I believe so. There was a house in London where Frederick lived with his aunt and an estate in Kent.'

Hilary could remember her sister saying that Edmund had gone south on business. He did it quite often, though what business it might be Hilary had not worked out before now.

'Frederick went to Eton and then to Cambridge. He is a fitting man to inherit his father's estates.'

How strange, Hilary thought, that her brother-in-law should have a child like that and then such difficult twins. She could not help being pleased at how difficult they had been. Had she been in a better humour she might have smiled. In the meantime Jessica had to be told.

Mr Flowers had more bombs to drop before he left.

'I have had instructions from Mr Waverley. Your sister-in-law and her children have a week and by then they must leave. The contents of the house and the jewellery belong to the estate so she must take nothing with her,' and Mr Flowers left.

Hilary could not help going after him as he walked through the hall. 'He couldn't let them live here even though he so clearly doesn't want it? It's dreadful. It's very bad indeed and he is a bad master and the folk who live and work here will be the worse for the way that it has been left, so negligent and so unfeeling.'

'The house is to be shut up. The servants will be found positions in various other places. The animals are to be sold.' Mr Flowers, having dropped his final bombshell, departed. Hilary had to stop herself from wanting to kick him into the North Sea.

Hilary went back and sat over the dining room table, wondering how on earth she would tell Jessica that she had nowhere to go, nothing to take from here and twenty pounds a year to bring up her children. How insulting that her brother-in-law had left them only that.

She swore she would send back the twenty pounds and tell Frederick to leave them alone, and then she knew that she wouldn't say anything of the kind. Who was to say that he might not change his mind and come north again? He had not seen his father before he died and that must be difficult. Also, as far as she could gather, he was not married so perhaps he had no one. Why not invite him to come to the village and see his stepmother and the two children? Not because of money but just because of family? Insults would achieve nothing.

Hilary felt cowardly about it all. She didn't want to have to take the responsibility for telling her sister what had been done here and that at the moment she could hope for nothing. Her husband had died, leaving her with two difficult children, and she had nothing to take and nowhere to go.

Jessica was alone in the drawing room. Hilary was inclined to ask where the twins were but then she did not want them around when she told her sister that she had lost everything. Jessica was looking a little less pale than previously. That wouldn't last, Hilary thought.

'I thought you must be about done,' Jessica said. 'Let me ring for some tea.'

A feeling of utter despondency hit Hilary now and she sat down with a thump on the closest chair. They were not sisters for nothing. Jessica eyed her and waited but Hilary wanted to put off the moment for as long as she could.

'What did Mr Flowers say?' Jessica asked when the silence was heading towards prolonged.

'Maybe the tea.'

'What did he say?'

Hilary couldn't look at her. She wondered whether her sister had ever fainted and might she do that now?

At that moment Julia bounded into the room. Why did such things always happen exactly at the moment when you didn't want them to, Hilary wondered, in exasperation. Julia did not understand about her father dying and kept asking where he was. Hilary had tried to explain that he had gone to heaven. She couldn't do with purgatory and to be fair she was starting to think that nobody needed it, things were so bad anyhow. However, Julia had no idea of heaven either. Thankfully now she merely said,

'Auntie Hilary' – Hilary was sometimes 'Auntie' and sometimes 'Sister', Julia not distinguishing between them, 'are you staying here with us now for always? And is Mr Blake coming? We could have a picnic on the beach and run into the sea.' She climbed on to Hilary's lap and sat there, smiling.

Ned came in too.

'Who was that man in the carriage who just left?' he said.

'That was a relative.'

'What sort of a relative?' Ned asked.

'Why don't you go to the kitchen and ask for some tea?' Hilary suggested.

'We have bells,' Ned said.

Jessica began to catch on.

'Cook is making ginger biscuits. I dare say they are just out of the oven,' she said and that sent the children scrambling away. 'You'd better tell me before they realize that I have just told a lie. We probably have three minutes.'

'That man was Edmund's only child from his first marriage. He inherits everything.'

Jessica didn't react. She didn't faint, she didn't say anything, and then to Hilary's astonishment she said,

'I knew there was something wrong.'

'Mama, you told a fib,' declared Julia, scuttling back into the room. 'They were cinnamon buns and I don't like them.'

One of the maids took the children to bed. They were quite excited at the idea, it seemed to Hilary. Julia was ecstatic and chatted, Ned was pale and said nothing. Hilary only hoped he would sleep because they would have to be told that they had lost their home and what she had thought was their inheritance.

Nobody spoke for a minute or two and it seemed to Hilary that time seemed to stretch endlessly before her such as it never had done before. It was like looking at the sea, knowing that there were a great many things beyond the horizon and you were scared because you hadn't met any of them before now.

'Nothing?' was all Jessica said.

'Nothing.'

'I don't understand.'

'Mr Flowers says it is very common that the first-born son should inherit everything.'

'But . . . there was no former marriage. There was no—' Jessica stopped there and gazed across the fire at her sister. 'He would have told me. He loved me, he . . . he loved only me.'

'I gather it was what you call a marriage of convenience. I suspect it was. He had looks and youth, she had money.'

'She was an heiress?'

'I think so. I don't know much. It's been such a shock. Maybe you should go and see Mr Flowers.'

'I don't think I could stand being in the same room with him,' Jessica said, shuddering. 'Why would Edmund have left me nothing? I have been his good and faithful wife.' Then a thought occurred to her. 'Do you think it was because we had an idiot child?'

The same thing had occurred to Hilary but she shook her head.

'But to have nothing? To be turned out of my own home with two children and with no money? How could he do that to me?'

'I don't think he would think of it like that.'

'Then how did he think of it?'

'I suppose he thought it was the right thing for a man to do.'

Jessica's eyes were bewildered and suddenly swam with tears.

'To make his wife and children homeless?'

'Perhaps he intended to alter it and then just . . . just forgot.'

The shock was too much for her sister, Hilary could see. She floundered for something to say.

'How could he have done that? How?'

'I don't know. I'm sure he didn't intend to hurt you.'

'Oh Hilary, what am I to do now?'

Hilary went over and took her sister into her arms, something she had not several days ago ever thought she would have to do again.

They sat over the fire until Jessica finally took herself off to bed. Hilary nearly offered to go with her because she didn't think her sister would sleep, but she had something she needed to do first, so she merely wished her goodnight and then went into the study and sat down in Edmund's chair behind the desk. She took thick cream notepaper, pen and ink and she wrote a letter to Maddy.

Dear Maddy – Hilary tried for formality and then couldn't manage it.

Things are awful here, the funeral was appalling and I have the most enormous boon to ask. I don't know whether Mother would approve but my sister and her children are now destitute, unless you count the twenty pounds a year she has been allowed. Edmund, God rot him — I'm sorry — has left everything to his first-born who is the spawn of his former marriage and the young man has given Jessica and the children a week to get out, which I thought was overwhelmingly kind. They are allowed to take nothing with them.

Would it be possible for you to ask Mr Gilbraith if he would hire some kind of conveyance so that Jessica and the children can come back to the village? I don't know what else to do. I know that we have very little space for any more children, never mind my entire wretched family, but hopefully it will be only a temporary measure. When my mind makes its way in the direction of normality I will think of something else to be done with them.

Jessica is amazingly calm. I assume she is in shock. Ned is horribly aware of what is going on and will have to be told at some point. There is no way that we can keep the news from him. Julia, of course, is in happy ignorance and still waiting for her father to return. Please send me a kind word. I feel so alone.

Ever,

Hilary.

Hilary had not underestimated Ned. He came softly into the library where she was just finishing her letter and he said,

'Auntie Hilary, when are you going to tell me what is going on? I know children aren't supposed to say anything in these matters but I worry more not knowing. I've never seen my mother like this, so calm and detached. Is this what happens when your husband dies?'

He looked around for a moment as though expecting his father to pop up from somewhere and then, sighing, he sat across the desk from her and looked straight at her. Hilary knew that she could put it off no longer.

'The man with the carriage, that was your half-brother, Frederick—'

Ned couldn't contain himself.

'A half-brother? But he didn't speak to me, he didn't come to Mama. Why not? I've always longed for a brother.'

'I think he felt quite wrong,' and that was appropriate, Hilary thought. Frederick Waverley was wrong all the way, just as his father had been, selfish, unfeeling, unseeing and mean.

Ned sat down and then stood up again, not knowing what to do, Hilary thought.

'Why did he come here then, if he didn't want to know us?'

What was the point in not telling him? Sooner or later he would have to know.

'He inherits the estate,' Hilary said.

There was no other way of putting it but she hated how stark it sounded.

Ned didn't say anything for so long that Hilary rather hoped Jessica would come back downstairs, but she didn't so there was nobody there to witness one of the most difficult moments of Hilary's and Ned's life.

She gazed at the little boy as he took in the information, rejected it, tried to accept it and then sat there, eyes widening. It seemed to Hilary that he put on several years as he did so. Children so often had to, she knew. Ned became an adult in those seconds and it was a horrible thing to see, yet she had witnessed it so many times by now. To have it happen to Ned was so very hard.

'But it's ours.'

'Yes, I know.'

Ned couldn't get his thinking beyond that he was a Darling in one way and that the estate had always been theirs, and Hilary was rather proud of the way that he reacted though she knew it would do no good.

'It belonged to the Darlings, Mama's family and yours too, didn't it?'

'Yes.'

'But he gets it because he was born first?'

'Something like that.'

'I still don't see why.'

'No, I know. It's supposed to be simpler.'

Had he been twelve he might have said,

'For whom?' but he didn't. It took a lot to silence Ned but she had managed it.

'Do we get to stay?' he asked, just when she was feeling like screaming into the silence.

This question she had anticipated and yet it was all the harder when it came from this young face with the disillusioned eyes.

'I'm afraid not.'

'Where are we to go?'

'We'll sort something out.'

'Will I go back to school?'

'I don't know yet.'

'And what about Julia? And Mama?'

'I don't suppose your father meant to hurt you.'

Ned looked long into the fire and then back at her face and that was when Hilary felt she must tell him what she had done. At least it would give him some idea of what came next.

'I have written to Sister Madeline and she will send us a horse and trap so that we can leave. We have a week.'

Ned went on sitting there until Hilary murmured,

'Shall I take you back to bed?'

He shook his head and left the room, walking like a little old man. It took all of Hilary's strength to watch him.

Thirty-Nine

Ned could not believe that he had to go. No matter how many times he had been told he was about to lose his home and everything which had belonged to it his mind rejected it as his stomach might reject bad food. He felt like throwing up.

That he was to be a pauper and go back to the little town where he had wanted to be with Julia seemed the hardest thing that he had ever had to do. He was finally to get what he wanted and now he understood the poison in such matters. He had been granted his wish and had had everything taken away from him.

His mother was now standing gazing out of the drawing room window, though he was certain she did not see it. He didn't think she saw anything. She no longer looked like his mother – that beautiful glittering woman was gone, and this wraith had taken over. She was almost see-through, he thought. Her face was so pale it was nearly lifeless, her eyes had gone dull and the black dress which had been made so hastily for her mourning did her no favours. But then wasn't that what mourning was supposed to look like? She was skinny and somehow almost shriveled, as though life had dealt her too many blows, and he was sure she felt like that, he did too. It was cruel to them all.

Ned felt guilty at every moment. He had got what he wanted and at what cost? It didn't matter what anyone said, he would never forget that he had caused his father's death and his mother's grief, and now they were to lose everything and go to that awful little town which he had thought would set him free. He had never felt less free now that he had no options.

They had to leave, his mother and Hilary had said it so many times that it had gone into his soul like he was being seared. He felt burnt, dried up, finished. He had no energy left, no will. His life was soured and spat out.

He went to his room when it was dark and he did not want to be with Julia any more. He became angry and the energy returned. It made him stamp and shout and cry from sheer frustration and self-hatred. He threw things at the walls but nobody protested. Nobody came to him. The servants were not his or his mother's any more, so if he rang a bell he felt as though there would be no response. No doubt they too felt as if their world had collapsed.

The days were both too quick and horribly slow, all at the same time, but he had thought of something so that he could take a kind of revenge. He had seen his mother and his auntie Hilary wrapping up the jewellery, none of which they were allowed to take with them.

He couldn't understand that. Surely his mother was entitled to the diamonds which had been his grandmother's and her mother's before her but no, he did understand. Frederick Waverley, whoever he married, would have the diamonds, even if they never lived there again, even when the servants were dismissed and the place allowed to fall down. Ned truly believed that that was what Frederick would do because he didn't care about it, he had no sense of responsibility for it. It was just a piece of ground to him.

Ned had heard the kitchen servants crying that day and he

was ashamed of his class. They were supposed to protect other people, to provide jobs, not treat them like dirt, or as things to be disposed of. The whole point of estates such as this was that it was a family, people were meant to be looked after, to be given jobs and houses and be a part of something. It was not about power or will, it was about carrying on and being there and being part of something all together, something which you cared so much about. That land was theirs.

Only it wasn't any more. His father had destroyed that because he had given it to a man who didn't belong here and might never show his face there again.

Ned had decided differently about the diamonds. He swore that whoever Frederick married would never have them. They would never leave the Northumbrian shores. They would stay there forever and ever, no matter who came and went, no matter what happened. He would do this one thing and nobody would be able to undo it and he would never tell anyone what he had done. He would have his revenge in one way, he would steal the diamonds and put them where nobody would ever find them.

He didn't put it off. There was no sense to it, and no need. That very night he waited upstairs in his bed until the house subsided into silence.

Julia went off to bed as usual but his aunt and his mother sat on and on as they had done every night since his father had died and his auntie Hilary had come to the house. They would sit over the fire and there he thought his auntie Hilary would try to comfort his mother. He was beginning to think that his auntie Hilary was the only person he really loved beside Julia.

It was almost one — he heard the grandfather clock in the hall strike the half hour and then the three-quarter when they came upstairs. Ned watched them from his door. His mother had done weeping by then for yet another day but his auntie Hilary had an arm around his mother. Ned watched it and admired her strength, she was there for them when nobody else cared.

Finally, when all was quiet and he had waited a good long time – he had no illusions about women going straight off to sleep in such circumstances – he put on his socks, carried his shoes and made his way as quietly down the stairs as he could. Luckily he knew those stairs so well he made no sound, and even at that moment he felt awful about leaving them for good.

He went into the library and unlocked and opened the desk where the jewellery was being held until they left the house and everything had been accounted for. It was not difficult and nobody would suspect it, everybody had other things to think about.

Finally he reached the hall and then he went into the back of the house, undid the bolts in the back door and, putting on his shoes, let himself into the yard.

Luckily it was a fine clear night, which was a big help when you were going to do something such as he was now.

Ned made his way down to the shore. It wasn't far and was one of the reasons why the farm had been built there so many hundred years ago. The land was sound and fertile and the fishing was good. He knew where the little boat lay, the one that they had always used. He had checked it earlier that day and knew that it was sound. He got into it, pushed it across the wet sand and then he rowed for a very long way until the land was barely to be seen in the distance.

There he paused, stowing his oars very carefully – it wouldn't do to lose them out here where the fog could get up within seconds and blind you – and when the wind was still and the sea was calm he put the diamonds over the side. He did not put the velvet case they had in with them, he dropped them over the side and had the satisfaction of seeing them sink, they were so heavy.

He rowed about half a mile further before he dropped the velvet case over the side and then he just hoped that nobody would ever find them. They were the Darling diamonds, they would never belong to anybody else.

Forty

Jay Gilbraith and Mr Nattrass came for them. Hilary was so grateful that she could not help going outside just as they arrived and telling Mr Gilbraith so. The fact that Mr Nattrass was there too made her feel so much better that she was ashamed at her joy. His face was nicely blank but she could not help going to him, after thanking Mr Gilbraith, and touching the front of his jacket while looking into his eyes and saying, through sudden tears,

'I'm so very glad you came. I needed you.'

Mr Gilbraith had tactfully gone a little way off and Mr Nattrass now looked deep into Hilary's eyes and saw the love there.

'I will always be there when you need me,' he said hoarsely.

'I shall never let you go anywhere without me,' she said so softly that nobody else could hear. She was half-ashamed because her sister's husband was dead but there is a time for everything, it said so in the Bible, and despite the circumstances and the problems Hilary felt as though her time was about to come, almost as though God thought she had earned it. She did hope so.

The four-wheeled carriage was beautiful. She could not think where they had got it from and for some reason it made her feel better. She felt so much less alone after Mr Nattrass and Jay got there and longed to confide in Jay the way that she knew Maddy did and indeed, when her sister was not about and the children could not hear, he said,

'I'm so sorry, it must have been a dreadful shock,' and Hilary said,

'It's been awful. Poor Jessica. I keep thinking she will falter but she doesn't. Why do people do such things?'

'I don't know.'

'The house has belonged to the Darling family for hundreds of years. Now it's gone. My parents must be turning in their graves. Well, we don't need to keep you. We have the clothes on our backs and little else. I'm so sorry to bring this burden to you.'

'Hey, we will be fine,' he said, 'don't worry. You and your family will never starve while I live.'

And he smiled such a good smile that Hilary took heart. He also smiled at the man by her side and nodded in acknowledgement.

'You are a very good man,' she said, squeezing his arm but moving just a little closer to Mr Nattrass, hoping that forever after he would be but a few yards away.

Keen to get back, Jay went to look for the children but they were not in the house or the grounds. He finally saw them on the beach and he knew then what a hard parting this was for them.

Nobody spoke. The twins didn't even turn from the waves when he got to them.

'You have to come now,' he said.

'Mr Blake will be here when the summer comes,' Julia said. 'It isn't that far away, is it now? We have to be here.'

In the end Jay picked her up and she clung to him, arms around his neck, and hid her face against his shoulder.

'Ned? Are you coming?' he said.

Ned could not believe that he was looking at his home for the last time. He had thought that he would never leave here. He could not understand why his father had not wanted this place for him when his mother's family had always lived there. Perhaps your mother's family meant nothing. Now, that last summer with Julia and Mr Blake would live in his memory as the last good summer of his life. As the carriage drew him away he looked back and back until his neck ached long after the house had gone from sight.

'I will get it back,' he promised himself, 'one day I will get it back.'

Julia was asking where they were going and whether Mr Blake would be there. Ned tried to close his ears.

When they reached the foundling school he didn't want to get down from the carriage. Was this to be all that he could wish for? They had been nothing but a burden to his father. He could have left them things, Ned felt sure. The estate must be worth a lot of money, yet here they were with nothing.

He thought longingly now of how good it had been to have a friend before he and Harry had become so hungry that they couldn't think. He thought about the last summer and Mr Blake and he wondered for how long he would have to live on those memories.

He had almost got what he wanted. He and Julia were here on the hill top at the foundling school for girls. Even the name made him want to groan. Now he had no tutor there was nobody to engage his mind in anything interesting and he dared say nothing.

The house they were given was tiny. Ned had never been in such a small place. It was on a terrace right in the middle and there were a lot of people all around when they arrived. Small children were playing outside, women were out washing windows and gossiping and they had all craned their necks to see his mother get down from the carriage in her black crepe dress followed by Julia, who was oblivious to everybody.

Mr Gilbraith had helped his mother down and now she stood at her front door. She had probably never seen such a front door or such a small house. She hesitated. He opened the door and ushered her inside and Ned and Julia followed.

It was a ghastly little house and barely furnished. It had two rooms downstairs and upstairs were two bedrooms, very small with nothing in them.

'There are no beds,' Julia said.

Trust Julia to be obvious, Ned thought.

'The men will be bringing them later.'

His mother stood as though stunned and then she tried to thank Mr Gilbraith. Ned walked out of the room in disgust, into the back street where washing was hanging on lines over the unmade road and the wind from the fell made you aware of the skin around your ankles and it smelled raw and sharp as it whistled its way past you.

He didn't think he had felt as bad as this since his father had died but at least he no longer felt responsible. His father's behaviour had hardened Ned's feelings. A man who could leave his family like this did not deserve the guilt which Ned had heaped upon his own shoulders. He no longer burned and felt responsible. He just felt lonely and empty and awful and nobody eased it for him, except that moments later Julia was there as usual bouncing around beside him. When had she become so irritating? She was still on about Mr Blake. Ned turned on her.

'Would you stop going on about him?'

Julia stared at him. Then she began to cry and Ned felt awful. He felt bad enough without her doing that.

'I want to go home,' she wept.

Ned felt like doing the same. He left her and went inside. His mother was walking about the rooms as though she thought it was a bad dream and if she wandered sufficiently it would go away.

As he stood there was a noise in the back lane and two men arrived with beds. They were ghastly things, tiny and iron and black, with thin mattresses such as he remembered from school.

Sister Hilary arrived, all brisk and energetic. Ned wanted to throw a large rock at her. She took linen from downstairs and began to make up the beds, encouraging Julia to go with her.

Julia liked her aunt so she cheered up and off they went upstairs. There was a chair in what they called the front room and his mother sat down in that, waiting for what Ned was not quite clear, but as though she did not know what to do. It was hardly surprising, she had never done anything in her life that he could recall. Perhaps she was waiting for a maid to make some tea and bring it to her.

That of course Sister Hilary did, setting light to the kitchen fire. After that Julia became even more enthusiastic. She liked the fire, he knew, she liked the brown bread and butter, helping Hilary put the kettle over the fire.

'If you want something to do—'

'I don't want something to do,' Ned told Hilary and stalked out.

Hilary, urging Julia to touch nothing, went out after him.

'I'm sorry,' she said promptly and to his back. Ned did not know he had been waiting for someone to notice. He turned to her.

'Do you know you are the only person who has said such a thing,' he managed, eyes blurred with unshed tears. 'And don't tell me it will get better. I suppose I deserve all this for not staying at school and for . . . for all the other things I did.'

'No, you don't.' Hilary moved nearer. Ned thought that if she put an arm around him he would hit her but she didn't.

'I do feel it was partly my fault,' Hilary said, 'urging you to come here and be with Julia. That worked well.'

Ned had never heard of irony but it made him smile and he turned to her. He said, and he couldn't help it,

'I do like you, Auntie Hilary.'

'I have to like you, Ned, you are my only decent male relative.'

He smiled even more at that.

'I feel like going down to London and killing Frederick,' And here Ned couldn't think of what Frederick was like so all he said was: 'He's a nasty pasty.'

Hilary urged him inside and she put a hand on his arm.

Ned went in with her and drank some tea, which he hated, just to show willing. His mother had not moved from her chair. The men came back with other chairs, a dining table of sorts which was very small and didn't stand straight so that they had to put paper under one leg. And then Sister Maddy arrived and Hilary introduced them. His mother sat there like she was stuffed and made very little sound.

She had Ella with her. Julia ignored Ella. She could only cope with Ned when anybody else was around, so Ned could have told Sister Maddy that it was a very bad idea. Ella kept close to Sister Maddy.

Ned had the horrible feeling he might be sent to live on Mr Nattrass's farm and do the sort of things his father had paid other people to do, and then he remembered what Mr Armstrong had said about him being selfish and didn't ask. At least he didn't have to go back to that awful school.

After Sister Maddy had drunk her tea she said softly to him, 'Will you come back see me later, Ned? I would like to talk to you.'

Ned felt sick again now and he recognized the feeling. Somebody was paying for him to go back to the school. Maybe it was Harry's father – perhaps having got over himself and wanting to send Harry he thought he would send the two boys off together. How ungrateful it would seem if Ned refused. If asked he saw now that he couldn't refuse, otherwise he would be a burden on the people here – his mother and his auntie Hilary and Sister Maddy.

He waited just a little while until the two nuns and Ella left. His mother was still sitting there. He thought he would go mad. He managed to avoid Julia, sneaking out the back way when she was showing her mother a picture book she had got from Auntie Hilary.

Ned legged it up to the foundling school and arrived breathless at Sister Maddy's door. She urged him inside and into a stout wooden chair across the desk from her. She looked serious. Oh dear.

'I have to go, don't I?'

Sister Maddy looked bemused.

'Go where?' she said.

'Back to . . . to that school.'

'Oh, no.' Her brow cleared. 'What made you think that?'

Ned, somewhat reassured, slumped into the chair.

'I thought Mr Naples might have offered to pay for me.'

She frowned.

'Oh dear me, no,' she said, 'you weren't hoping?'

'Of course I wasn't,' Ned said.

He was offended that Mr Naples had not offered but of course he didn't want to go. Though maybe if Harry had been there it would have been much better. Ned hadn't had a real friend before but he knew that Harry would not want to be friends with him now since Ned had scorned him. They had not spoken to one another in so long and not written. Ned could not bear to think of Harry and how lucky he was on his estate which he would inherit from his father – at least unless his father had behaved badly and already been married and had other sons. Ned hoped he had not. He liked Harry, he was taken aback at how much he did. Harry had courage and, despite everything, given the chance they might have been real friends.

'I'm not surprised,' Sister Maddy said.

He was always amazed at the way that nuns said exactly what was on their minds. They were not like the people he knew and he rather liked it – but then what was the problem?

'I have had a letter from Mr Flowers,' she said.

She picked up the thick cream paper and Ned knew exactly what it was about. How on earth would he lie to her? Then he decided that he wouldn't lie. There was nothing anybody could do.

'He says that there is some jewellery they cannot find and I didn't like to ask your mother about it.'

'Does Mr Flowers think my mother would go off with

something she had been told she was not entitled to?' Ned said scathingly.

'Diamonds,' Sister Maddy said, neatly evading the question. 'They are family heirlooms, he says.'

'I don't know anything about precious stones,' Ned told her.

'I expect one of your ancestors took to diamond mining,' she said.

Now that was a comforting thought. He had not imagined his family going off to other places to do something adventurous and exciting.

'I understand that they are worth a great deal of money.' Sister Maddy stopped here, looking at him. She thought pausing would get him to tell her what she wanted to know but Ned knew that one and merely looked back at her. Eventually she gave in.

'Do you know anything about them?'

'My mother used to wear them at parties. Julia and I would sit on the landing and watch the glitter of all those women wearing coloured gemstones.'

'Ladies?'

'Some of them had titles, I expect,' Ned said, feeling cool and calm.

'So you don't know anything about the diamonds?' Sister Maddy, he thought, was not the kind of person who gave in easily.

'I know they belong to the Darling family.'

'That's just it,' she said, 'they don't belong to the Darling family any more.'

That nearly clinched it. Ned would have bitten out his tongue rather than admit to anything.

'I suppose that depends on how you look at it,' he said.

'What do you mean?'

'Well, they were passed down as the Darling men gave them to their wives and my father gave them to my mother because he had to so you could say that they were hers rather than belonging to other people since she was from the Darling family and he wasn't. The head of the family always gave them to his bride. My father did at one point want to put them in a safe in Mr Flowers' office but my mother loved to wear them so much and, after all, what is the point in having jewellery if you don't get to wear it, she would say. She did look very pretty in them, though I can remember handling the necklace once and it was very heavy and my mother is so very small.'

Sister Maddy was giving him the hard stare Mr Blake had been so good at sometimes. Ned wished Mr Blake was with them – Julia was right, he had been a huge loss.

'A family heirloom isn't the same thing as a woman owning jewellery,' Sister Maddy said, 'and I'm sorry to ask you this but did you steal them?'

'Do you see anything on me? I wasn't even allowed to take my favourite books and they meant a lot more to me than any jewellery. Can you imagine Frederick wanting to read about elves and pixies?'

'You like to read about those things?'

'Not particularly.'

'So you hid the diamonds on the property?'

'I didn't.'

Sister Maddy sighed and then she said frankly,

'Well, I will have to write to Mr Flowers and tell him so.'

And Ned went off feeling better.

*

Maddy went to Jay. She liked to go and visit his big house on the fell. His office was on the fell side of the building and got the worst of the weather, which she knew he loved, but it was a calm day, no wind across the bleakness, and when she told him the problem he said,

'Do you want me to turn him upside down and hope the diamonds fall out of his pockets?'

'I don't think he's telling me the truth.'

'Evading the question isn't quite the same thing. I think Ned must be exceptionally clever.'

'He is. He's also very bitter. I think he's done something with them.'

'Does it matter?'

'I think it will to Frederick Waverley. When you think something's all yours you can get worked up about small things.'

'Small things?'

'Well they are,' she said.

Hilary had rather reluctantly told Maddy that she and Mr Nattrass would be married.

'I feel that we should wait until Jessica is out of mourning but I don't want to.'

'I don't see why you should. You've done so much for your family already they can hardly begrudge you your happiness.'

'I could have them to live with us.'

'That is the worst idea of all,' Maddy said with such heat that Hilary was pleased.

'Jessica has her own life to lead and although it will be difficult for her now she will have to get on with it, just as everybody else has to. You should not sacrifice a moment of your happiness for her sake.'

'It seems unchristian.'

'I don't think it is. Besides, for all the rest of us it would be lovely to have a wedding. We need something to cheer us.'

'You always manage to say the right thing. I don't know how I'll ever make any decisions without you.'

Maddy smiled.

'Neither of us is going far,' she said, 'and a lot of your decisions from now on will be quite different and you will have your husband to advise you.'

'There is something else as well,' Hilary said. 'I think I should write to Frederick Waverley via Mr Flowers and ask if he would come to the wedding, despite his mourning.'

'That is a very good idea,' Maddy said.

> To Frederick Waverley
> c/o Mr A.S. Flowers
> 22 Northumberland Street
> Newcastle upon Tyne

Dear Mr Waverley

I hope you are not in despair at your father's death though it would hardly be surprising if you felt you had lost everything. My sister and I thought it was so very civil of you to be there at his funeral when you live so many miles away.

I know it seems tactless but I am about to leave the sisterhood and be married.

I have waited a very long time for this to happen and so you will have to forgive me the hasty way I appear to have gone about this.

The man I am to marry, Mr Nattrass, has a small farm here. We would very much appreciate it if you could be there on the day, even just for a few hours. I will ask Mr Gilbraith to put you up in his house and I know that he will be more than willing. I think it would be a huge favour not only to my sister but to her two children to meet their half-brother. Ned has always longed for a brother and I feel that they would be happy to have you among them and so would I on this so special day. We have no family but you, please do come, you will be made very welcome and my sister would have somebody to talk to about her husband. These things are important and she will want to know about your life in London and Kent. She loves the south so very much. It would make all the difference to her to have you near her.

Your aunt,

Hilary Darling

Forty-One

It was almost six weeks after Ella came back that she was called to Sister Madeline's office one Saturday morning and found her mother and the Fancy Man standing in front of Sister Madeline's desk. Her mother was smiling at her. At that moment Ella's first instinct was to run away. She didn't think she had seen her mother smile before, it was unnatural and it could not last.

Her mother — and Ella had to remind herself again that this woman was her aunt and not her mother, for it was hard to think of her in any new way — looked almost like her grandma when she did that but Ella didn't trust it and didn't close the door.

Sister Maddy came to her, smiling and greeting her kindly, the way she always did with everybody. She closed the door and urged Ella forward, saying that her parents had come especially that day to see her and she was now going to go and give them just a little time to say hello.

Ella turned and watched as the sister went out and then she gazed longingly at the door. Her mother was still smiling but it seemed a little bit forced, Ella thought, when she managed to look at her.

The Fancy Man got down on one knee to her and she remembered how much she had liked him.

'We want you to come home with us. Do you think you might manage that?'

'I want to go back to my grandma. It was the best things could ever be.'

And then her mother chimed in.

'We could take you home with us just for a day or two if you like. Sister Madeline says you could come for a visit and then come back here if you change your mind,' she said.

Ella looked straight at her.

'I don't know,' she said.

'We thought that if you come home with us now we could take you to church tomorrow like your grandma did,' said the Fancy Man. 'And we could go and see the people who are in her house. They have just had a baby and they said we could take you to see it if you like.'

'And I'll make Sunday dinner,' her mother promised.

'What if you fight?' Ella said.

'We won't,' the Fancy Man said. 'We have made a pact that we won't do that again, that we will try to do better so that you will want to come and stay with us. Will you trust us, just for two days?'

Ella hesitated. This was not what she wanted. On the other hand she couldn't have what she wanted so maybe this might do. She had not forgotten how afraid she had been when they fought but she had learned a lot since then. She had learned a lot by running away – what mattered, how not to make friends – and she thought of all those children at the safe house in Newcastle and how much worse off so many of them were.

'You can come back here any time you please,' the Fancy Man said. 'If it's during the week your mam will bring you because I will be at work but I promise you any time you aren't happy you will come back here, Sister Madeline has promised us.'

At that point Sister Madeline appeared like a good fairy and agreed with what had been said and so Ella went off with them on a horse and cart. She was a bit worried about what would happen now but she liked the horse and cart and she did not look back at the foundling school.

When she got home to Consett there was a big pile of books on the kitchen table, all tied up with a red ribbon, and when she ventured upstairs her horse brasses had been put on the walls.

On Sunday they took her to church where she thought a lot about her grandma and put in a special prayer for her, just in case God was taking her grandma for granted, though how anybody could she was not sure. Grandma would make her presence felt wherever she went, at least that was what her mam said, and that evening Ella sat by the fire and felt as though she belonged here for the very first time.

Forty-Two

Jessica had been in the little hilltop town for several weeks and had barely stirred from the chair she was sitting in. Ned had come to loathe that chair. Had it not been for his auntie Hilary they would have starved. At first she came and made meals, though his mother ate nothing, but after the first few days, when his aunt had tried and been unsuccessful at getting Jessica to do anything, she took the children to eat at the school. The beds were made up and they slept here but spent very little time in the house.

Ned hated it and now that he had got what he wanted he hated everything about it, but most of all he hated that Julia seemed happy and was no longer following him around.

He didn't understand how she had moved on. He thought it might be something to do with the fact that she thought they would be going home and was treating this as a kind of special holiday. Also she liked having their mother nearby. They had never seen anything of her and now she was a novelty, always to be found in the sitting room of their house, doing nothing so that Julia could always find her.

Ned had tried to get his mother to talk to him but she didn't seem to hear him. He would have asked Auntie Hilary to help but he knew that she was well aware of the situation. The other nuns came to the little house and in despair they cleaned and gave the children clothes so that they could take the others to be washed. Life did not go on at the little house, Ned thought, it was as though time had stopped after they left their home.

Auntie Hilary did everything she could to shift Ned's mother though she did not stir from the chair. In the end his aunt brought the local doctor in to see her. His mother calmly got up and left the room and went upstairs for the first time, which was all his visit accomplished as far as Ned could see. She did not come downstairs after that for several days. Ned began to think that he was to lose his second parent so shortly after losing the first. It was as though parenting was not allowed to he and Julia in any way. In the end he went upstairs and the sight of her lying there, not moving, reminded him of his father dying and his heart clutched and bumped as he watched her.

'Mother?' She didn't respond until he said it again and then she turned over so that she was facing him. 'Mother, could you come downstairs? I need you to.' She said nothing and he wasn't convinced that she heard him. He sat down on the edge of the nasty little bed and it creaked.

'It's such a hard bed,' she said and he knew that it was nothing to do with the bed, or rather it was because she had always slept in a double bed with her husband and she would never do so again. It was as if she thought she was condemned to this life forever and he began to think they both were. For the first time that he could remember he began to cry so hard that she sat up.

'Why, Ned, Ned,' she managed and then she reached forward and put her arms around him and Ned sobbed the more because she had hold of him.

'It's my fault that Father died. This is all my fault.'

Then she pulled him into her arms and she said in the most sensible voice he thought he had ever heard,

'Nothing of the sort. How could this be your fault? You're just a little boy, even though you think you aren't.'

From the safety of the warm and sweet smell of her, Ned confessed.

'Mother, I stole the diamonds.'

She let go of him but instead of the reproving glance he expected to see her eyes were sparkling.

'Did you, my darling boy, did you really?' and she started to laugh. 'Tell me all about it.'

So he did.

That was the day that Jessica began to try to help herself. She had three goes to get the fire lit but when she finally succeeded she was pleased with herself. Then she carried water to the boiler and she got the kettle going and by the time Hilary came for her daily visit Jessica was feeling a lot more in charge.

She didn't tell Hilary about the diamonds, and she wasn't even sure she was pleased about her small secret, but at the moment she thought anything would do.

She was pouring out the first pot of tea she had ever made when Hilary told her about the wedding.

'I didn't like to tell you before,' she said.

'Why ever not?' They were seated at the kitchen table and Hilary said nothing.

'Oh Hilary, you didn't really think I was so selfish that I would begrudge you some happiness? I have been so very happy.' Jessica began to cry but just a little, she felt all cried out.

'It comes so soon after your loss.'

'I think Mr Nattrass is a lovely man. He came this morning and brought butter and milk and eggs and several different vegetables, some of which I barely recognized,' Jessica said and they both began to laugh and then they sipped their tea.

'I will help you with the vegetables,' Hilary promised and then she said,

'I've got another confession to make. I do hope you won't mind and even if you do it's too late to change it now. I have written to Frederick and asked him to the wedding.'

Jessica stared at her.

'What do you think?'

Jessica was determined not to cry but she looked hard into her teacup and she said hoarsely,

'It's just so typical of you, Hilary, so very kind, trying to scrape us all up as you go.'

'It's what nuns do. You don't think I've overstepped the mark then?'

'I think if you had told me first I might have objected purely on the grounds that he took everything from me. But I think I am beginning to come to terms with that and . . . and Julia is happy here. I don't think Ned is though . . .'

'He may be in time. He can spend a lot of time at the farm with us, I think he will like that. We will all have to accept what has happened. Julia has gained from this, though it hurts me to say it, and I think Ned will in time. In the meantime we are all together so that's something important.'

'Did Frederick reply?'

'He didn't. I have told Mr Gilbraith, having been large about saying to Frederick that he could stay there, and he seems to think it a good idea.'

'And does Sister Maddy think so?'

'We are keeping our fingers crossed.'

'Most unnunlike,' Jessica said, taking another sip of tea.

It was predictably a freezing cold day in summer when Hilary married Mr Nattrass and the whole village turned out. The wind screamed across the fell so that everybody was nithered. They all told one another how unusual it was that it was cold in June but it wasn't true. Flaming June had never been true of County Durham, the locals just pretended that it was always hot here. In June it could rain for a week while sometimes in April it was scorching, but up on the tops you almost always needed a coat. As the saying went: 'In Durham we have nine months of winter and three months of bad weather but who cares. There is lots of coal to keep us warm.'

So Hilary and Mr Nattrass were married and that day there was hail, falling sideways, to mark the occasion. Everybody was there – the children from the school, parents and grandmas and grandpas, aunts and uncles – and they had put tables all over the place to try and make certain there was food and drink for them all. Hilary had insisted that everybody she knew would be at the wedding and she was so well loved that everybody came.

In the afternoon the sun got out and there was music and dancing and Hilary was as happy as she could be considering that her only wish, to have Frederick there, was not granted.

They were married in the morning and the feasting went on all day. Lots of people came up from Wolsingham in the afternoon and since the sun barely sets in the north in June it was halfway through the evening by the time Ned got bored and went off in search of something interesting.

His sister was by her mother's side. She had barely left her since they had moved there. He missed Julia following him around. How ridiculous. Nothing made him happy. His thoughts were always with his home now. He thought of how hard he had tried to get away and now he couldn't get back. How very trying it all was. He heard someone behind him and turned, thinking that it must be Julia, but it was Ella, and she looked happier than he had seen her. She and her parents had come for the wedding and were staying with Mr Gilbraith.

'You seem all right,' he said to her.

'I am. I miss my grandma. I suppose I will always miss her and my mam still has a house which is far too clean but we've sort of given in, Bill and me.'

'You like him?'

'Oh, he's lovely,' she said. 'I have to be careful because my mam isn't very good at sharing people, especially him. He buys books for me. My mam thinks my bedroom is a big clutter but she says also that it's my clutter and I must keep it tidy if I want it cleaning, so now and then I do tidy up a bit. We go to church too.' Ella pulled a happy face and smiled.

As they stood there a very large and rather politely plain carriage drew up pulled by four shiny black horses. Such things never happened. Ned was astonished. Ella stared.

The men got off it and let down the steps and from it descended a tall young man who Ned had to admit looked rather like himself and even more like his father. The man, slender and not very old, came to him but obviously not quite sure what to say, merely said,

'Good evening.'

Ella said nothing, the incident had taken her voice, Ned thought, and hardly surprising.

'Hello, Frederick,' he said, 'I am Ned.'

It took Ned all his breath to say anything. Nobody had told him that his half-brother might turn up. Nobody had said anything, but who else could it be, looking exactly like their father and wearing expensive clothes?

'I did think you might be. I was given an invitation to come here.'

'This is Ella. Ella, this is my half-brother who inherited everything.'

Frederick flinched. Ned was pleased.

'I got a letter from your auntie Hilary and she says that Mr Gilbraith has asked me to stay,' Frederick said.

'He's like that, doesn't care who he asks. Have you come for your diamonds? I don't have them on me.'

'No,' said the young man looking him straight in the eyes. 'I have come here to meet you and my stepmother and my half-sister. Will you take me to them?'

'It would be a pleasure,' Ned offered and he guided the young man in the direction of the foundling school where the wedding festivities were taking place outside. Ella stood on the far side of Frederick so that they were like an escort as they showed him the way, winding their way past where local musicians were playing music and everybody was gathered around big tables. It was very noisy, what with the joyful dance music and everybody talking and laughing and people were dancing with their children in big rings at that point.

Ella ran over to her parents and Ned took his half-brother to where his mother and Julia sat at the table, next to Mr Gilbraith. Mr Gilbraith was never slow at these things. He got to his feet straight away and came forward, a big smile on his face and his hand outstretched in welcome.

'Mr Waverley, what a pleasant sight and what timing. Say hello to your stepmother and your half-sister and then sit down. Your aunt is married to Mr Nattrass, no doubt he will take you to see his farm later and introduce you to Dobber and Bonny, his sheepdogs, and then your day will be complete.'

Frederick saw the bride. She looked nothing like she had when she was a nun. She was dressed in white and as he stood there she beamed at him and then she came across, ignoring everybody, and she said,

'Oh Frederick, I hoped and prayed that you would come.'

'Auntie Hilary,' the young man said with a slight smile. He also bent over and kissed Jessica, who said nothing but nodded at him. Julia clung to her mother.

'Do sit down, Frederick,' Hilary told him. 'This is my very new husband, Mr Nattrass.' Mr Nattrass also seemed very pleased to see Frederick and pumped his hand and smiled sunnily at him.

So Frederick sat down and was given beer and ham sandwiches, not his usual fare but he was so glad to be there that he felt his heart ease in his chest. He had never been as cold in his life as during the long journey here as he came further and further north and he had a feeling he would have to get used to it.

He did talk to his stepmother that afternoon and said that he would make sure Ned got to go to a good school and that he hoped she would forgive him for his ill manners.

Ned groaned but not aloud.

He knew now that he would be sent off to that wretched boarding school, there was no hope left for him. He also had the feeling that although Sister Maddy might ask Julia to stay at the foundling school, Julia would go back with her mother and her half-brother to visit the old place and soon Frederick would be running up the sands with her.

However, Ned thought it was time that somebody else did. He needed to move on. He did say to himself that Frederick might ask Harry to come and stay if they were to have a visit back to Northumberland. Perhaps, if Harry's father was not too horrified at what they had done, and if Harry could go to school with him, it would not be nearly so bad as it had been.

Frederick went to stay at Mr Gilbraith's and Mr Gilbraith asked Ned if he wanted to go and stay too. Ned felt that he ought to refuse but he discovered that he longed to be where his brother was. He was almost ashamed at the feeling. He was ready to like Frederick, especially when his half-brother said to him later,

'I wish you would call me Freddie. What was it about the diamonds?'

Ned wanted to lie but he didn't want to start off with such a stupid untruth so they sat outside and the sun tried to go down, which of course it doesn't at that time of the year, and when he came to the end of his story Frederick – Freddie – started to laugh.

Ned was rather pleased that Freddie swore when there was just the two of them – that he didn't give a damn about any diamonds. Freddie wanted to go back to the hall and he wanted Ned to teach him to row and he wanted them to ride their horses up and down the beach. Ned went on and on about the beaches, about how clean they were, how long and wide and pale, and about the long spiky grass which grew in the sand dunes, how the sunlight rose above the sea's horizon and how he and Julia had long since trodden pathways between the house and the beach.

'We could go fishing,' Ned offered.

'I never did that.'

'There are lots of fish out there and the local men put lobster pots out and there are crabs and winkles and—'

'Winkles?'

'You don't have those in Kent?'

'I don't know. I never got involved before.'

'They come in shells. You boil them and then you eat them out of the shell.'

'I've had snails.'

'Oh, right then,' Ned said, feeling slightly as if he had been bettered.

They talked about fishing and boats for so long that even the sun had given up and gone down, so it was late and almost chilly when they went back to the house where Mr Gilbraith was waiting for them.

Freddie and Mr Gilbraith sat over the fire and Ned fell asleep to the sound of their soft conversation. Even then he was making plans for Harry to come and visit and even perhaps ride over on his pony. And for Ella to be there as well, if her parents would let her, so that there would be four of them. He fell asleep with happy thoughts in his head and the Darling diamonds passed out of his thinking forever.

Acknowledgements

I would like to thank my wonderful and hard-working editors, Emma Capron and Celine Kelly and Rhian, for all the time, energy and expertise that they have spent pulling this book into shape. It's wonderful how some editors know instinctively what to change and what to leave alone and how the book is so dear to the writer's heart. These are great talents and they have them so largely. Their enthusiasm is such a big help, that's what encourages writers to go on. Thanks so much.

Also, as ever, to everybody at Quercus. I feel very proud to belong.

If you enjoyed *The Runaway Children*, discover the first
book in the series:

The Foundling School for Girls

After Ruth Dixon's mother deserts her on Christmas Eve,
her father comes home drunk and commits an unthinkable act.
Without money or friends she has nowhere to go, but when he
hurts her a second time, she knows what she must do.

Ruth is rescued by Jay, a businessman, who takes her to the convent where she meets Sister Madeline. Along with the rest of the
nuns, Maddy provides food, shelter and education for orphans.

Ruth comes to see her new friends as family and things
are finally looking up. But then a pit accident changes everything,
and they all stand to lose something –
or someone – they love . . .

Available now in paperback, eBook and audio.

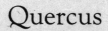

A Widow's Hope

Is everyone given a second chance?

Ten years after the death of her husband, Faith Norman
is surprised to see her brother-in-law, Rob Berkeley,
return to their small Durham town.

Rob is determined to bring the family business, the foundering
steelworks, back to full strength. But for Faith, the resemblance
he bears to his brother is a painful reminder of all she has lost.

As they get to know each other once more, the likeness
gradually becomes more welcome to her healing heart.
This may be their one last chance, but the road to
happiness is never straight nor smooth . . .

**A gripping saga about guilt, secrets and enduring love.
Perfect for fans of Dilly Court, Maggie Hope
and Nadine Dorries.**

Available now in paperback and eBook.

Quercus

Orphan Boy

Will he ever find the life he longs for?

Born to a mother who died in childbirth and an uninterested father, Niall McAndrew grows up a solitary child, without a home to call his own. His only friend is Bridget, a young girl forced prematurely into womanhood.

Niall has brains, spirit and ambition, as well as being blessed with handsome good looks. But his loveless childhood has left its mark. Can he ever find the happiness he yearns for?

A moving rags-to-riches tale of a young boy with big dreams.

Available now in paperback and eBook.

Quercus

The
Pit Girl

To make a home, she will risk everything . . .

When Kate's father dies, she loses everything. Forced to leave
London, Kate moves to a remote mining village in County
Durham to live with an uncle she barely knows.

Isolated, out of place, and suffocated by the restrictions of polite
society, Kate does the unthinkable: she takes a job in her uncle's
office. The scandal could be either her salvation or her undoing.

When a sudden pit disaster puts everything at risk,
Kate will find out if she has the will and courage
not simply to survive, but to triumph . . .

An emotional read about love in the face of hardship.

Available now in hardback, audio and eBook.

Quercus